MW00639666

Violent Mistake, Blackrose Brotherhood #2

Ariana Nash - ***Dark Fantasy Author***

Subscribe to Ariana's mailing list & get the exclusive story 'Sealed with a Kiss' free.

Join the Ariana Nash Facebook group for all the news, as it happens.

Edited by No Stone Unturned / Proofreader Arrowhead Editing

Edited in US English.

Special Hardcover Edition Version 1 - September 2023

www.ariananashbooks.com

ARIANA NASH

VIOLENT Mistake

BLACKROSE BROTHERHOOD #2

Felix

Kazimir

CHAPTER 1

elix

MUSIC THUMPED his chest and filled his head, muffling his thoughts. The club's lights were too bright and the drink—Felix lifted whatever cocktail concoction he'd ordered—the drinks were expensive. Everyone around him seemed too young to be drinking. He wasn't *old*. Twenty-eight wasn't old. But places like this with its too-loud, sparkly millennials and drink menus he needed a loan to buy from made him feel as though he came from another world.

He sipped the awful cocktail, removed a tattered notebook from his pocket and scribbled a few notes. The atmosphere here was an important part of setting the scene later, when he recorded the next episode of the *Unexplained in Maine* podcast. He wasn't in Maine. That was just where it had all begun. Tonight, he was in midtown Manhattan, working a target. A target seated right across the bar.

Kazimir Skokan.

The bastard leaned against the bar, surrounded by men and women as bright and as loud as him. They all wanted a piece of the internet sensation, wanted to feature on his feed and have their picture appear to over one hundred million of his followers.

Felix raised his tall, thin cocktail glass and teased it between his fingers, pretending to admire the drink. Instead, he watched Kazimir's face, warped through the glass. Famous for looking pretty? What a joke. Kazimir was tall and pale, with jaw-length black hair that held a hint of a wave. He had one of those faces that was probably classified as ugly in high school, with too many sharp lines, pouting lips and a feminine glamor to his eyes. Even Felix could admit the prick was pretty. His smile lit up the damn room. And his laugh... Well, fuck. That was just another reason to hate him.

Kazimir laughed now, as though he'd heard Felix's thoughts, and Felix fought to suppress a snarl.

He'd never hated a man more.

Kazimir was the reason he'd lost his job, his wife, his kid, his fucking home. But that was okay, because Kazimir Skokan had secrets, and Felix was going to reveal every single one—see how his rabid fans turned on him then.

Kazimir's gaze skipped across the bar, landing straight on Felix, even through the glass. The man's larger-than-life smile, still half-laughing from something one of his fans had said, slipped sideways, turning sly. He stroked a finger along his jaw and glanced down, as though bashful. Felix should have looked away, but the damage was done. He lowered his cocktail glass, no longer pretending not to see him.

Yeah, see me, you asshole.

Kazimir tipped his own glass, acknowledging Felix, then threw the drink back in one gulp and turned to his adoring crowd. They hadn't seen in those few seconds, with his blue eyes locked on Felix, how his personality had changed. It had been subtle, a hint of what lay beneath, but Felix had seen it. Kazimir was a liar. Worse than that, he was a killer, and Felix was the only damn person who saw it.

Soon, everyone would see him. Everyone would know. And maybe then Felix could have his life back.

CHAPTER 2

azi

The reporter-turned-true-crime-podcaster had returned, stalking him again. As Kazi had planned. He'd made sure to broadcast exactly where he'd be, at what time, and with whom, hoping Felix Quaid would be as predictable as he'd been for the past three months, like a persistent blip on Kazi's radar.

Quaid should have stayed away. But no, he was here, and that was the last of the man's chances used up.

Mikalis had given the order. Felix Quaid was a dead man. Quaid just didn't know it yet.

Damn shame he had to die, because he was hot. All that hate burning in his eyes every time he fixed Kazi in his sights. Meatbags with passion always got Kazi's ancient heart racing, but it had been a while since any of them, man or woman, had made his pulse race like Quaid did. Hate like his took time to fester, like a wound rotting from the inside. Quaid blamed Kazi for his life's downward spiral. It was his own fault. He should have learned not to go poking into Brotherhood affairs. Should have backed off when Mikalis had killed Quaid's story before "Vampires Are Real" could be splashed all over the *New York Times*. Should have walked the fuck away, but no, Quaid couldn't let it go. So what happened now was Quaid's own fault.

The woman who'd been hanging on Kazi's arm all evening plastered herself to his side and muttered about going back to his place. Carol, Maggie, Lucy? She'd be fun for an hour or two, but then she'd probably ask to come around again, and Kazi had a one-night-only rule. Any more than that and the Brotherhood noticed. That was when shit got complicated.

He hated complicated.

Lucy slipped her hand down the back of his pants, cupped his ass, and whispered in his ear all the ways she was wet for him.

He flashed her a smile but plucked her hand free. "Hold that thought. I'll be right back." He could swing by and pick her up later, after he'd taken the trash out. She'd make a convenient alibi. Murder and sex made for an okay evening. Better than being alone.

As he made motions to leave, the group of people clustered around him—he hadn't bothered to remember their names—crooned and complained, trying to bribe him to stay with offers of drinks and more than a few salacious glances. He laughed them off, told them all he'd be back, and called the bartender over.

"That guy over there?" Kazi asked, nodding toward Quaid quietly simmering in his own hatred. "I'll settle his tab."

"Sure." The bartender held out the card machine and Kazi waved his all-black credit card over the device. Paying for Quaid's drinks seemed the least he could do. It just so happened the black card was connected to Atlas, the Brotherhood's artificial intelligence central hub. Atlas would track the payment and wipe it from all records. Should the cops come calling, there would be no official record that Felix had ever been at the bar.

He pushed from the crowd, threw on his long coat, and sauntered from the rowdy club, stepping out onto the sidewalk. A bite of frost touched his face. He liked the colder months when the air was harsh. It reminded him of a land he hadn't returned to in almost a thousand years. Some of the Brotherhood preferred to forget their ancient history. Not Kazi. On nights like this, he recalled precisely the smell of woodsmoke and pine, the crackle of a campfire after the hunt, and the feel of soft animal furs against his skin. A time when he'd been human. He'd had a heart back then and felt things deeply. That old heart had long ago turned to stone.

"Want me to call a cab?" a bouncer asked.

Kazi blinked back into the moment. He'd lost himself for a while and hadn't seen the man guarding the club's entrance. "No, I'm good. Thanks."

"Gonna be a cold one." He blew into his cupped hands.

"I hope so." Kazi flicked his coat collar up, buried his hands in his pockets, and started off toward the parking lot where he'd left the car. Like the credit card, the car's plates had a habit of disappearing off official records. It was capable of moving through New York like a ghost. Seen, and then forgotten.

A few cameras caught his stroll as he ambled by some storefronts. That footage would need to be erased later. If everything went to plan, he didn't leave the bar at—he checked his watch—a quarter past midnight. Officially, he'd be there all night. He'd return later and post something brilliant on Instagram, providing a convenient timestamp. It was probably overkill. But he hadn't climbed his way to the top of the Brotherhood by being sloppy, like Zaine. It was a mystery how that love-struck dumbass was even breathing—him and his meatbag NYPD detective lover, Eric. Eric was clearly the smart one of the couple.

The sound of a second pair of footfalls joined Kazi's, far enough behind that most human hearing wouldn't have picked it up under the drone of the city's background noise. He knew Quaid's gait. This wasn't the first time the ex-reporter had followed him. Technically, they'd never met, besides the dagger-like stares Quaid threw his way and that one time Quaid must have had too much to drink and left a voicemail on Kazi's phone telling him he'd better come clean, or Quaid would expose what he'd done to the world.

The man was an idiot.

This was a fucking mercy.

The parking lot lights flicked on as he walked down the ramp, lighting the way to the black car in the far corner. One camera angled toward the exit noted his arrival. A few steps and he was outside its fixed view.

Was Quaid stupid enough to follow Kazi into the lot?

He blipped the car's alarm, disarming it, and turned to lean against the door and wait. Quaid had gone quiet wherever he was. Maybe he wasn't the fool Kazi had assumed him to be. Some humans listened to their instincts, and it could be that Quaid's were telling him that walking into a poorly lit parking lot alone with a man he suspected of heinous crimes was a terrible idea.

Then Quaid appeared, swaggering down the ramp, thinking he could take Kazi if this got physical. In a fair fight, he might have—if Kazi had been human.

"Felix Quaid." Kazi folded his arms, watching him approach. He had an easy gait, his steps confident, and although he'd gone for the scruffy, hobo appearance, clothes all creased and a few days' worth of beard growth shadowing his face, he wore it well. "I listened to your podcast," Kazi said. "*Unsolved in Maine*."

"Unexplained *in Maine*," Quaid sneered. "What are you doing out here, Kazimir? Huh? You waiting for me?"

"Just walking to my car. Last I checked, it's not a crime."

"You wanna talk about your crimes?" Quaid smirked, and that anger thinned his smile, turning it cruel. "Have you got all night?"

"I'm beginning to suspect you really don't like me, Mister Quaid."

"You're fuckin' right." Quaid stopped a stride away, his body language all come-at-me-bro. "I know what you did."

"Hmm, I've done a few things, some of them a little risqué. It's good for views, yah know?"

Quaid stepped closer, within reach. A foot shorter than Kazi, he had to look up to land his sneer. "That's not who you are, and we both know it."

There had been a time, long ago, when Kazi would have wrapped this man in his arms, driven his teeth into his neck and made those his final words. Quaid stood so close that he wouldn't see the attack coming. Kazi would make him like it too. He'd die with a smile on his face and his cock hard. Unfortunately, that wasn't how the Brotherhood did things. Not least because blood from the vein was one of the surefire ways to lose control, and losing control put a nyktelios on the wrong side of Mikalis, where nobody in their right mind wanted to be. Which meant Felix Quaid's death was going to be dull in comparison. Such a damn shame. Kazi was so fuckin' bored.

Quaid squared up to him. "You took everything from me, you suave prick."

Interesting insult. Curiously complimentary.

Kazi thrust out a hand, locked his fingers around Quaid's neck and pivoted, switching places. He slammed Quaid against the car, moving so fast it left Quaid gasping and disorientated.

He leaned in, plastering himself to Quaid's stocky body, and tilted his head with a closed smile. Quaid's heart raced, like a rabbit's tiny little heart, the animal caught in a wolf's jaw, moments away from death. His body would be pumping his veins full of adrenaline, preparing him for the fight of his life, not knowing he'd already lost. The ancient part of Kazi thrust two pairs of fangs into his mouth, one to pump his victim full of venom, the other to drink him down. Neither would be happening—he never lost control—but Kazi could relish the fantasy all the same.

"You should have run, Felix. We gave you chances. We warned you."

Quaid's eyes blew wide. He'd seen the fangs, probably saw the shimmer of silver in Kazi's eyes too. He'd know, somewhere in that primeval part of his mind, that he was at the bottom of the food chain, looking death in the eye. The nyktelios were far older than humans, brought forth by the goddess of chaos and darkness, Nyx herself. Part of Kazi came from her—the part hungering for Quaid's blood, the part that wanted to rip the man to shreds and bathe in his blood.

Kazi bowed his head and tasted Quaid's fear, parting his lips to draw the man's scent across his tongue. "I was a prince in an ancient land, a prince worshipped like a god. Dying by my hand is an honor, Felix." He swallowed, committing everything about the man to memory: how he resisted, the strong *thump-thump* of his heart, how the hate still raged in his eyes. "Thank me in whatever hell we'll eventually see each other in."

A jolt slammed into him.

A hundred thousand volts danced through his muscles, landing like a sledgehammer, then setting his veins on fire. Kazi couldn't do a damn thing but drop Quaid and buckle, folding in on himself in an effort to resist the onslaught. Shouts rebounded around the parking lot, engines revved, tires squealed. *Attack. He was under attack*. He dropped the reins on his control and a surge of dark power pushed the Taser's debilitating shock from his body. He straightened, the Taser still clicking in the man's hand, still trying to knock Kazi out cold.

Whoever had just fucked up his evening was about to get a crash course in what happened when you pissed off a Brotherhood vampire mid-monologue.

More prongs struck like vipers, piercing his clothes and him. Enough volts rolled into him to light up a small city.

The world went dark.

CHAPTER 3

Felix

THE WORLD HAD LOST its mind, or he had. Kazimir had him in his grip, his strength that of ten men. It wasn't possible. Then he saw the teeth, curved and sharp. And this couldn't be real. None of it.

A van screeched into the parking lot. Cops, it had to be. He was saved! The door flew open, and a swarm of black-clad people poured out.

Not cops.

One of the people fired a Taser at Kazimir, suddenly freeing Felix. He gasped, filling his lungs with precious air, and blinked tears from his eyes. Kazimir writhed on the floor. He had no idea who these people were, but he owed them his life.

They struck Kazimir again with more Tasers. Enough to kill a man. He lay still, probably not dead. Felix wasn't that lucky.

But they'd seen what he was. They'd seen it too. Felix wasn't alone in knowing the truth. Whatever the truth was... Fangs. He'd had fangs. Actual fuckin' curved teeth, straight out of a horror movie. Four, not two.

He hadn't imagined it. And Kazimir's eyes, they'd turned a cruel, cold silver.

Someone barked an order at him.

Felix opened his mouth to thank them.

The Taser struck. He dropped—didn't feel the asphalt rush up to meet him. Everything was on fire, his body, his lungs. His jaw locked. Blood spilled into his mouth. His vision blurred, split, and blurred again. If he could speak, he could tell them they had the wrong man, but his vision fizzed and his jaw wouldn't unclamp. It felt like hours until the Taser stopped, leaving him a panting wreck.

Several people bundled Kazimir's limp body into the back of their van.

Maybe they'd leave now that they had their prize.

But then they lunged, grabbed Felix, and hauled him onto numb legs. Something sharp and cold jabbed him in the neck. The world tilted around him, collapsing in on itself, leaving him drifting, not asleep but not awake. He dreamed of his body lying next to Kazimir's on the van floor. The doors slammed, the engine rumbled, and everything faded until there was nothing but the sense of drifting alone in an ocean of darkness.

He shifted into a sitting position, made all the more difficult by the ropes chafing his wrists. His whole body protested, aching as though he'd been used as a punching bag. A strip of dirty cloth blocked his teeth and tongue. He worked it free and used his shoulder to drag the gag down over his chin, letting it hang around his neck instead.

He'd been out long enough to be transferred to some kind of metal container. But the container rocked and clattered, sounding as though he'd been dumped inside a train car. He'd have been more concerned about being kidnapped if it hadn't been for the man sharing the container with him.

Pinpricks in the metal sent shafts of needle-like beams toward the floor, where Kazimir lay. He'd been gagged and bound by the wrists too and remained unconscious.

If he didn't get out of the container and away from Kazimir, he'd be fucked.

He'd known the man was a monster, but not a literal one. Not an actual fucking *vampire*. Although, weirdly, now he knew that, much of the rest he knew made sense. People vanished around Kazimir, all his social media posts and posed photos had been taken at night, and shit, he even kinda looked like a vampire, if the movies could be believed. Take away all the designer brands and throw him in a period outfit—pale skin, long black hair, viciously cold eyes—it *worked.*

Felix laughed at his own thoughts, and then cut off that laugh, fearing he sounded insane.

He was going to die in this container if he didn't kill Kazimir first, or escape. Kazimir had thrown him around like a doll. He was a lot stronger than he pretended to be. How was Felix supposed to kill him? Sunlight? That was a thing in the myths, right? Garlic? Crosses?

The inside of the container was dark. Getting the door open would let in sunlight, but there didn't appear to be any kind of latch on the doors, no handle either.

It was madness. *This* was madness. There had to be another explanation.

What if he *was* mad?

If he was, he'd know soon enough, when Kazimir woke up.

He got his feet under him, stood, and shuffled to the doors, keeping Kazimir in the corner of his vision. No latch, no lock, nothing. He was only getting out when whoever had caught them unlocked the container from the outside.

He might be dead before then.

He eyed Kazimir again... His hair, always so perfectly tousled, had lost some of its luster and lay in a mop around his head. His cheekbones were damn sharp enough to cut glass. And that jaw... All the pretty made sense now. That was how he trapped his victims. He used his good looks to *hunt*.

Although he didn't appear monstrous while sleeping.

A thousand questions ran through Felix's head, fueled by a hundred different vampire movies and books and their lore. If he'd known they were real, he'd have paid more attention.

He chuckled again, swallowed a sob and slid down the container wall to slump on the floor.

A secret like that... Kazimir would never let Felix live through this. He was going to have to figure out how to kill a vampire, and do it fast.

The train rumbled on.

What if he just... strangled him?

He shuffled toward the unconscious Kazimir and knelt close. Felix's wrists were tied, but he could still get his fingers around Kazimir's throat. He angled his hands toward Kazimir's slim neck. He could do this. He had to—just spread his fingers, and clamp on, and squeeze—

He grabbed the man's neck. And crushed his fingers closed.

Panic tried to loosen his grip. He'd never killed anyone before. He turned away, panted through his teeth, fought the churn in his gut, and then looked back to find Kazimir's deep blue eyes fixed on him. With a yelp, Felix lurched backward and slammed into the container wall, plastering himself against the cold metal. *Shit, shit, shit...*

Kazimir moved slowly, unfurling like a sleepy cat, then brought his bound wrists down to his lap and snapped the ropes as though they were nothing but paper.

Fuck.

Kazimir yanked the gag free, tossed it aside, then casually got to his feet and brushed the dirt from his coat and clothes. Straightening, he ran his fingers through his loose hair and gave his head a shake.

"I'm going to assume your gentle caress was an attempt to kill me and not something more intimate?"

There were a lot of words in that sentence, none of which Felix heard from behind the thudding of his heart. He'd worked for the *New York Times*, reported from war zones, been shot at, had to run for his life on more than one occasion, but he'd never really experienced fear. Until now. Wars, battles, bullets—all those things were real. He could fight those. But vampires?

Kazimir tilted his head, stretching his muscles with a click. "I guess not. For what it's worth, I don't want to kill you."

"What *do* you want?" Felix heard himself ask. He didn't sound as terrified as he felt. Maybe he had that going for him. If Kazimir didn't see his fear, maybe he'd think Felix had good reason *not* to be afraid.

"Out of this container. The rest we'll get to." He flashed a quick smile his fans probably would have swooned over. Felix glared and stayed stuck to the container wall, as far away from Kazimir as possible.

"I take it the people who captured us aren't friends of yours?" Kazimir asked.

"What? No." The people with the vans. He hadn't even thought about them. He'd assumed, since they'd attacked Kazimir first, they were part of *his* world. Although why they'd brought Felix along, he had no idea. They could have killed him if it was about keeping him quiet. But presumably, they could have killed Kazimir too and hadn't.

Kazimir cruised around the inside of the container, and when he drew near, Felix scooted to the opposite side, making the vampire chuckle. "Relax. I'm not going to kill you here."

"Why not?" Would Kazimir hear the quiver in his voice? "You were before."

He sighed, tipped his head back and closed his eyes. Felix's gaze roamed, absorbing how his long coat framed his lean body. Felix had spent a few years as a photographer, before discovering he much preferred to be investigating the stories than observing them.

Kazimir had the kind of presence that demanded to be captured by a camera lens. His every angle was a potential pose. It was no wonder social media loved him. Maybe somewhere in all of that, people knew there was something different about him, something as alluring as it was repelling. How else was Felix supposed to explain that when the shafts of light caught Kazimir's face, he wished he'd had a camera on him to capture the way light stroked over his dark lashes, a light that appeared to crease his brow, making his eyes narrow. So sunlight *did* hurt him, but not enough to give Felix much of an advantage.

"Until I know who we're dealing with, I'm keeping you alive."

"What difference does it make if you kill me now or later?"

Kazimir shrugged. "Paperwork, mostly. I hate it. It's such a bore. If I kill you now and it turns out our destination happens to be a very public station, there will be questions."

Whether he lived or died right now came down to *paperwork*? "At least I know where I stand." He was going to die and soon. Knowing that, he wished he'd done more. It didn't seem fair or right. He'd fucked everything up, and now he'd never be able to fix it. "Nobody will even miss me."

Kazimir propped himself against the opposite wall, arms folded, and peered across the vacant space between them. "You're wrong."

"Huh?"

"Your wife, for one. You have a daughter too. Rosa. She's four—"

"If you fuckin' touch them..." Felix's heart raced again. How did he know so much about Felix's life?

Kazimir smirked. "What are you going to do, hmm? Attempt to kill me like you did earlier? If that's what that was? Let's both stop pretending we're anything other than what we are. You can't stop me from doing anything I please. And I've been doing exactly that for a very long time."

"How long?" he asked carefully.

"A thousand years, give or take a few."

"Shit," he gasped. The thing in front of him was not a man, even when his mind tried to tell him over and over he was. A thousand-year-old monster. But he didn't look any older than Felix. "Are there more like you?"

Kazimir dropped his gaze to the container floor. "If we go down this path"—he flicked his gaze up—"you asking questions, me answering—you're not going to find a happy ending. It's better you don't know."

Maybe that was true. But if he could somehow escape, he might need that information to keep himself alive. He slumped to the floor, thoughts in freefall.

They rode in silence, listening to the clattering wheels, and as much as he tried to stay awake, when the light outside the container faded and the temperature dropped, he drifted, half asleep, occasionally jolting awake to keep an eye on his traveling companion.

Kazimir didn't move at all. The only sign he was a living thing was the occasional blink.

The clatter of chains and the jolt of the train car stopping flung Felix awake. Light crept into the container at the seams, but he couldn't tell if it was daylight or floodlights.

Kazimir positioned himself at the back of the container, his glare on the door. "Best get to your feet, Quaid. We've got company."

Maybe the people outside would realize their mistake and save him? He dragged one of his bound hands down his face, rubbing the dreariness of sleep away, and staggered to his feet. At least he'd get out of the metal container and away from the monster.

More chains clunked, and then the door rumbled open.

A blur shot by Felix's shoulder, accompanied by a burnt amber scent. In less than a second, Kazimir was outside. But he didn't make it far. He dropped, as though someone had pulled the plug, and groaned on his hands and knees.

Confused and blinded, Felix raised his hands, shading his eyes.

A circle of hooded people closed in, their faces hidden in shadow.

Kazimir shuddered in pain. But from what?

One of the people moved forward. He guessed a woman from how the all-black gown fell from her shoulders. She knelt on one knee in front of Kazimir. "Welcome home, prince," she said, her voice strangely accented. European? "We've waited a long time for this."

Good or bad, Felix had seen enough.

Nobody seemed to be paying him any attention, and he was done with this circus.

He bolted, dropped from the train car and made a dash toward the trees. A few hooded people moved in, cutting off his escape route. He reeled, spun and met more of them, all hooded, all with shadows for faces. "Wait..." He held up his hands. "Stop. There's been a mistake."

"Are you the prince's feeder?"

"A w-what?"

"You were found with the prince, engaged in the act of feeding. Were you not?"

He couldn't see the man's face beneath the hood, but he sounded young, maybe early twenties. Was it a good thing to be a feeder? "I er..." Felix cleared his throat. "I think you got the wrong guy."

"No mistake." The new voice belonged to an older man. He swooped in and grabbed Felix's arms. "He's the feeder or he'd be dead. It's that simple. Throw him in with the prince. He's going to need him."

"What—" Felix dug his heels in. "No, listen, there's been a mistake." More people crowded in, grabbing at him. "Stop, please... I shouldn't be here." They marched him toward the sprawling front deck of a long, timber-clad building. It resembled a church, with a small central spire over a pitched roof. "Wait, please... I don't know anything. You can let me go. I haven't seen anything!" he rambled, repeating the same words over and over. None of them listened.

Fuck them, then. He wasn't dying for some mad vampire-worshipping cult. He kicked and bucked. One of them freed his right arm, giving him room to swing. He bucked again, tore free, and ran. He ran so damn hard, blind with fear—just ran, legs pumping and lungs ablaze, toward the trees.

A single shot rang out.

His shoulder burst into a blaze of fiery agony, spinning him around. He tripped, sprawled in the dirt. No, no, he wasn't dying here. They couldn't do this.

A hooded figure stepped in front of him. The gun leveled at his face. "We'll find other feeders if you're not his?"

Felix panted and clutched his shoulder with his tied hands. Warm wetness trickled between his fingers. "Yeah, sure. I'm his feeder." He wasn't going to argue with a man who had a gun to his head. He'd be whatever the fuck he wanted him to be, just as long as it wasn't dead.

"Get up," the gunman urged, jerking the weapon.

Felix staggered to his feet. His shoulder pulsed, hot and heavy. Damn, this was fucked up. "Who are you?"

The man stayed quiet and escorted him back through the brush.

Kazimir was gone by the time they returned to the church, which was both a relief and a concern. If he didn't know where Kazimir was, he'd have no idea what the bastard was plotting.

The armed man guided Felix up the building's front steps, but instead of entering using the large arched front doors, he was led down the deck and inside a smaller, less grand entrance.

The people inside weren't hooded and stared as though Felix was the one with fangs. All of them wore the same dark purple uniform with a silver dagger and eye motif on their left breasts. What kind of cult was this? Every mute person he passed glared without saying a single word.

Maybe he'd be safer with Kazimir?

Ahead, a lock clanged. A heavy metal door swung open. Hands shoved him inside the small cell, and the door slammed shut behind him, plunging him into near darkness.

"Hey?" His voice echoed in the tiny space. "You can't fucking do this!"

He brought his hand away from his shoulder. Blood glistened. His vision spun. His gut heaved. "I'm bleeding here!"

"If you are worthy, the prince will bestow his gift upon you shortly."

Felix stared at the door, wondering again if he'd lost his mind. "What gift?" He didn't need a gift. He needed a fucking doctor. "Hey!"

Nobody answered.

CHAPTER 4

azi

WHAT HAD BEGUN as a simple hit on Felix Quaid had turned into something very different. "*Vyjebaný*," Kazi swore. The hooded people, whoever they were, had begun to test his patience.

Back to being tied, this time to a metal chair bolted to the floor in a cell-like room with no windows, he pulled at the chains, clamping his wrists behind him. Somewhere low in his spine, a clever little device sizzled a warning.

While he'd been unconscious, the hooded ones had inserted a microchip beneath his skin, nestling it against his spine. When triggered, it delivered a debilitating shock to his nervous system, like the one he'd been dealt when he'd dashed from the container.

But the chip was designed to debilitate, not to kill.

So what was this?

They'd called him a prince. Why then was he their prisoner?

At least the problem of Quaid had been dealt with. He'd seen the man run into the woods and heard the shot. Kazimir would have preferred to kill him himself as Mikalis had ordered, but the outcome was the same.

How long had it been since he'd left the club? At least twenty-four hours. It wasn't unusual for a Brotherhood member to go dark during a mission, calling on backup only when required. Storm would be the first to notice Kazi was missing. He'd check the club and find the car, unless the hooded ones had moved it. Which if they had any sense, they would have, further delaying any Brotherhood investigation.

For now, Kazi was on his own.

The door rattled, swung open on screaming hinges, and three men shoved Quaid into the room. The fact he was alive quickly became an afterthought behind the fact he was *bleeding*.

"Feed, prince. We'll talk later," the female said.

The door slammed closed.

Quaid hung back, bracing his shoulder with a hand. They'd untied him. His disheveled appearance blurred in Kazi's vision. *Blood.* It sang to him, calling, seducing. He hadn't expected it, but he could resist. It did, however, make Felix's presence even more irritating.

"I thought you were dead," Kazi growled.

Quaid's eyebrows lifted. "I might be if they don't get me a doctor."

Sweat glistened on his face. He was suffering. Strange that they'd put him in with Kazi already wounded. Did they *want* him to die?

"They called me a feeder," Quaid said. "You know what that is?"

Kazi chuckled, although he was far from amused. "It means this is a game."

"Well, I'm not playing."

"Doesn't look as though either of us has a choice, does it?"

Quaid swayed, then slid down the wall to the floor, leaving streaks of blood on the white paint.

Kazi blinked at the smears, then tore his gaze away. He tried not to breathe in the sweet scent, tried to push its effect from his mind and somewhat succeeded. Quaid had no idea how tempting he was: wounded prey, the best kind. In another life, he'd have been the one chasing Felix Quaid into the woods. Hunting him down. He'd have made his prey run, until it tired, and watched as terror filled its eyes. Fear was an elixir. He smelled it on Felix now.

"You all right?" Quaid asked.

Kazi laughed again. "I'm tied to a chair at the mercy of questionable hosts."

"Can't you just... break out?"

"Oh wait," he drawled, "why didn't I think of that?"

Felix winced. "I just... In the container, you broke the ropes, so..."

"They've tagged me with an inhibitor. As soon as I begin to exert any kind of significant strength, it triggers a bolt of agony. It's... unpleasant. I'd prefer to avoid it happening again."

Quaid sighed and thumped his head against the wall. "I am so done with this shit."

"Unfortunately, this shit is not done with you."

The man eyed him curiously. He had soft, intelligent eyes, now that they weren't filled with rage. Perhaps he'd forgotten his hate since he had greater concerns, such as staying alive. As Kazi watched, his lashes fluttered closed and his heart rate slowed. Already low on blood, he'd bleed out within the hour. He'd die in this room, as was his fate.

Kazi wet his lips. "Quaid?"

"Hmm."

"I can stop the bleeding. And seal the wound."

"Right," he drawled, and a small smile tugged at the corner of his mouth. "By killing me quicker?"

What was Kazi thinking? Quaid dead—that was the whole point of his mission. Sure, it had gone awry, but that didn't change what needed to be done. Still, when Kazi settled his gaze on the dying man, a sense of panic tripped his heart. Quaid had followed him like a shadow for months. The man despised him, Kazi knew that, but he could appreciate his passion. Quaid had lost everything, but he'd fought on, probably knowing he shouldn't, knowing what would happen if he didn't let the news story go.

Quaid had known something was wrong with the world, and despite everything working against him, he'd dug deeper and deeper. So deep he'd uncovered the Brotherhood.

Kazi admired a man who didn't give up, even when he should.

Perhaps he'd let his prey run, just for a little longer.

"Come here."

"No, I'm good right here," Quaid mumbled. His glassy-eyed gaze wavered over Kazi's face.

"Quaid, if you do not do as I say, you will soon lose consciousness and die in less than an hour."

"Isn't that what you want?"

"Yes, but—" He cut himself off, slowing his heart and calming his tone lest it give his own surprising sense of panic away. "I need you to help me escape whatever this is. Do that, and I'll grant you a favor."

He perked up at that. "Like letting me live?"

"Such as... giving you a head start."

Quaid shifted forward and draped his arms over his spread knees, no longer concerned about the wound, which likely meant his body had numbed it. Next, he'd grow cold, then he'd fall asleep. "What do you want me to do?"

"Come here. Kneel next to me."

Quaid narrowed his eyes.

"I'm fixed to this chair. My wrists are bound. I can't hurt you. I'm trying to save you."

"And you'll give me a head start? You'll let me live?"

Kazi nodded.

Reluctantly, Quaid crawled forward, his movements slow and cumbersome. He rested next to Kazi's leg. "Now what?"

"Pull my collar down." Again, he didn't move. "If you continue to delay, you won't have the strength to save yourself."

Slowly, too slowly, he reached up, slipped his warm fingers into Kazi's shirt collar and pulled. It didn't move far. "The buttons,"

Kazi said, no longer bothering to hide his concern. "Undo the buttons, Quaid."

Quaid blinked, mumbled something about not knowing why he was undressing Kazimir Skokan, and fought with the buttons holding Kazi's shirt close to his neck. Kazi watched Quaid's face, watched his soft lips twist as he concentrated and how his dark lashes framed caring eyes.

His lashes fluttered closed. Quaid slumped against him.

"Quaid?"

Nothing.

"Felix!"

He startled awake and muttered, "Fuck, it's cold..."

Kazi wet his lips. "Listen. You must do this and do it fast. Do not think about it. Just do it. Understand?"

His eyelids were closing again. *Damn him!*

"Felix, pull my collar away from my shoulder. Do it now." Kazi's fangs extended into his mouth, and saliva pooled in anticipation.

For all his control and his decades of restraint, there was no denying the ancient creature inside wanted to feed and fuck and gorge itself.

Quaid yanked the collar down over Kazi's shoulder, exposing it to cool air.

Kazi shifted his arm forward, bowed his head and scraped his teeth across his own shoulder, zipping it open. Blood bloomed in the cut and dribbled down his skin. "Drink." Quaid balked. "Felix, drink... It won't hurt you, much. It'll save you. *Drink it*." He forced some weight behind the order, using a power the Brotherhood forbade, but it worked. Quaid bent his head, sealed his lips over the cut and sucked.

Instincts clamored through Kazi, demanding more. His dick hardened, painfully erect. His fangs leaked, spilling bitter venom into his mouth where Quaid's blood should have been running but wasn't. Part of him screamed silently, roaring its fury at being denied sustenance. He squeezed his eyes closed and imagined dragging Quaid into his arms and sinking his teeth into his neck while

Quaid drank from his veins. He'd bury his cock in the man, ride him hard, make him moan and claw and scream for more, make him come in body and mind until his whole world was Kazi and nobody else.

Quaid's tongue lapped at the healing cut and slid up the wound, seeking more. He moaned, and it was all Kazi could do not to spill in his trousers. The cut healed, and Quaid slumped half on Kazi's lap, half on the floor, clinging to the threads of life.

Multiple doses of nyktelios blood shared carefully over time would turn him. But a little, like this, would protect him.

And mark him as Kazi's.

CHAPTER 5

azi

THEY TOOK QUAID AWAY. Kazi breathed hard, bared his fangs at the hooded figures, and made sure every one of the fiends saw who they were toying with. But after they'd left, and with Quaid gone, the rage, lust and madness waned, leaving him cold, his crotch damp, and his heart ragged.

He should have let Quaid die. It would have been easier to do nothing and watch him bleed out. So why hadn't he?

Now he'd shared blood and marked him as owned. An act the Brotherhood never allowed. But it wouldn't matter. By the time Mikalis got involved, Kazi would have killed Quaid. Nothing about the mission had changed. Just the circumstances surrounding it.

WHEN THE DOOR NEXT OPENED, the woman who had greeted him on arrival, while he'd been on his knees, entered his cell.

She closed the door, faced Kazi and dropped the hood of her gown, revealing a distinct Romani face framed by tightly cropped black hair. Black liner enhanced dark eyes, and blood-red lipstick made her lips shine. The Romani were of ancient blood and lineage, a people steeped in tradition, a people who originated near his old land. Kazi stilled, intrigued.

"Prince Kazimierz Skokan, son of Kazimierz, King of the Slovaks, born some thirteen hundred years ago."

Interesting. Few knew who he was, at least none he'd left alive. If she knew his ancestry, then she likely knew about the Brotherhood. That made her fascinating, and dangerous. And likely next on Mikalis's hit list.

"And you are?"

She crouched. Sultry eyes studied his face. "Under the eye of the eternal goddess, we welcome you to our community."

The language was modern, but the sentiment remained the same as always. The eye and dagger motif on their uniforms, their organized attack—he knew them. "You worship Nyx?"

She straightened and came forward, almost touching his knees. She grasped his chin in her thin fingers and lifted his head, making him look into her eyes. "You, my prince, will be our salvation."

He very much doubted that. He'd been working on saving his own soul for over a thousand years and wasn't there yet. "There's only one way this ends for you and your acolytes, and that's by the points of the Brotherhood's fangs."

She smiled. "Nobody is coming, Kazimir." She leaned forward, and her face filled his vision. "We'll make you a god again. Isn't that what you really want?"

He tore his chin free. "Let me go and I'll petition Mikalis for leniency. He'll kill you quickly instead of torturing you."

She laughed, backed away, and rippled her fingers in goodbye. "You were never his, sweet prince."

He snarled at the door after she'd left. Damn Nyx worshippers. Unfortunately, they had cropped up through the centuries, evolving and adapting with each new generation like a virus. This group had done well to recruit so many to their cause without Atlas picking up their electronic chatter. Like the primal goddess they worshipped, they thrived on chaos and carnage, convinced the dark queen could be resurrected.

Their last revival had been centuries ago in Russia. Storm had dealt with them then. He'd clearly missed a few, allowing their doctrine to be passed down to their children.

And now they were Kazi's problem.

At least he knew who and what he was dealing with. Now he just had to outmaneuver them, escape, and gut their coven, beginning with their leader.

Felix Quaid's death could wait.

CHAPTER 6

elix

HE BLINKED awake in a bed that was not his own, in a room a whole lot cleaner and tidier than his cramped, cluttered Sunnyside studio apartment. Sunlight streamed through the slatted blinds. It might have been the perfect morning if not for the headache trying to thump his brain matter out of his ears and the cuffs fixing him to the bed's side rails.

"I apologize for the restraints, but you've already tried to run once. Trust must be earned."

The woman who spoke had a sharp Eastern European accent he couldn't pin down to a region. When not wearing the dark purple gown, she almost looked *normal* in torn jeans and a V-neck black sweater.

Her short hair had been cropped close to her skull, giving her a sleek, professional appearance. She stood from the bedside chair, unlocked the cuffs and set them aside on a bedside cabinet. "The door is locked," she added, returning to her seat.

She'd been the one to call Kazimir *prince* when they'd first arrived. Much of what happened after was a blur, but she was clearly some kind of leader.

He rubbed at his wrist, trying to recall the last few hours. He'd been shot. He reached for his bare shoulder—only now realizing he was almost naked beneath the sheets, apart from a pair of shorts. A small red welt was all that remained of what he was sure had been a gunshot wound.

Had he dreamed it?

"Lady," he croaked, "I can't be here. You have to let me go."

She blinked slowly, untroubled. "You aren't his feeder, are you?"

"I don't know what that is," he admitted. "I just want to go home. I won't tell anyone what I've seen."

"Unfortunately, we both know that's not true, Mister Quaid." She opened her phone and showed him the *Unexplained in Maine* podcast logo. "Seems you have quite the following. Not as many as Kazimir, but enough to be a concern."

He dropped his head into the pillow and blinked at the ceiling. The last day and night, or however long it had been, he'd ricocheted from one crisis to another. He had no idea who these people were, why they'd cuffed him to a bed, or what he was going to do about Kazimir...

Wait, earlier... he'd been inside a room. He remembered that much.

Kazimir had been there, chained to a chair. He'd struck a deal with him. It was all a blur, but he'd definitely promised to give Felix a chance at survival if he'd—

He covered his mouth with a hand. Shock scattered his thoughts. Had he... He'd been so afraid he'd never see his daughter again—he'd been *dying*—that he'd obeyed Kazimir's order to drink his blood.

He wet his lips. He didn't taste blood. He probed his teeth with his tongue, then, with his free hand, poked a stunted canine tooth. No fangs. Had he dreamed putting his mouth on Kazimir's shoulder? Was any of this place fucking real?

"I'm beginning to wonder if you're not a part of this world, Mister Quaid."

He could have sobbed with relief. "I'm not. This isn't—I don't know what's happening." She might be the only person to understand what he was going through, and if she understood, then maybe she'd let him go.

"Hmm." She smiled sympathetically. "Wrong place, wrong time? Yes. Well. We cannot change what has already been done, but we can change the future. And isn't that a marvelous thing?"

"What?" Marvelous? There was nothing marvelous or amazing about any of this.

She got up from the chair. She was leaving, and he still didn't have any answers. "Wait. Tell me what's happening. Why do you have me here? Where's Kazimir?"

"Safe."

He tried to sit up, but the room spun. "C'mon, you can let me go now? I did the thing... you wanted."

"No, not yet." Her smile was shallow again. "Behave and we'll perhaps reconsider."

"This is a mistake!" Why wouldn't anyone listen!

"For you, perhaps. Not for us." She opened the door, and he caught a glimpse of a corridor outside, its walls painted black with a gold rail.

"He'll kill you," he blurted. "He'll kill everyone here. Don't you know what he is!"

"Oh yes, Mister Quaid, we know exactly who and what our prince is. And I'm counting on him to do exactly as you suggested."

A YOUNG MAN pushed a service cart into the room and refused to answer any questions or look at Felix. After he'd left, Felix eyed the lidded platters. Anything could be under them. Food, severed heads—who knew with these guys.

He lifted the lid off one, half-wincing away. Fried eggs, tomatoes, toast, juice, sausage, bacon... And if that wasn't enough, they'd provided fruit, milk and a pot of coffee. It could have been a five-star hotel spread if not for the locked door and bars over the windows.

His stomach grumbled. If they wanted to feed him, he wouldn't say no.

He ate a little, but his nerves were too shot for him to wolf down everything. The coffee though, that was bliss. He padded around the room in his underwear, sipping coffee, feeling a little better, less shivery and cold. He had some strength back too.

What did he know so far? Kazimir was... not human. He'd been planning on killing Felix. But he'd also admitted he didn't want to. Back in New York, before they'd been taken, he'd mentioned a *we*, so there were more like him.

How far did it go?

He drank the hot coffee and leaned against the wall by the window. Outside, the trees were splashes of red and brown. They could have been in Maine or Montana. He had no idea.

His shoulder twinged. He gave it a rub and rolled it back and forth, working out a lingering soreness.

If Kazimir wanted him dead, why help him live? He'd said something about needing him, but what could Felix offer a monster?

And a monster was exactly what Kazimir was. He'd been right under everyone's noses for years. Millions of followers, all of them worshipping him with likes and comments. If they knew the truth, if Felix broadcast it to the world, Kazimir would be destroyed.

But so would Felix. Kazimir and the others of his kind would come for him. But what else was there? What was the point of his wretched life? He'd lost everything anyway. He could do this one good thing, tell the world about the monsters, even if it was the last thing he ever did.

Except he didn't want to die. His wife had given up on him, and he couldn't blame her for that—he'd never been a present husband, always chasing the next story, traveling to the next war zone. But little Rosa, his sweet daughter? Maybe it was better she forgot him so he couldn't break her heart too?

The door rattled and opened, and two men entered. One placed a pile of clothes on the bed. "Get dressed. We'll be back in fifteen minutes."

"Back for what?"

They left, and the door lock clunked over again. He dressed in the plain slacks and shirt, and when they returned, he dutifully followed them, keen to get a look at his surroundings. His guards walked him deeper into what appeared to be a sprawling building, much larger than the church-like frontage suggested. Doors led to silent offices. Windows revealed dark rooms. If this was a workplace of some kind, there weren't many people around.

They rode the elevator down a level and stepped into a corridor immediately bustling with the straight-faced, uniform-clad people he'd seen before. They glanced over, more curious than hostile. Some wore the dagger-and-eye pins on their shirts.

His guards opened a door into a large, sumptuous office lined with bookshelves. The woman who had been at his bedside smiled a welcome. She waved a hand, and the guards left.

"You know this is kidnapping, right?" he said.

"In your world. In ours, it's preservation."

"My world? What does that even mean?"

She ignored his question and plucked a few books from her shelves, then set them down on her desk. She opened them at various pages and pushed the books toward him. "Your world is a lie, a thin veneer over a hidden truth. There's a battle waging around you. It's been raging for millennia."

He glanced at the pages of elaborate drawings of fanged creatures engaged in vicious fighting. The language on the adjacent pages was made up of symbols, perhaps ancient Greek or older?

"The goddess Nyx was the beginning of all things. Her union with her brother, Erebus, created the primordial beings of Time and Order, and the world as you and I know it sprang into existence."

He frowned, not wanting to upset her beliefs, but that wasn't how life had begun on Earth. But sure, whatever, he wasn't going to argue with the people who'd already shot him once and had a vampire chained in their basement.

"Erebus, however, was darkness, and as with all darkness, he was hungry. He wanted more. He wanted to swallow chaos—Our Goddess, Nyx. Wanted to consume her." She blinked, eyeing Felix as if waiting for comment. "He raped her repeatedly. Predictably, she grew tired of his shit and created the nyktelios, her guardians, her protectors. Vicious, unstoppable beings, made of thirst and madness, that devoured Erebus right back, chasing him into a prison made of sunlight, forever trapping him. With her nyktelios at her side, Our Goddess grew powerful. Her spawn, Time and Order, crafted the world we know today. With the nyktelios, she'll make our world hers." She turned the pages, revealing more and more artwork to fit her fairy tale.

"What happened to her?" Felix asked. "Where is she now?"

"The nyktelios learned how to reproduce, and with each new generation, they spread across every corner of the globe, consuming and feeding in the name of Our Goddess."

"That doesn't sound like the world we're in..."

"A betrayer festered within the nyktelios, one of their own working against them, against Nyx. He gathered more nyktelios to his cause, and slowly, irrevocably, he began to undermine Nyx's reign, weakening her until she, too, vanished the way of Erebus, hidden between dawn and dusk, and her nyktelios, her servants, forever search for her."

She clearly believed her story, the way most religious zealots did, leaving no room for discussion or doubt. Felix scanned the pictures again. "These nyktelios... they're vampires?"

"There are many words for them. Vampire is one."

"Kazimir is a vampire," he said, looking again at the fanged creatures in the book. Some were winged with claws, more demonic than the suave, charming man Kazimir appeared to be, but perhaps that was one of many guises he could take?

"No," the woman said. "He's nyktelios, but he's not one of them. He's Brotherhood. He's a traitor."

"A traitor?" Felix echoed. Then that meant he and his kind—the Brotherhood—were working *against* this goddess of chaos, trying to stop her from turning the world into darkness? That seemed like a good thing, if he believed any of this.

"You don't seem to like Kazimir, Mister Quaid."

He snorted. "What gave you that idea?"

"Yet he saved you?"

"Yeah." He swallowed and dragged a hand down the back of his neck. "I haven't figured out why yet."

"We'd like to know the answer to that too."

He side-eyed the cult leader. Kazimir was obviously dangerous, but this woman... She appeared to be a friend, but she had the same underlying predatory aura that Kazimir had. "Are you like him, a vampire?"

"No," she laughed. "You and I are the same. The difference is, I have my eyes wide open."

So maybe she was a friend? "What do you want from me?"

"Kazimir is about to undergo a difficult ordeal. It will make him vulnerable. We'd like you to get close to him."

"Me?" Felix laughed and closed the nearest book with a *thump*. "He's not going to talk to me. And if I start asking questions, he'll know it's coming from you."

She propped herself on the edge of her desk and folded her hands over her knee. "Mister Quaid, the Blackrose Brotherhood nyktelios adhere to a strict code. They never bleed for mortals. But last night, Prince Kazimir broke those rules and saved your life by sharing his blood, despite the fact you are not his feeder."

He wasn't sure he liked where this was going. "What *is* a feeder?"

"A human a nyktelios uses for sustenance. They fuck and feed from their feeders in a symbiotic relationship. They get blood, and the feeder falls in love."

That sounded terrible. A feeder was a slave. And they'd thought he was Kazimir's feeder. Every new piece of information he learned about Kazimir made the man so much worse.

"Whatever you feel for Kazimir, he has an interest in you." As she went on, she produced a tattered notebook from her desk drawer and tossed it among the other books. Felix's hate-filled notes on Kazimir. He had months and months of research between those pages. "We're about to hurt him," she said. "He will suffer. Do you want that?"

Trying to bring down Kazimir Skokan had killed Felix's career, his prospects, his marriage. Everything. Did he want to hurt him? "Yes."

She smiled. "Then do as we say, Mister Quaid. And you'll have your revenge."

CHAPTER 7

azi

A PAIR of hooded ones entered the room, unlocked the chains at his wrists, and lifted him from the chair.

"No trouble and we won't have to hurt you, prince."

Pain, he could endure. Especially as the price for knowledge. To kill his enemy, he had to know his enemy. And he couldn't learn from his cell.

They walked him down a narrow, dark corridor, deeper into a colder, darker area of the building and then into an elevator that carried them down several levels. The doors opened, revealing another long corridor painted black and purple, with an occasional dagger-and-eye motif.

The fine hairs on the back of Kazi's neck lifted. If this was about Nyx, the chaos goddess and progenitor of the nyktelios race, then whatever they had planned was unlikely to be pleasant.

Rhythmic chanting sounded up ahead, growing louder with every step.

Kazi lifted his chin. The hearts of those holding him raced, either from nerves, arousal or fear. Perhaps all three. Kazi could incapacitate two of them before the inhibitor chip kicked in and dropped him to his knees.

What if they planned to sacrifice him to Nyx? Sacrifices had happened before. The Nyxians had trapped a nyk, chained it to a pillar in the sunlight and made it bake until the sun had scorched all the fight right out of it, until it was weak, starved, beyond madness. Then they'd taken its head. He knew because he'd been part of the clean-up.

Kazi was hard to kill, but only when conscious. Unconscious, he might never see the final blow coming.

Fuck this.

He yanked his bound arms down, jerking the guards off balance. He swung his chained wrists up, smacking the man on the right under the chin and knocking him backward. Fangs sprang free, venom primed. He whirled on the second man, bared his teeth—

Fire rolled up his spine.

He cried out, but the shout never made it past his lips. He collapsed onto his side, fighting unconsciousness. He had to stay present, stay in the moment.

The pain receded, leaving him limp and gasping, and the remaining two guards hauled him back to his feet.

The chanting grew louder.

His head hung, too heavy to lift.

As the door ahead opened, he hauled his gaze up enough to see the crowd gathered around a black granite altar. Granite pillars jutted toward a domed ceiling. Twelve in total, like numbers on a clock face. They dragged him over channels in the floor. The glossy black altar had grooves carved in it too.

The men hauled him against it. He dug his heels in, resisting. Blood. He should have known. Why else would they have kept him alive? The channels in the stone were for collecting blood. *His* blood.

"No."

"Prince, if you fight again, there will be more pain," the Polish male said.

Kazi breathed hard, nostrils flaring. He couldn't do this. It spat in the face of everything the Brotherhood stood for. If Mikalis discovered what he'd done, there would be no forgiveness.

A weight slammed into his back, tipping him forward over the altar—a fist, a bat, didn't matter. A dozen hands were on him, shoving, heaving, pulling. Instincts to protect himself tore a growl free, and with it came the rush of power—triggering a new flood of pain.

The chanting, the pounding of his heart, and the hearts of the hundreds of people here, all swirled in a heady fog, trying to drown him.

Cold granite dug into his shoulders and back.

His coat was gone. His shirt torn free. The chains around his wrists vanished, and his arms were pulled open—their Christ on a cross.

He clamped his jaw shut. Venom spilled between his lips. Damn them! Damn them all! The chanting lapped at him, threatening to wash him away. Cold, sharp steel sliced up both forearms, and warm blood streamed. The chanting grew rapturous. The smell of human lust and hunger filled the air. He bucked, roared, but more chains held him down, and when the beast inside tried to rip free, the whole world exploded in jagged agony, plunging him into oblivion.

He shivered in the cold metal chair. They'd taken too much from him and unraveled his threads of control with it. He couldn't hide the fangs, couldn't pretend anymore. There was nobody to pretend for anyway. Just his own sanity.

He'd kill them.

Every single one of them.

He'd drink them down and bathe in their blood if that was what they wanted. Because that was the only way this ended. If they wanted a fucking nyktelios, then they were going the right way about it. One more visit to the altar and it wouldn't matter that he had a chip in his spine; he'd be too lost to feel anything.

For over a thousand years, he'd held absolute control.

Over a thousand years spent keeping his primal needs wrapped in mental chains.

But now the Nyxians were undoing it all, turning him back into the monster he'd fought so hard, and for so long, to be free of.

Where was Storm? Why hadn't they come for him?

The door opened, and Quaid stepped into the room, stopping abruptly, keeping his distance. His eyes widened. He looked away, his mouth curling in disgust.

Kazi straightened. They'd cleaned him up since the ritual, but left him shirtless. The savage slashes in his forearms had healed, leaving the skin pale and vulnerable. Eventually, even those scars would fade, but not the ones inside.

As Quaid leaned against the wall, his face turned away, a strange sense of shame cinched Kazi's heart. He hadn't orchestrated this, he hadn't wanted any of this, yet guilt squirmed inside, as though it had been his fault. Even after all this time, human emotions held their sway. "Why are you here?" His voice sounded gruff, broken.

"I think they're hoping you'll feed from me."

Kazi snarled and dropped his gaze to his lap. His vision splintered. Part of him liked the idea of taking Quaid and drinking his fill. His fangs throbbed. It took too much effort to hide them, another sign he was losing his grip on control. "They'll get you killed."

"But not you? You want me alive, after wanting me dead. So which is it?"

Kazi rolled his eyes. "There's more at stake here than your pathetic life."

Quaid's glare accused him of a thousand crimes. There was a stillness to him that Kazi hadn't noticed before. A solid confidence. Something or someone had given him that confidence. They'd probably told him all about Kazimir Skokan, told him what a monster he was, how evil he was, and how he deserved to suffer.

"You've seen the fangs and a hundred vampire movies and you think you know me. You think you know us? You have no idea."

"You don't think I'm aware of how little I know?" He crouched and tilted his head, eyeing Kazi. His gaze took in his bare chest, and if Kazi wasn't mistaken, there was an interest there that went beyond simple curiosity. He'd read the file Atlas had supplied on Felix Quaid. The man was a mess. Failed marriage, fucked-up life, but it had begun before his story on Kazi had tipped him over the edge. Buried deep in his high school records, there had been a brief rebellious phase, including drugs, alcohol, and male partners. Maybe he'd gotten those sexual encounters out of his system, but the way he admired Kazi now suggested more than casual interest.

A wicked, irritated part of Kazi sought to make Quaid hurt too. A few sharp words would do it, but he didn't have the heart. Quaid was too easy a target.

Quaid looked away again. His jaw worked, cheek twitching. "This whole thing is pretty fucked up," he muttered, half to himself.

"We agree in that."

"I don't know what's going on here. Some cult shit and vampires and fuck knows what else. Kazimir, I'm just trying to survive."

He believed him. "I can help with that."

"Yeah, I remember your kinda help." The man rolled his eyes. "I'm not into that, but thanks."

He'd been into it when his life had depended on it. "We made a deal."

"Yeah, you'd save me and give me a head start, I remember."

They were using him, just like they were using Kazi. He wasn't ever getting out of here. "Quaid, they're not letting you go. You've seen too much. Neither of us is getting out of this if we don't work together."

Quaid pulled a knee up and draped his arm over it. "Work together how?"

Kazi hadn't figured that part out yet. Every time he tried to overpower them, the chip disabled him. "I need to get their inhibitor out of me."

"Where it is?"

"Somewhere in my lower back."

"Shit."

"If you can smuggle a knife in here—"

He recoiled. "No way. I'm not cutting into your spine."

"I'll heal the damage you do."

He grimaced and shook his head. "And then what? You'll kill everyone here."

"Yes."

Quaid's smirk was almost charming. "I can't let you do that. They might be religious nuts, but they don't deserve to die."

How had it come to this? Kazi's survival relying on a fool? "You don't know what they're doing."

"You're a vampire. I'm not helping you kill them."

"Forget the vampire shit. You don't know anything, just what you've seen with your own eyes. Quaid, look at me. Look at the marks on my arms. They chained me down, cut open my veins, and bled me. I don't expect you to know what that means, but it's not good for anyone."

"Why? Huh?" he demanded, growing angrier by the second. "Why should I believe anything you say?"

He had no idea why Quaid should believe him. Whether it was Kazi trying to convince him or the cult, neither would save him.

"You didn't even tell me about the Brotherhood," he sneered. "I don't know anything because you won't tell me."

He chuckled. The Nyxians had probably revealed just enough to twist Felix against Kazi. "What did she tell you about us?"

Quaid winced and rubbed at his forehead. "I don't know, stories... She said Nyx made the nyktelios, and the Brotherhood work against them."

"We do. I exist to rid the world of nyktelios. It's all I've lived for for many, many centuries."

"But you're like them."

"No, I'm not. I have control. A nyktelios is... It's all of your human stories about vampires but a hundred times worse. They are mindless, vicious killing machines. But the worst of them, the oldest and most dangerous, are able to conceal that part of them. They slaughter humans, gorging themselves on chaos. We thought we were beating them, but lately, their numbers have been growing again. The Brotherhood does what's necessary to eradicate them, keeping humans safe in the process."

"What's the difference between you and the nyktelios? Huh? You're not selling me on the whole *you're good* thing. So tell me why I should help you, Kazimir?"

"I have orders to kill you because you got too close to me, to what I am. You got too close to the Brotherhood. If we're exposed, it'll make our job a thousand times harder. We don't need humans getting in the way. It only makes our task worse. We protect the Brotherhood at all costs, because without it, you had better believe the world you know would be a very different place."

"How different?" Quaid asked quietly.

"The nyktelios are a hungry plague. Like locusts, they'd swarm and feast until there was nothing left. Their only belief is that humans are slaves, put on this earth to feed on and satisfy their needs. They are ruthless, almost immortal, and they need to be stopped."

Quaid wasn't a fool. He could see the logic in all of this.

While Quaid thought it over, Kazi rested his head back and closed his eyes. Quaid's heartbeat was a strong, steady beat, and a siren song to Kazi's hunger. He did need to feed if he'd have any hope of keeping control of himself, but Quaid would never allow it, and he had no desire to force him to obey again.

"What makes the Brotherhood so different?"

"We have rules. We never feed from the vein, we never create feeders or others like us, and we never care. We do what must be done."

"All right, say I believe you. If I escape and call someone at your brotherhood? Then what?"

Kazi winced. "They'd come, and they'd free me."

"But?"

"Everything that's happening here, it must all be destroyed. Nothing can escape."

"They'll kill me too."

Kazi nodded.

"Fuck them, then," Quaid snorted

Kazi felt his own smile lift his mood a little. Quaid was taking this all remarkably well.

"So let me get this straight." Quaid took a breath. "My options are—one, I feed information about you back to the cult leader, and she kills me when they've learned whatever they want to about you, or two, I help you escape and you kill me right after. I'm starting to think I'm fucked whichever way this ends."

"The Nyxians must be stopped. The rest... I can delay."

His eyes sparkled with a touch of ironic humor. "Their leader said the same about the Brotherhood. She really doesn't like you."

"As you can see"—he rattled his chains—"we don't get along."

Quaid huffed a humorless laugh and shook his head. "And I thought you were just a pretty face." He seemed to catch his own meaning and winced. "I mean, you know... all those Instagram posts." He coughed, clearing his throat.

Kazi narrowed his eyes. He could have let it slide, but since Quaid had mentioned it... "You think I'm pretty, Felix?"

"No," he denied and snorted. "But a lot of people do." His gaze skipped everywhere except back to Kazi. "All suckered into your bad-boy charisma."

Bad-boy charisma. "I'm not interested in them."

Quaid's glance met Kazi's. There it was again, a spark of interest. A curious little flicker of hunger. It had been there at the bar too, right before Kazi had lured him away to kill him. Felix Quaid was hot for him.

Quaid turned away, shoved to his feet and knocked on the door. With his back to Kazi, he didn't see how Kazi admired his fine physique, even in the cult's loose, unflattering clothes. He knew Quaid had muscle. He'd had more before his downfall, but his strength was still in there. Beneath all that self-doubt and reeling guilt was a man of honor, a man of integrity. If the fight back in the parking lot had been a fair one, Kazi would have enjoyed sparring with him.

"Quaid?"

He glanced over his shoulder.

"I trust you'll do the right thing."

Quaid's soft eyes narrowed. He gave a curt nod, then left. Kazi was alone again. The cold returned. He hadn't felt cold with Quaid close, hadn't felt so alone, so vulnerable. A part of him ached to have him back, even if it was just to talk. With the cuts aching and his hunger gnawing on his mind, he feared what might become of him if the Nyxians bled him again.

CHAPTER 8

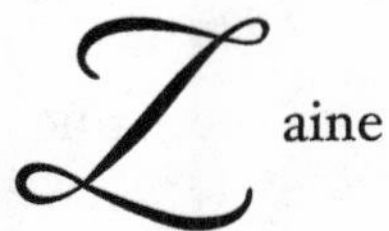aine

THE HOLOSCREEN HOVERING above the smart table blinked with Kazi's last known location in midtown Manhattan. The timestamp was over four days ago. Deleted CCTV footage showed Kazi leaving the club and his target, Felix Quaid, leaving moments after him.

The ex-journalist was just a man. No threat to Kazi.

But Kazi hadn't checked in.

"Hey," Storm grumbled, joining Zaine next to the table. "What have you got?"

Zaine pinched the air, zooming in on Quaid's outline, then swiped that image away and flicked his fingers, bringing up a cascade of more deleted footage from the nearby cameras. "Kazi leads him away." He pointed at the picture of Kazi in his long coat. Even on grainy CCTV footage, the prick was handsome. Shame about his personality. "To the nearby parking lot. My guess is he planned to overpower Quaid, dump him in the trunk and drop the body where he'd never be found. But..."

Storm folded his muscular arms. "Go on."

"CCTV footage catches Kazi, then Quaid, and then—" He clicked his finger, and the screen went dark.

"What?"

He shrugged. "Nothing."

"I can see that, Zaine. What does *nothing* mean?"

"It means, whatever happened, Atlas didn't capture it."

"A glitch?"

"I had Octavius go over it. No glitch. Atlas is missing fifteen minutes of footage. When the feed comes back—" Zaine flicked his fingers again, sweeping the new images onto the screen. They showed the parking lot ramp, but nothing of interest, just the jump in time from the timestamp.

Storm unfolded his arms and braced himself on the table, peering closer. "Atlas never glitches."

"Which is what Octavius said. He got all snarly and bent out of shape about it. He says he's running diagnostics to see if someone got into the system somehow."

"Someone got into Atlas?" Storm asked, eyebrows raised.

"Let's hope not." If they had, then the whole Brotherhood was compromised. Which was probably why Octavius was losing his shit. "Kazi's car was still there. Aiko's bringing it back now. Kazi's not answering his phone, and we know it's permanently attached to his hip. The people he met at the bar said he was due to go back but never showed up."

"Fuck." Storm straightened.

"Quaid's missing too. He was scheduled to upload a new podcast episode two nights ago, but he's gone dark. His listeners have started a thread on Reddit. They think he's been kidnapped because of a story he was working on about an influencer..."

Storm growled, a sound that always shivered through Zaine, and not for good reasons. "Could this Quaid have gotten the drop on Kazi somehow?"

"Eric's taking a look at the man's apartment in Sunnyside, but he doesn't seem like much." Zaine switched screens, bringing up all of Atlas's files on Felix Quaid. "Ex-war reporter. He's got family. No criminal record. Nothing to suggest he's a threat beyond, you know, asking too many questions about Kazi. There's no way a man like him outwits Kazimir."

"If this was you, I'd think you'd dropped the body and taken yourself off for some R&R."

"Yeah, but this is perfect Kazi. He's the dick who does everything by the Brotherhood playbook."

"This is out of character," Storm growled. "Bring everyone in." He pulled his phone from his pocket, probably dialing Mikalis. "Someone has one of our own, and they're about to fuckin' wish they'd picked a different way to die."

CHAPTER 9

elix

HE DIDN'T GO ANYWHERE without an escort, and they kept his door locked. For all the free food and free reading material, he was a prisoner, although a well-fed one. Breakfast, lunch, and dinner like clockwork. He hadn't eaten so well in years. It wasn't charity though. He figured they expected him to be Kazimir's feeder, and he was damned if he was hanging around long enough to become his bloodslave.

The hoods collected him again and walked the same route to the leader's office. He still didn't know her name, and when he'd asked, she'd merely smiled.

She greeted him this time by sliding a tatty leather-bound book across her desk. He sat, opened the book, and frowned at the foreign words, all handwritten. "I can't read that."

"It's Slavic. A chronicle of medieval kings, in fact. Including the Kazimierz." She produced a stack of printed pages. "The translation. The section you'll be interested in is on page three hundred."

"A king? But you all call him prince?"

"Kazimir was never a king." She smiled at his confusion and headed for the door. "You'll understand more when you read it. This door will be locked behind me. Read and learn about the true Kazimir."

After she'd left, he immediately rummaged through her other books and documents on the desk, then examined everything in her drawers. No computer. His efforts revealed nothing of use, and weary from all their cryptic bullshit, he dropped into the desk chair and dragged his hands down his face. "Fine, I'll read your propaganda, lady."

He prepared himself for the worst, but nothing could have prepared him for the horror of Kazimir's past.

CHAPTER 10

Kazi

WHEN THEY CAME AGAIN, he knew not to fight, but as soon as they escorted him to the room where the acolytes chanted, Kazi fought anyway—and failed, earning himself a blast from the inhibitor.

Like before, chains swung down, pinning him to the altar. They spread his arms and cut...

Rabid with disgust and indignation, he let his head fall to the side and looked at each of them. Hoods hid most of their faces, but some he'd recognize later. They would be the first to die when he got free.

The wounds healed, his body fighting, and so they cut again. He'd missed that the first time, having fallen unconscious, and he almost wished he'd missed it this time too.

Their blades came down a third time, slicing him open. Blood ran in scarlet rivulets, painting a pattern across the floor and filling concentric circles, then spilled over an edge, disappearing somewhere below.

The chanting made him sick with rage.

They'd destroy him, who he was, who he'd made himself since Mikalis had found him, saved him.

He couldn't let them have his control. He had to hold on.

A face among the hoods caught his eye. Hard jaw, lips pressed into a thin line, and when he tipped his head up, the hood shifted, revealing Felix.

No...

Kazi blinked, and his vision swam, tears leaking from his eyes. When he looked again, someone else stood in Quaid's place. He hoped he'd imagined him there. Quaid wouldn't be a part of this. He hated Kazi, but this was worse than hate. This was wrong.

His control slipped away with every drop of blood.

He didn't want to be that creature again. He didn't want to be the prince history had torn from its pages, his sins too terrible to transcribe. He didn't want to let the others down, let Mikalis down... He didn't want to be the monster Quaid believed him to be.

But the truth was, he always had been.

CHAPTER 11

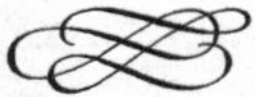

elix

HE COULDN'T WATCH ANYMORE. When they'd brought him there, he'd thought he'd wanted to see it, see Kazimir punished, see him sprawled on that altar, but he knew he'd been wrong as soon as he'd stepped into the room. All of it was wrong. It didn't matter what he'd read about Kazimir—bleeding him like an animal couldn't ever be right.

Nobody noticed him slip out—they were all too hypnotized by the ritual to care.

He hurried along, keeping his borrowed hood up and his head down. Not too fast. He couldn't look suspicious.

Maybe he could just keep on walking, walk right out the front door? His heart was so damn loud everyone probably heard it. Although there didn't seem to be anyone around. They were all back in that room... bleeding a man for reasons he didn't understand.

A man who had slaughtered whole villages...

He wasn't thinking about those books and the things he'd read about Kazimir.

Sickness flopped in Quaid's gut. He'd seen terrible things, reported from the aftermath of battles, but being a part of that ritual was a whole different level of fucked up. He had to get out of here. Get far away from everything. Find Julia, kiss Rosa, hear her laugh, and then maybe never see them again to save them from the monsters that might follow him home.

The large arched doors loomed ahead.

He rushed toward them, put his hands on the wood, ready to push... Nobody was going to stop him. He was alone. He could shove through and run into the woods.

But then what?

Was he going to run forever? If what Kazimir had said was true, the Brotherhood would find him and kill him. It could be a few days, a few weeks, months maybe, but they'd find him. If he ran from this, he'd die. But he'd die if he stayed.

And then there was Kazimir...

The things he'd done... whole villages murdered. He'd slaughtered anyone and everyone—men, women, children. He *deserved* to be tortured.

If he believed it.

But the whole truth was rarely reported, especially in history. Bias was everything.

Kazimir was more than the cult books had made him out to be. There were always two sides to every news story. And history was written by the winners.

Could Kazimir have done those things? Yes, he probably had. But the Kazimir chained to the chair, the thousand-year-old man who believed in stopping monsters just like him? Maybe Felix was a fool, but he didn't believe that Kazimir was the same as the prince from the history books.

Quaid couldn't run from this story. He had to see it through to its end.

He stepped back from the door, turned on his heel and headed back into the building, with no real idea where he was going.

Head down, he walked in, striding along as though he had every right to be wandering around. He needed to find a kitchen, somewhere with cutlery and knives... something to get that chip out of Kazimir. He'd help him and make him promise not to kill everyone. The cops could deal with it all, a court of law, real justice. The Brotherhood might need more convincing to keep Felix alive, but if he saved their brother, they'd thank him. Maybe.

He nodded at a few people dressed in uniform, not in their gowns. The gowns marked him as some kind of disciple. After reading the books, he'd told the leader he wanted to see Kazimir punished, and that was when she'd handed him a gown and told him to join them.

They'd be searching for him soon, if they weren't already.

If he could find a knife and get back to his room without anyone seeing, then ask to visit Kazi, that was when he'd cut the inhibitor out of him.

He pushed through a pair of swinging double doors into a dining hall. A few people at the counters noticed his arrival. Ignoring them, Felix veered toward the cutlery station and grabbed a knife.

"Hey, you..."

Shit.

"You're not supposed to be up here."

"Yeah, yeah, sorry," Felix mumbled. "Is the, er, bathroom around here?" He slipped the knife up his sleeve.

The doors flew open. "Stop him!"

He bolted and made it halfway across the dining hall in seconds. But they were gaining on him. He flung a chair behind him, vaulted a table, and dashed for the nearest door—straight into two uniform-clad cultists. A punch flew at him, striking his jaw, snapping his head away. He sprawled into waiting arms and kicked out, catching one of the men in the knee hard enough to make him buckle, and then there were six of them on him all at once. He dropped and hugged himself against an onslaught of kicks.

A bark in a foreign language stopped the beating, leaving Felix panting on the floor.

The leader crouched. "That was foolish." She swept a drop of blood from his bottom lip and brought it to her mouth. "We do not give second chances."

Her men grabbed him and lifted him to his feet.

"You people are insane," he snapped, kicking out. "This is all fuckin' insane!" He heaved and bucked, unbalancing his guards but not by enough.

The nameless woman laughed. "Throw him in with Kazimir. Maybe he'll survive."

They marched him from the dining hall, down different corridors again, turning left and right as though to deliberately confuse him, until they came to an ominous metal door full of bolts and one tiny slitted window. That wasn't a room. It was a damn cage for an animal.

"Wait..." He tried to dig his feet into the floor.

They heaved the door open and threw him into a wall of thick, wet darkness.

The door clanged shut. Bolts slammed home.

And Quaid froze.

Shit, it was so damn dark he couldn't see his fingers in front of his face. He blinked fast, trying to see something, *anything*.

Lights suddenly flooded on, sending a spear of agony to the back of his head. He hissed and staggered back into a corner.

The light had chased away every single shadow and illuminated Kazimir chained upright, his back to the wall and his arms spread, as though this were some kind of medieval torture chamber.

"God..." Felix gasped.

Kazimir's head drooped, chin on his chest. The curtain of dark hair hid his face. Wet trousers clung to him. Puddles pooled around the floor, below where his feet dangled, barely touching the floor.

They'd washed him, washed the blood off. The cuts on his arms had healed, but the lines glowed pale, almost translucent.

Quaid shuffled back to the door. There didn't seem to be any cameras, but there had to be some, right?

Shit, what was he supposed to do now?

He dabbed at his split lip and winced away the aches in his side from the kicks they'd dealt him.

A small, thick chuckle fell from Kazimir's lips. Then the laughter rumbled, turning darker. That wasn't his typical laugh, the laugh Quaid hated to hear but always fuckin' played over and over on YouTube or deliberately searched for on an Instagram reel.

Kazimir lifted his head. His smile pulled his lips thin over sharp fangs. His eyes, a cool blue before, shone silver now.

Fuck. They'd thrown Felix in with the monster.

At least he was chained. Were they strong enough?

"Hey," he called, hoping someone outside could hear. "Hey? What am I supposed to do?"

"Feed him," a gruff voice replied. "And pray to whatever god you worship that he doesn't kill you."

He'd never really put much stock in religion. Maybe now would've been a good time to be a believer. "Feed him," Quaid muttered. "Fuck." He raised his hands, and Kazimir tracked the motion. "You're still in there, right? That's how this works? I mean, I don't know much, but I know you're normally in control of... this, and right now, that's not working out for you, right?"

The vampire stared, unblinking. There wasn't much of the laughing, sassy, smart-ass Kazimir in his eyes now, none of the bitchy humor, the smarter-than-thou attitude, none of that slyness that ticked all the bad-boy boxes his fans swooned over. Quaid almost wished for that man back, just a piece of him, because the thing looking at him now wasn't a man at all. And he was pretty sure if he went anywhere near it, it would tear his throat out.

"This doesn't get better for you, right? Unless you feed?" He wasn't sure how it all worked, but everyone else seemed to, and they all wanted him to open a vein for a blood-hungry mass murderer.

"Kazi." He stepped closer, hands still raised. "You don't mind if I call you Kazi, right? Look, here's the thing, I don't want to die here, okay? I got a little girl who needs her daddy, despite me being a dick for most of her life. I'd like to be around to make that right. Maybe you can help with that?"

Kazimir blinked, and that might have been the first time since Felix had entered the room. Was that a good thing? Kazimir's chest heaved, dripping wet and lean, with a defined six-pack of muscles Felix had noticed a few times before. The fact he was gorgeous was damn hard to miss when he threw it in everyone's faces.

How to feed a hungry vampire without dying?

He should have paid more attention when Julia had made him watch *Twilight*. Although he didn't remember the vampires being savage and mindless like this.

He was going to have to get this done, and with Kazimir rabid, it would be a bloodbath. He had to find a way to reach the man behind the monster.

"You asked me if I thought you were pretty? I denied it because..." Felix licked his lips. "It's complicated, all right? Always has been. I mean, I like women, but... Then there's you, and yeah, okay, you're pretty, and a sonofabitch, because you know you're pretty and you're making me fuckin' say it. I hate that about you too, by the way. You're so fuckin' gorgeous, and all this time, I've hated you for destroying my life, and then I catch myself rewatching your video interviews like a hardcore fan, and I can tell myself it's research, but it's not. And I hate you for that too."

Kazi blinked again. His breaths shuddered, their see-sawing rhythm easing. Maybe that was a sign he was getting through to him.

"I mean, it's not like I've jerked off to your pictures or anything..."

Okay, maybe that had been too much information. Hopefully, Kazimir wouldn't remember this conversation. Or maybe Felix would be dead, and it wouldn't matter anyway.

Kazimir's brow creased, pinching. His nostrils flared, and his chin jerked. He moved like an animal, all jagged and instinctual, a predator tracking its prey. Shit, that made Felix the prey. But as he watched, those jerking twitches smoothed, and the man shuddered, making the chains at his wrists clink.

"Those people outside this room, they're trying really hard to get me to hate you even more. They want me to think you deserve this. But I'm not one of their brainwashed cult members. I'm a reporter. Or I was. I report the facts, and I see you now, fighting with that thing inside you. You're trying to get it under control. I see that, Kazi. Okay? I see you. And I figure you maybe need to hear that right now. Maybe it helps. Because I really need you not to kill me..."

Kazimir thumped his head back against the wall. He swallowed, long and slow. "Help me."

"I want to. I do. But I'm not gonna lie. I'm scared."

"I know. *I smell it on you.*" His fangs gleamed, dripping with some kind of glistening substance.

Quaid pursed his lips. "You're not helpful."

"*I'm trying...*"

"Yeah, okay, I get that." He moved closer again, and Kazi dropped his head, fixing his stare on Quaid, pinning him to the spot. "Is it going to hurt?"

Kazi ground his teeth. "If you want it to."

"What? No. Fuck. Never mind." He squeezed his eyes shut. He was really going to do this. "Will you promise me this isn't going to kill me? Tell me that."

"I... promise. I will not kill you."

He dropped the steak knife into his hand. "You see this? Fuck with me and I'll stab you in the heart, okay?"

Kazi's smile bloomed, the brilliant but fake one. "Come here, Felix," he growled.

Felix swallowed and shuffled a little closer. Kazi was taller than him, but they'd slung him by the chains so he could just rest his toes on the floor. He'd lost his shoes. Although why Felix noticed that now, he wasn't sure. Probably because he didn't want to gaze into his eyes and see their shining ice-blueness, because that blue meant Kazi was back under control, and *that* meant Felix had to let the vampire sink his fangs into some part of him and *feed*.

"Do this, and I will protect you," Kazi whispered. Felix watched his lips move, forming the words. "Help me and I will fight for you, against them, against the Brotherhood. I don't want to lose myself, Felix. I can't be the blood prince again. Save me from that and I'll save you from them."

Felix looked up into startlingly beautiful eyes. "Who is going to save me from you?"

He had no answer, but his eyes promised terrible, wonderful things. Felix absolutely did not want to do this, but some primal part of him hungered for it, as though an ancient part of Felix recognized something rare and wonderful in Kazi and wanted it.

"Don't make me regret this, you asshole." Felix closed the final step between them and turned his face away, exposing his neck. His heart raced, and his head told him to run. He clutched the knife like a religious talisman, as though it could save him.

The shock came—not from the bite—but from Kazi locking his legs around Felix's thighs. He jerked close, groin to hard groin.

Felix got a hand between them and tried to push at Kazi's chest, but Kazi struck. His teeth tore in, and pain boiled through Felix's veins. He gasped, but as quickly as the agony had come, it receded, leaving him lightheaded and detached. It should have hurt; the fangs pulled, widening the wound. Kazi's mouth scorched Felix's skin, his tongue teasing blood from the bite—but with each new stroke from Kazi's tongue, each swallow that rolled through the vampire, Felix wanted *more*.

The hand he'd wedged between them to push Kazi away—he used it to dig his blunt fingernails in, clinging on to ensure Kazi didn't stop. He moaned, overcome. His cock ached hot, tingling to be touched. He rolled his hips, grinding his dick against Kazi's firm thigh. The vampire grunted, then made some kind of resisting moan of his own and shifted his hips. The hot rod now rubbing Felix's dick could only be Kazi's cock. He wanted him too, like *that*.

Felix rubbed faster, jerking, driving himself harder and harder, needing more friction, more heat, more of Kazi's delicious dick rubbing his own. It was like the times he'd pumped himself breathless to Kazi's pictures. Hating him, but wanting to fuck him too. Only, this time, Kazi had him in his grip, his teeth in his neck, his cock dry-fucking Felix's, and it was a thousand times better than any hate-filled fantasy.

"Harder," Felix grunted, digging his fingers into Kazi's chest while clamping down with his other hand on Kazi's restrained arm, around one of Kazi's quivering biceps.

Felix was out of his mind, mad and drunk all at once. But he didn't care. He needed to come against Kazi's cock, with Kazi's teeth in his throat, his tongue stroking his neck. Every tug on the wound tugged on his cock too. "Fuck, more..." His hips thrust. If he could just get his dick right next to Kazi's heat, right there—he moaned, so close to coming he couldn't breathe, couldn't think. Fuck—he needed this. He'd needed it for years, to lose himself completely, to fuck another man and be allowed to relish it. "Ugh, goddamn." Pleasure pumped through him, deep into his dick. He came, spilling in pulses into his underwear, pumping slick heat so close to Kazi's dick that he had to feel it too. He wanted that, wanted Kazi to know what this was.

The vampire's fangs were no longer in his neck.

That was good, probably.

Sleepy, fucked, and wrecked, he turned his head and looked into Kazi's eyes. His mouth was right there, his lips full and hot. Felix knew that because he was kissing them, teasing them, tasting Kazi and blood and...

He pulled back. His heart had found its way to his head and was thudding too hard and too fast, pulling blackness in front of the edges of his sight. "I think... I'm gonna..."

"Guards!" Kazi yelled.

He couldn't pass out. He couldn't.

"I'm sorry," Kazi whispered. "I'm sorry. Felix... stay awake."

There were others in the room. They had their hands on him.

He tried to fight them off, but the walls fell, tipping him sideways. They caught him, walked him forward. Why wasn't his body working? What the fuck had Kazi done to him? He stole a glance behind him and caught sight of Kazimir still chained to the wall. His skin was flushed, his eyes bright, his cock hard, but his expression was full of regret, as though the world were ending, and he'd caused it.

CHAPTER 12

azi

THE DOOR SLAMMED SHUT, but the lights stayed on, burning the shadows away. He was so fucking hard all he would have to do was think about Quaid and he'd come, but that was the problem. He hadn't meant to take so much, hadn't meant to pour more than enough venom into him to turn him into a love-struck feeder, probably forever. He should have taken a small amount, but he'd been starved, and as soon as his fangs had pierced warm, ripe flesh, he'd been lost.

For centuries, he'd resisted.

The Brotherhood drank blood from bags, never from the vein, because it made it so much harder to resist doing it again and again and again, until men and women like Felix had no choice but to submit and spill their blood. He'd taken that choice from Felix, and he'd fucking known it even as he had devoured him. He could have stopped sooner. Should have let him go. But he'd wanted to feast on him, to fuck him, and when he'd responded like he had, moaning and bucking, demanding more until he'd spilled against Kazi's dick... Kazi was a man too, and he'd wanted Felix in those carnal ways.

By Nyx, he'd tasted so good...

More than good. He'd tasted like every brilliant climax at once. If he hadn't been restrained, he'd have taken Felix on the floor, then against the wall, sucked him, and fucked him, and made him writhe in all the best ways.

Kazi hadn't felt desire like he did for Felix in... He wasn't sure he ever had. It had been different, more maddening, yet somehow *easier*. It didn't make any sense, and he lacked the knowledge to understand it, which in itself was a surprise. Over a thousand years and he'd never tasted anyone like Felix Quaid.

The Nyxian leader entered the room, her expression smug. "Well done. You kept him alive. I didn't think you'd last." She dropped her gaze to the erection tenting his trousers. "In more ways than one."

He bared his teeth. "With every hour you keep me here, the Brotherhood gets closer."

"It's already too late, prince. Their downfall, and yours, is in motion and has been for some time."

She couldn't have gotten to them. She was just the head of one group. And mortal. The Brotherhood was eternal. Although he knew that not to be true. They'd lost brothers, lost battles. And this nameless woman had a confidence about her, warning of more than he was seeing. "What have you done?"

"Don't worry yourself. Rest, replenish. We'll need one more bleeding ritual from you, and then it'll be over." She wet her lips and gazed at his dick again, her thoughts all over her face. She took a step closer and brushed the back of her hand over his cock, sending rippling shivers down his spine. "I can relieve that for you, prince."

"Move closer, then, witch. I promise not to tear out your throat when I come."

Her laugh was a wicked tease that swirled around the room long after she'd gone.

What she hadn't noticed, and neither had the guards, was the glint of Felix's steak knife lying on the floor near the wall.

Kazi smiled. "Clever Felix."

And now that Kazi had downed his fill of fresh blood, right from the vein, he might be able to withstand the temporary agony the chip delivered long enough to dislocate his thumbs and slip through the chains holding his wrists.

There was one way to find out...

THEY COLLECTED him two days later. At least, it felt like two days—hard to know in the windowless cell. This time, he didn't fight. And when they approached the altar room with its incessant chanting, he secretly smiled.

As they marched him through their congregation toward the altar, he gave them no resistance. What he was about to do, it was dangerous. Control went both ways. He could have it taken from him or lose it himself. And if everything went to plan, control was going to be his biggest battle.

They laid him on his back over cold granite and draped heavy chains over him.

And then she came, the witch.

Her hood framed her smiling face. "It has been an honor, prince."

They planned to kill him. If it hadn't been for Felix's knife, these moments might have been his last.

"What's your name?" he asked.

"Vesna Dragovic of the Dragovic tribe. My village and its people were wiped from the map by a monster some twelve hundred years ago." She spoke calmly, as though she were reporting on the weather, but an ancient vengeance pulled a wicked smile to her lips.

"Of course, I'm not that old, but my mother said I had an old soul. She died with your name on her lips, as did her mother before her, and so on. As far back as the little girl you missed, hiding in the burning debris of her home, hiding from the monster who killed everyone she knew, drank their blood and strung their bodies from the oldest village trees. He was the blood prince, she told her daughters, and his name was Kazimir." Vesna leaned over him. "That name has been whispered over the lips of generations since her. I should thank you, prince. You see, if it weren't for you, I wouldn't know about Nyx, your goddess. Nor would I know that the only way to resurrect her is to destroy the Brotherhood who betrayed her."

Old guilt hardened his heart. He did not recall her village or her people. But he didn't doubt her words. Telling her he'd changed, that the Brotherhood had saved him, would mean little. Hers was an old vengeance, the kind etched in stone. "You can't destroy the Brotherhood. It's more than me, more than even Mikalis."

"Watch me." She spun, fanning her cloak, and nodded to her assistants.

The hoods moved in.

"Vesna, wait." Kazi fixed the leader in his sights. "The Brotherhood protects people like your family. We stop the nyks. I was... Back then, I was a nyk."

She laughed. "That's just what he tells you, Kazimir. They're lies." She descended the steps and joined her chanting acolytes.

Two hooded figures approached, gleaming knives raised, and the chanting built toward its crescendo. Whatever their motives, whatever they needed his blood for, it ended now.

He just hoped Felix wasn't here to witness it.

They raised their blades in unison, like mirror images on either side of Kazi's prone body. He fought the desperate instinct to attack. They leaned over him, blades turned downward. And he knew all too well the feel of the metal slicing him open.

Never again.

He thrust his fists up, snapped the chains and struck the

acolytes. Bones shattered. They reeled, screaming, and for a few moments, silence fell over the room.

Perhaps they didn't understand what they were seeing, or worse, they did and knew what came next.

Kazi tore the chains free, scattering fragments into the crowd, and leaped from the altar. His vision funneled, his target clear. Vesna. She knew it too—fear widened her eyes—she knew he was coming for her.

CHAPTER 13

Felix

AFTER KAZI HAD FED, they'd bundled Felix back to his room, hooked him up to an intravenous drip, and put him under.

He woke sometime later. Maybe days, he wasn't sure. The days and nights had all bled into one—but he came around feeling pretty damn good. He should have been disgusted but wasn't. When he touched his neck, where Kazi had bitten, the feeling wasn't grotesque. The shivers felt... good. Felt right. What did that say about him?

He'd helped a man—mostly a man—in trouble, and he'd struck a deal that meant he got to live. It was that simple. Kazi had said he'd protect him, and right now, he needed it. Although he'd lost the knife, so how he was going to get Kazi out of that room was a whole other problem.

They came, unhooked the drip, and told him to dress, then handed him a ritual gown.

He obeyed, if only to get out of the room he'd been trapped in for days.

He didn't trust Kazi, but he trusted he wanted to escape. He could rely on that. Everything else around him was a fucking nightmare.

Like before, they escorted him toward the altar room. The chanting was building to its crescendo, which meant they were late. If he hadn't lost the knife, he could have saved Kazi from this torture. When he stepped through those doors, he knew what he'd see: a man being bled against his will. Vampire or not, it was fucking wrong.

He'd have to watch it. Then they'd make him feed him again, and around and around it would go.

His guards shoved him through the doors.

The chanting cut off.

A murmur rippled through the crowd. Felix tried to get a look at the altar. Were they too late? Kazi leaped into the air, arms spread, teeth bared, his hair wild and eyes silver.

"Shit!" The guard at Felix's right lurched forward, but the guard at his left turned on his heel. "Oh, hell no."

The crowd erupted in a surge of bodies, all of them heading toward the exit—and Felix. He bolted left, out of the way, but still got tangled in a crush. Hands tugged at him, trying to pull him back. Panic bleached their horror-filled faces.

Then the screaming started. He knew those screams. He'd heard them in the midst of gunfire and booming shells. The wounded had howled. Some had screamed because they'd seen friends blown to pieces. There were no bombs here and no guns, only Kazimir tearing into them.

Kazimir moved fast from one to the next to the next, crippling each of them in a single, bone-breaking blow. Then the crowd surged again, trying to sweep Felix with them in their panic. He shoved back, fought a path through and stumbled out one side.

This was chaos. And a bloodbath.

"Kazi!"

Kazi whipped his head up. A man dangled from his grip. He didn't appear to have been bitten, but there was madness in Kazi's silver eyes that suggested the bite would come next. If Kazi was all about control, then he was losing.

"Kazi..." Felix raised his hands. He just had to figure out how to placate a millennia-old, pissed-off vampire without getting his own throat torn out—and figure it out fast. "Hey, hi... It's me. Fuck—" He dropped his hood, forgetting he was wearing the damn thing.

The growl that rumbled from Kazi wasn't the good kind. Felix's heart hiccupped, tripping over a sudden bout of panic. And then Kazi dropped his prey and came straight for Felix like a shark through water.

"Oh shit..." He backed away—Kazi was almost on him—backed up faster, tripped, fell against a wall and froze with Kazi a statue of furious male inches in front of him. Kazi seethed, breathing like a rabid animal.

"Hey," the word fell out of him. "Please don't kill me? You promised."

Kazi blinked, snarled, then caught sight of the desperate people all trying to squeeze through the doors. When he faced Felix again, his glare softened. "What the fuck are you doing?" Kazi growled.

He sounded more reasonable than his rabid appearance suggested.

"Stopping you from making a mistake?"

"I'm not making a mistake. These people butchered and bled me. They deserve—"

"Maybe—"

Kazi lunged and thrust his forearm under Felix's chin, pinning him to the wall. His silvery eyes filled Felix's vision. "*Maybe*?" he repeated. But with each passing second, the madness faded from his eyes. He blinked in quick succession and pulled back an inch, taking his weight off Felix's neck. He was clearly battling with his own thoughts, and he wasn't the only one. The chaos, the carnage, and now Kazi as close as they'd been when he'd bitten Felix...

Kazi withdrew suddenly, taking himself back several steps. "Damn them... and you, Felix."

Felix slumped. "What did I do?"

Kazi huffed and ran a hand through his ragged hair. He turned his gaze to the fleeing people. "Stopped me from making a mistake."

"That didn't sound like a thank you, but I'll take it."

"It wasn't a fuckin' thank you. I lost Vesna in the panic." Kazi jogged back to the altar, then crouched at its edge, apparently forgetting the acolytes, some of whom had noticed he was no longer tearing into them.

Some hung back, watching... waiting.

"Hey!" Felix barked. Did they want to die? "Get out of here!" The last of them scurried off, leaving him alone with a calmer Kazimir. He approached his side and watched as he skimmed his fingers around a groove in the floor. Intermittent holes had delivered his blood to the floor below, another sub-ground basement.

"We need to get down there," Kazi said.

"Yeah." Felix shifted from foot to foot and checked the doors. "Or we could just leave before they come back with guns."

Kazi flashed his photogenic smile. "Then can I kill them?"

"Fuck. Are you joking?" Kazi blinked. He wasn't joking, but Felix laughed as though he were, or maybe as though he were losing his mind right here, in this room. Kazi, though, wasn't laughing. But he had kept his smile.

"You have a lovely laugh, Quaid."

Felix choked on his laugh, cutting it off. He cleared his throat. He was definitely losing his mind, because as wild and vicious as Kazi looked, he wasn't afraid of him. Kazimir wouldn't hurt him. They'd made a deal. "I, er... We should..." A broken chain link caught his eye, and then the rest, all scattered around the altar. "How did you get out?"

"I used the knife you left and cut out the inhibitor chip."

Holy shit, then Kazi was free from the pain device. He could do anything, kill anyone, kill them all. But he hadn't. And when Felix recalled seeing the bodies fall, Kazi hadn't bitten them. He'd lashed out, but none lay on the ground now. This wasn't the aftermath of a battle, like so many Felix had seen in war zones. Kazi had hurt them, but they'd all escaped. He'd let them live.

"Do not worry." Kazi straightened, and Felix found himself too close to the man. Again. And that same urge to reach out and touch him almost had him doing exactly that. To touch his face, skim those sharp lines, taste his lips.

"I promised to protect you, and I will." His eyes glittered their stunning blue. "You're mine now, Felix Quaid." He turned on his heel and strode toward the doors.

Definitely losing his mind, because the sway in Kazi's hips held some kind of hypnotic power over Felix's reeling thoughts, funneling all his attention into admiring the roll of muscle down the man's back. Then his thoughts caught up with Kazi's words. "Kazi, wait... 'Mine' how exactly?" He hurried behind him. "Mine like... I don't know, like we're friends or something, because I didn't sign up for that. We're not friends."

"Friends?" Kazi opened the door, checked the way was clear and strode down the corridor. "No." He frowned, glancing behind him. "Not that."

At least he seemed as troubled by that idea as Felix was. "We're in the middle of nowhere with a bunch of psychos who can't decide if they want to worship you or kill you. Can we just... get out of here?"

"This isn't about me, despite what Vesna says. It's about blood, and I need to know why they've been harvesting mine."

An elevator waited ahead. They both stepped inside, and Kazi hit the down button, not up and the way out. Did he *want* them to recapture him? "One look downstairs and then we go, right?"

Kazi half-nodded or shrugged a shoulder. It wasn't clear.

"Kazimir?"

"Yes, Quaid?"

Had he always said his name like that, with a rumbling sultriness that shivered beneath Felix's skin? "We're leaving after this."

"Fine, I won't kill anyone."

"That's not what I said."

"No, but you were thinking it." He smiled a million-likes smile.

Felix spluttered a laugh. Could he be warming up to this asshole? "I hate you." That felt better, as though he'd rebalanced the sliding scale of hatred and loathing between them.

"I am aware."

The elevator pinged, and the doors rumbled open. A plastic sheet hung from the ceiling. Kazi swept it aside. The lights were dim, like emergency lighting. Tubes dangled from the ceiling, attached to six-foot-high glass-fronted pods—thirty man-sized containers at a quick count. A central bank of screens and monitoring equipment ran like a spine down the middle of the room and into thick darkness at the far end. More plastic sheets blocked the view of whatever was back there.

Cool air whispered over Felix's neck, lifting fine hairs, and goosebumps sprinkled down his arms. His breath misted. It was damn cold.

Kazi had wandered a few meters ahead, taking in the unexpected sight of a well-equipped medical lab. Felix's mouth dried. His heart thudded too loudly. Okay, he knew this feeling. It was a get-the-fuck-out feeling. It was a feeling that a hundred things were wrong with this picture, an ambush feeling.

Kazi froze.

"Go," he whispered, then took a single step back toward Felix. "Go."

Was that panic in his voice?

Felix peered into the gloom at the far end of the lab. Something clattered. Something scraped. The sheets rippled, disturbed by movement. Someone was back there.

"Go!" Kazi spun, grabbed him by the shoulder and shoved. Felix lurched into a sprint, dashed into the elevator and jabbed the buttons, any button—up, down, it didn't matter. Kazi blurred to a stop in front of him, blocking his view. The growl that rumbled out of him wasn't like any of the others. "We're not going to make it."

The elevator door began to close. Kazi stepped forward, out of the car.

"Wait!"

"Get outside. Run. Don't stop."

Behind him... there were—

The doors clunked shut, and the car jolted. Felix jabbed at the open button, but the car was already rising. A heavy weight slammed into the doors. Felix jerked back. The elevator continued to climb.

"Shit, shit, shit... What the hell was that?"

Behind Kazi, he'd seen a storm coming for him.... a churning mass of silver eyes and dagger-like fangs.

Nyktelios.

CHAPTER 14

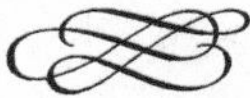

azi

NYKS WASHED toward him in a wave of claws and fangs. He bared his own fangs and plowed into them, fists swinging. Nothing human showed in the countless wide, silver eyes. Only the desperation to kill. Kazi punched them down, kicked them away. Some he grabbed and sank his fangs into their necks, piercing the artery and delivering a deadly dose of venom—one of the few ways they could be killed. Hands clawed at him, whipping him around. Teeth grazed his arms, jaws opened wide, fangs gleaming. He fought, landing blow after blow. They had to die. None could escape, even if he had to die here with them.

He spun, landing savage kicks. They flew back, crashing through tables and smashing the pods, but in their rabid madness, broken bones weren't enough to stop them, just slow them down. There wasn't time to bite every one—for each of them he dropped, another took its place. He couldn't hold them off forever.

Teeth caught his neck, and venom sizzled too close to his veins. He roared, grabbed the nyk, threw him over his shoulder and slammed him to the floor.

A *danger of death* sign caught his eye, fixed to a gray electrical terminal box. If he could start a fire, he might have a chance to destroy this place with the nyks in it. The broken pods leaked gasses from breathing tubes. If there were enough explosive gasses in the lab, a spark could kill them all.

He vaulted a table, skidded off its edge and sprang for the box. The cover tore free in his hand, exposing an organized spaghetti of wires. He hesitated, thoughts screeching to a halt. This could be his end. *Memento mori*—remember, you must die. The Blackrose Brotherhood's creed. Death came for everyone eventually, even the Brotherhood. If he died here, he'd take a fuckload of nyks with him. There was no better way to go, and perhaps his death would balance the scales he'd been fighting against since Mikalis had saved him.

He grabbed a bunch of wires and ripped them free. Sparks danced. The back of his neck tingled a warning. He grabbed the inbound nyk and plunged his face into the wires. Electricity fizzled and smoked, and the nyk's hair burst into flames. Fire danced down his clothes. But mad and desperate from turning, the creature grabbed for Kazi, still needing the kill, even as his skin sizzled from his face.

Kazi lurched back. He threw tables and chairs behind him, slowing their approach. The flaming nyk dashed forward with the rest of its pack, dripping flames, spreading fire to the others like a virus.

He lured them deeper into the darkness they'd come from.

Cuts on his arms and neck sizzled and wept blood. Venom poured like acid through his veins. Quaid would have gotten out by now. He'd have run for the trees. And that was good. It was the only good thing in all of this. With Kazi gone, Quaid might be free of the Brotherhood, and maybe Mikalis wouldn't pursue him. Maybe he'd let him live.

He'd have liked to have gotten to know Felix better.

Gasses swirled. Flames crawled up the walls, and the nyks surged again, screaming their rage.

Kazi faced death, and smiled.

CHAPTER 15

elix

He ran into the night with the others. They fled and cried, and nobody noticed him running among them.

Kazi was back there, fighting those creatures, and Quaid couldn't do a damn thing to help him. He couldn't fight nyks. This wasn't his world, his fight. He didn't have a gun, no weapon, just his fists, and those beasts would tear through him. But Kazi was back there... He could have fled too and saved himself, but instead, he'd thrown Felix into the elevator and held back the tide.

Felix slowed. Kazi had saved him.

He turned, walking backward through long, wet grass. The building they'd all fled from loomed in the mist, its windows blazing into the night.

Kazi would stop those monsters. Felix knew little else, but he knew that. He believed it too. Whatever Kazimir had been, he'd changed. He wasn't the monster Vesna had tried to make him out to be.

A blast erupted from the building, tearing its guts out in a huge mushroom of rolling fire and heat. The blast slammed into him, and for a few breathless seconds, there was nothing, just a high-pitched ringing in his ears and the touch of wet grass against his face.

Get up. He had to move... to get away. This was his chance to finally escape the pit of insanity he'd somehow fallen into. Run, like Kazi had said.

He got a knee under him, then a foot, and stumbled upright.

Where a building had been before, a gaping hole smoked. Steel girders had buckled like broken bones. Flames poured into the night sky, reaching for the stars, spluttering and crackling.

A twitching, lumbering figure emerged, a thick, hulking shadow of a man. Felix's heart leaped. Kazi? He stepped toward him. The figure fell into a loping run and rumbled a growl. In the dark, its eyes flashed.

That wasn't Kazi.

It was one of the monsters.

"Shit." Felix bolted.

Maybe, if he could make it to the trees—

The creature slammed into him. He sprawled face-first in the grass, tasting dirt and scuffing his chin on rocks.

Hands caught his shoulders, and knees dug into his back. He flung a desperate glance over his shoulder and saw the nyk's open jaws coming for him, firelight gleaming off its fangs. "No!"

He roared and twisted, bucking in the creature's iron grip.

The monster's weight vanished.

Felix rolled onto his ass and scurried backward.

Kazi had the writhing nyk in his arms. He plunged his teeth into the monster's neck and snarled, locking it in his deadly embrace. Felix froze, unable to look away. A river of glowing, fiery ants raced through the nyk's veins, burning it up from the inside out. Its skin sizzled off its bones, and with a silent scream, it turned to dust, leaving Kazi swaying on his feet.

Felix blinked.

Kazi dropped to his knees. Blood ran from the wounds in his neck and dribbled from deep gouges in his arms and chest. Half his flesh was burned and shriveled.

"God..."

Kazi pitched forward. Felix lunged in, catching him by the arm and swinging him into his grip. How was he even breathing? "Kazi?" Felix cupped his cheek, the only place on him that wasn't cut up or bloody. Kazi blinked, and the silver retreated from his eyes, returning them to their fascinating blue.

"Any... more?" Kazi rasped.

"What?"

"Nyks?"

He scanned the grounds around them, lit by shifting flame. There wasn't any movement. "No. I don't know. I don't think so. Shit, Kazi... you need a doctor."

Kazi's mouth ticked into a broken smile. "Move..." He pulled from Felix's grip, crawled, and then staggered to his feet. "We have to move." He started toward the tree line, twitching and limping like a broken puppet. His right shoulder hung lower than it should, and blood gleamed down his back.

What was he supposed to do, let him die alone in the woods somewhere?

Felix folded an arm around Kazi's waist. "Hold on to me." Kazi's arm flopped around Felix's shoulders. They plodded on. "You need help."

"S'fine," Kazi mumbled.

Fine? He looked as though he'd been shoved through a wood chipper. "You're not fine." Felix could fix this, couldn't he? Share blood like they had before? "We could—"

"No," Kazi said, as clear as day.

He helped him walk on, the pair of them stumbling and tripping over uneven ground. The forest closed in around them and turned cold now they'd left the raging flames. If anyone else had gotten out, Felix didn't see any sign of them. He had no idea where they were or where they were going, just *away*. Away seemed to be enough for Kazi.

Rain began to patter on the leaves and drip-drip to the ground.

"D-did you get them?" Felix asked quietly. He'd begun to shiver and couldn't seem to stop. His body was going into shock. He'd live. Kazi might not. What did immortal mean, really? He'd lived a thousand years, but that didn't mean he couldn't die, right?

Kazi's breath hitched. "I got them," he growled around his fangs. He'd have hidden those deadly weapons by now if he could have, which meant all his efforts were focused on keeping himself upright.

"You could just take a little of my blood, right?"

"Can't," Kazi grumbled. "Stop offering."

But he needed it. Felix could spare a pint, surely? He *wanted* to help him. Kazi had just killed countless monsters, probably saved a whole bunch of lives. If those things had gotten free, they'd have been running amok in the forest, killing anything and everyone they found, including Felix.

Kazi had saved Felix's life. Again. The least he could do was give him some blood. "Listen, you said you'd protect me, but who's protecting you, huh?"

"Felix, please—you don't understand." Kazi licked his lips, and when he turned his head, the molten silver had begun to creep back into his eyes. "If I drink... I already... I've already made that mistake."

"Okay." He wasn't going to win this. "Just know that I'll do it."

Kazi huffed a silent laugh and leaned a little heavier into Felix's side. "What happened to hating me?"

"That's still a thing. Just because you've saved my ass a few times doesn't change that."

He chuckled again. "You have a very fine ass, Quaid."

Heat warmed Felix's face, and he was grateful for the dark so Kazi couldn't see him blushing like a teen.

~

THEY STUMBLED and staggered for what felt like hours. The outline of a timber barn came into sight. Felix propped Kazi against a tree and checked inside, making sure they were alone, then helped him limp into the dry interior.

A few frayed couches had been positioned around an old wood-burning stove. Someone probably used the barn as an outpost. Felix deposited Kazi on the couch and focused on getting the fire lit. He could do that, at least.

The stacked wood was dry and lit easily with the lighter he'd discovered beside it. Warming his hands, he finally began to thaw the shivers.

Kazi lay slumped on the couch, eyes closed, body limp. He breathed through slightly parted lips. Dark lashes fluttered against his pale cheeks. What did vampires dream of? His chest was a mess of claw marks and missing chunks of skin. He'd heal, wouldn't he? Even without Felix's blood?

He had to be in agony. But if he could sleep, then maybe it wasn't as bad as it all seemed. Or maybe Kazimir was so damn exhausted he'd passed out.

Felix tore his gaze away and rubbed his face. Okay, so they were safe and dry and warm. That was a start. He spotted a folded blanket on a shelf and collected it. The fabric was about as soft as wire wool, but it was clean. He draped it over Kazi, careful not to wake him, then carefully sat beside him and watched the fire, then watched Kazi's sleeping face.

Prince Kazimir Skokan.

The blood prince. History had wiped him from its pages. The Brotherhood had probably had something to do with that. From what he'd read, Kazimir had slaughtered thousands. Maybe he'd been a nyktelios back then, or maybe he'd been a mass-murdering nobleman, but something had happened to stop all that, something to change his fate, something that had turned him into the man he was today. The man who *saved* lives.

That something was the Brotherhood too. The reporter in Felix ached to know more about the forgotten prince and the people he worked for. Not the awful parts Vesna had been hell-bent on showing him, but the parts she'd forgotten to mention. Clearly, there was a lot more to Kazi than the shallow Instagram model striving for more likes as though they were the blood he needed to survive. Maybe he did. Maybe his ego was that fragile.

Asleep, dreaming, he looked at peace.

Felix propped an elbow on the back of the couch, angled himself toward Kazi and studied his blood-smeared face. The memories of sharing his blood were all messed up in his head, but he was pretty sure he'd kissed those soft-looking lips. He couldn't deny he'd wanted to. Desiring another man was... not as much of a surprise as it should have been. He'd loved his wife, and he'd naively thought he could make it work, but his heart hadn't been in it.

And then he'd discovered Kazimir Skokan.

Kazimir's picture was everywhere, and more than curious, Felix had wanted to study the man everyone seemed to be talking about, sensing a story there. Kazimir had always been too handsome, too popular, too much. Nobody was *that* perfect.

A few years back, when Kazimir had posted he was in Maine, Felix had figured it was too good an opportunity to miss. He'd followed him and seen something... something he shouldn't have: a secret meeting with Kazi and three men, two of whom had vanished like smoke right in front of him. He knew what he'd seen, knew it was real, and that had begun the obsession to discover the truth. The more he'd studied Kazimir Skokan's life, the shadier it had become. People went missing in towns he showed up in. Bodies turned up, unsolved John Does.

And now here he was, sitting on a moth-infested couch in a stranger's barn, next to Kazimir Skokan, who'd be dead if he wasn't something supernatural.

Felix's whole world was a lie.

Maybe he should have left the story alone, but he'd known it had teeth—he just hadn't realized how accurate he'd been.

He couldn't walk away. Not least because there was something about Kazimir that kept pulling him back. Some part of Felix wanted to know him, to spend more time with him, to talk with him, be with him. It wasn't the thrill of lust he felt whenever Kazi laid eyes on him either, although there was plenty of that.

He'd always wanted to fuck him, just hadn't wanted to admit it. Now there was no escaping it.

Christ, he was so messed up.

He flopped his head back and closed his eyes.

When two people experienced traumatic events together, they formed a bond. This was that. A psychological break. He'd get over him.

Maybe they should fuck and get it over with, get it out of his system.

He opened his eyes and admired Kazi's dark lashes, the way his hair fell across his face, how his jaw demanded to be stroked. If he hadn't been wounded, if they'd been two men on a couch, he'd have tasted his lips by now, might have woken him up, would have kissed him slowly, straddled his legs, and taken his face in his hands, making it clear how much he wanted him.

But that couldn't happen.

It was a fantasy. It had always been a fantasy.

And tomorrow, whatever this feeling was, he'd banish it. Because Kazimir was a dream he could not have.

Even if he'd never desired a man more.

KAZI WAS STILL out cold in the morning, but with the sun shining through cobweb-covered windows, there wouldn't be a better time to scout around outside and make sure they were alone.

Felix wedged the barn door shut behind him, blew into his hands to keep the cold at bay and picked a direction that might or might not be north. There was no use in trekking too far. He'd get lost. All he needed was to get the lay of the land. By the time he got back, Kazi would be awake.

He stomped through cool shadows. Autumn had its chokehold on the forest, and most of the golden-brown leaves had already fallen and lay in a soft, wet mulch underfoot. The ground undulated in gentle hills, reminding him of Maine, but there were a thousand places like it in the US. If he could get to a road, find a sign, he'd know where they were.

After walking for half an hour one way and finding nothing, he turned, followed his tracks back, and tried another direction, always keeping the barn behind him. It was damn easy to get turned around in the trees.

The sun rose higher, but cold air bit at his fingers. The cult's lightweight clothes did nothing to keep him warm. But at least he was out of that wretched place, even if he was freezing his balls off.

A low droning hummed ahead. He stopped, leaned against a tree and listened. The sound faded away, then rumbled back again.

A car? Which meant a road. And normal people.

Back to reality. Finally.

He pushed on and caught glimpses of the strip of asphalt, then a gas station. Hunkering down in the brush, he scanned the forecourt and spotted an advertising board. Some notices appeared to be in French, but before panic could set in, he caught sight of an *Eagle Lake's Autumn Garage Sale!* poster.

They were at the northern edge of rural Maine. A long way from New York, but a whole lot closer to home than France.

The gas station would have a phone. He could call the police, tell them he'd been kidnapped, and end this fucking nightmare.

Then what? How was he going to explain the explosion? As soon as he started spouting stories about fanged men and women, they'd think him nuts. And then there was Kazi. He doubted Kazi's people and cops mixed.

So, he couldn't call the cops. But what if he called the Brotherhood?

He had no idea how to do that. It wasn't as though they were listed under *dial a fucking vampire*. Besides, all he knew about them suggested he'd make Felix disappear alongside this mess. And he wasn't ready for that.

Or he could walk down the road and hitchhike. He could be home by tomorrow. And all of this—the cult, vampires, Kazimir—would be a hideous nightmare.

CHAPTER 16

Kazi

THE OLD BLANKET tucked around him itched. Kazi frowned at it. He didn't remember grabbing it, but he'd also been out of it after they'd found the barn.

Logs crackled in a wood-burning stove. That had to be Felix's doing...

He lifted his head. Sunlight fought with the cobwebs and gloom, but the window was far enough away that it didn't irritate. And Felix wasn't here.

Kazi's heart sank. It made sense that he'd go. He'd left the second Kazi had closed his eyes. It was the sensible thing to do. Run, disappear, survive.

But his absence dug a hole in Kazi's heart, cutting deeper than the rest of his wounds. He hardly knew the man, and whatever his own feelings, much of it was the venom's work, trying to bond them together as feeder and master. But knowing why he liked to have Felix close didn't make his absence hurt any less.

He'd thought, perhaps naively, they had something. A spark. A connection. He knew Quaid hated him, but he'd been sure there was more to it than that. He'd seen it in his long glances and heavy silences, in the things he didn't say. And then there was the feeding session, when Felix had come undone in his arms. A mistake, for sure, but a delicious one.

And that couldn't happen again.

Felix Quaid had already sampled too much of Kazi. Any more and things got... complicated.

It was good he'd left.

For the best.

Still hurt though.

He shoved the blanket down and winced at the still-healing mess of his chest. His arms were worse, all cut up from nyk teeth. He shivered, so damn cold. Their venom was trying to drag him down, make him weak, easy prey.

He *was* weak.

He hadn't fought and killed that many nyks alone in a long time.

The barn door rattled.

Kazi shot from the couch, grabbed the intruder and slammed him against the rattling barn wall. *Kill him*, instincts roared. Felix's sweet scent coiled around his wrecked mind, soothing the madness, switching it from the rabid need to defend himself to a different need, but no less potent.

"It's me." Felix swallowed, making his throat undulate, drawing Kazi's eye to his neck where his pulse beat hot and heavy. The man's body was a beacon of life, strumming with blood and warmth. A surge of hunger and lust demanded he take him, sink his teeth in, drink him down, make himself strong again, use the feeder for exactly what feeders were good for—

Kazi whirled away.

He needed to get a grip, get the urges back under control. But his own blood ran hot, his body was broken, and he *needed* Felix in all ways. Some of them good, all of them selfish.

"Hey... you all right?"

He waved his concerns away, because that made it worse. He sounded as though he cared, and it was easier to live with what he'd done to him if they still hated each other. Felix didn't know the truth. They'd shared blood. Kazi had sunk his teeth into him, let him drink his blood, marked him. Felix was a feeder and already addicted to Kazi. It was still early though, and they'd technically only shared blood once. He could probably shake off the thrall with enough therapy. And drugs.

Maybe. Most didn't though.

The Brotherhood would finish him off anyway for his own good. He knew too much, had seen too much, tasted too much. Kazi caught himself growling under his breath and swallowed the possessive rage. He was so fucked. They both were.

Maybe he *should* just kill him and get it over with. It was going to end that way eventually. It always did.

"Kazi?"

He looked over his shoulder. Felix wore loose sweats, and his face had gained a shadow from a few days' worth of beard. That face, though, when he wasn't snarling at Kazi or glaring in hatred, that face was a picture Kazi wanted to keep close to his heart. Slightly pouting lips ticked sideways now, trying to smile and failing, because he knew he was treading on ice. His brown eyes were quick to narrow, sometimes bright with intelligence, and often soft with humor. His hair was a mess, and better for it. Kazi liked him like this, bedraggled and unhinged, frightened, and something else too... defiant, hopeful. Strong enough to know the truth.

"My offer stands, you know," Felix said, hand out as though he were approaching a wild animal. "You saved my life last night. If you need blood, take it."

He only offered because he didn't know the repercussions.

But Kazi *did* need him. And wasn't it already too late? What was another taste?

Felix approached as though he wasn't afraid when they both knew he was. Desire warmed his gaze too. His body remembered how Kazi could make him feel, and he wanted that again—Kazi's venom made him impossible to resist.

By Nyx, Kazi was weak for him.

He scooped Felix's face into his hands, and in that moment, he blinked up, wide-eyed and expectant. Kazi wanted this—their connection was a lie, but he still wanted it. If Kazi had been good, he'd have turned away, told him to leave, told him it was all just chemicals, just hormones, just a vampire's way of capturing its prey. If he had been good, he'd have told him the truth. And maybe he would... later.

Kazi hovered his mouth over Felix's, so close to kissing him, his control hanging by a thread. If he took him now, Felix would relish it, then hate him. Hate him worse than he already did.

Fuck it.

Felix's mouth was soft and sweet. Kazi teased it open with his tongue, slipping inside, and when Felix moaned into the kiss, he knew he had him, could do anything to him. Could feast, fuck, make him come, and kill him with a smile on his face. Kill him, as he'd been ordered to.

The kiss turned heated and rough. Kazi folded the man close, needing to feel his warmth. Felix plunged his hands down Kazi's back, cupped his ass and roughly yanked him tight against him. The kiss broke, and then Felix's soft, warm mouth was on Kazi's jaw, his neck, his shoulder.

Blunt teeth bit in, and Kazi tilted his head back, letting Felix explore. Kazi was hard, a fact Felix discovered when he brought his hand between them. His fingers molded close through Kazi's trousers, stroking him harder.

Felix swooped back in to claim Kazi's mouth in a furious kiss that staggered Kazi backward. Yes, Kazi needed this, needed him. The backs of Kazi's legs hit the couch, and Felix shoved, all hands and mouth and tongue, and the hard press of his cock jutting against Kazi's thigh. He dropped his head, and his wet tongue swirled around Kazi's nipple, flicking and sucking.

He grabbed a fistful of Felix's hair and jerked his head back, exposing his throat for the bite his fangs throbbed for.

Felix's snarled, "Do it."

It was all the permission he needed. He struck, biting hard, pumped venom, and then withdrew just enough to allow his blood to flow over his tongue. The beast within sang its relief, spilling power and strength through muscle and bone. He wanted all of Felix, every last drop, but that would kill him, and despite Mikalis's orders, despite the Brotherhood being his life, he wasn't losing Felix that way. He'd given the man his word. Felix was his, for better or worse. Mostly worse, but they were both damned anyway.

He tore free and swept his tongue over the wound, healing it. Before Felix could protest, or hesitate, or realize his mistake, Kazi dropped to his knees, held him by a hip and unfastened the tie on his sweats. His dick jutted, so damn eager to be freed. Kazi plucked it from his trousers, pulled it into his mouth, between his fangs, and swallowed him deep.

Felix bucked and thrust, driving himself between Kazi's lips. He clutched Kazi's hair. "Sweet fuck, your teeth..." He must have liked how Kazi's fangs bracketed his thick length, because he rocked his hips, pulsing in and out. Felix moaned and shuddered as he mindlessly fucked Kazi's mouth, his grip twisting and pulling.

"Ugh... yes..."

Kazi rocked with him, and then Felix stopped, jerking Kazi's head back and his dick out. Panting, he peered down at Kazi. "If you don't want me to come down your throat, you gotta stop."

"Baby, you can come anywhere you like."

A peculiar expression crossed his face, half humor, half confusion. Whatever his thoughts, Kazi didn't see the rest of them on his face, because he grabbed his erection, held him back, keeping him still, and sucked, sliding his tongue to pump Felix's cock deep between his fangs, deeper down his throat. Felix's jagged breathing and shuddering thighs gave his failing resistance away. He wasn't going to last, wasn't trying to. Kazi wanted it, wanted him, wanted to taste him in every way.

Felix's grunts grew louder. His grip tightened, bobbing Kazi's head. He sucked and tongued, so damn hard and hungry that Kazi thought he might come without being touched. And then Felix's groaning growl of a shout lurched out of him, his cock shuddered, and salty cum slipped down Kazi's throat.

Felix freed his hands from Kazi's hair and thrust his fingers into his own hair, scrunching it around his head. *"Fuuuuck,"* he breathed, back arched, cock still pulsing and spilling.

Kazi took it all, and when Felix was done, he wrapped his fingers around the man's dick and licked from balls to tip, burning for him as soon as their eyes met. This was their spark, their connection. It wasn't just sex; it was more primal, more wild. Kazi knew sex, and it didn't compare to this, at least not for him.

Felix sank to his knees. He peered through his lashes, and almost shyly, his warm, rough fingers began to work at Kazi's trouser fly.

"How long have you been dreaming of fucking my mouth?" Kazi drawled.

Felix chuckled. "Longer than is right." He slipped his hand inside and dove his fingers around Kazi's dick. All the air puffed from Kazi's lungs. He leaned back, chin up, giving himself over to the man who might be his undoing.

"You like that, hmm?" Felix purred, adding a hint of slyness that set Kazi's heart racing. Felix gathered a sweep of pre-cum and used it to slick his fingers, then pumped, sliding Kazi's dick over his palm and wrist.

He wouldn't last. He was already teetering on the edge of pure ecstasy, having tasted the man's blood and cum, consuming Felix, making him his again. Kazi lost his mind to the wicked pleasure and burning desire. His fangs ached, leaking, seeking more, and when Felix tilted his head, exposing the healed bite, Kazi struck a second time. He plunged his teeth in and thrust his dick through Felix's grip. The pleasure was a blast of electricity down his spine, burning through his veins. He swallowed blood and fucked Felix's hand, knowing he was too lost to last. Pleasure crested, then spilled over.

He came hard—would have shouted if he hadn't had his teeth in Felix's neck—and climaxed so damn violently he might never come back down from the high.

It took a few moments of breathless bliss before realizing he still had Felix's throat locked between his teeth. He withdrew, sealing the wound with a swirl of saliva. "By Nyx, are you all right? Did I hurt you?"

Felix blinked. "No, fuck... no. You didn't hurt me." He spluttered a laugh. "I just... I've er... It's been a long time since I've been able to do that."

"Do what?"

"Make a man come," he said, trailing off and darting his gaze away.

Kazi kissed him, hard and fast, messy and raw, fangs retracted so he didn't accidentally take more blood. Then he kissed him slowly and wrapped his arms around him, kissed him like he meant it, because he needed him to know... he did mean it.

With yet more nervous little laughs, Felix wriggled free, discreetly wiping his hand on the blanket draped over the couch. "I guess you get laid every weekend, huh?"

"Most nights, actually. Men. Women. I don't care."

Felix threw him a dirty look, but it didn't have any weight behind it. "You're such a fuckin' attention whore."

Kazi lunged, recapturing his escaping prey, and bent him over the couch. "They aren't this, like it is with you." He could have said more, but Felix tensed, and he feared he'd already said too much. "Let me do this again, slower... *better*."

"Better?" Felix snorted. "If you think you can top that."

"I can." He pinned Felix under his glare. "*Top* that."

The man smirked. "Oh yeah?"

He stroked Felix's back, over his shirt, then slid his hands beneath the fabric, over his warm skin. He wanted him naked and writhing on this couch, now. He wanted to bury himself inside him. Kiss him. Taste him. He wanted all of him, all at once. Wanted him so much it hurt.

"Okay..." Felix gave him a small shove. "All right, just give me some room for a second, huh? I just need a minute..."

"Why?"

He dropped onto the couch. "I just got fucked and fed from." He dabbed at his own neck, frowning when his hand came away clean. "Just a second to catch my breath... This is er... This is new for me." His smile flopped sideways, and when Kazi sat next to him, he slumped against his side. "Can we sit like this... a while?"

He couldn't risk taking more blood, not where they were—wherever that was.

Kazi draped an arm around Felix and tucked him close. "Rest, baby. I've got you."

"Hmm..." Felix's lashes fluttered closed, and Kazi listened to the mellow but strong beat of his heart. He was out like a light in seconds, all warm and firm and Felix.

Shit.

Kazi huffed through his nose. Somehow, in all of the chaos, Felix Quaid had gotten under his skin in a way that mattered. Perhaps it was the master and feeder dynamic. Perhaps it was a lie. It didn't matter though, because Kazi couldn't ever complete the mission. He was never killing Felix. Which meant Mikalis would come for him. For them both.

The mistake had been made, and it was too late to take it back.

CHAPTER 17

elix

He woke tucked into the crook of Kazi's arm like an idiot. Some long, distant sense of guilt and shame tried to jerk him free and pretend everything he'd done *with a man* hadn't happened. But if it was so wrong, why did it feel so damn good to sit with him?

"You okay, baby?" Kazi's voice rumbled.

"That name..."

He arched a dark eyebrow. "'Baby'? You don't like it?"

It was complicated and too much to sort through in a stranger's barn after escaping a mad cult. A sense of pride said he should hate the silly name. But he didn't. "No, I kinda do," he admitted, liking that he could admit that without hating himself.

Maybe it was too soon, but who he was right now felt like someone he might want to be. He'd spent so long drowning in hate that he'd forgotten what it was like not to have all that hate weighing him down.

Kazi's touch skimmed his arm, spilling little shivers through him. Waking up next to him felt good. Kazi twisted, angling his body toward Felix to look down at him. His eyes entranced him. Those eyes had seen over a thousand years. He'd lived countless lifetimes. Why would someone like Kazimir vow to protect him?

It had to be the deal between them. Kazi needed blood, and that was all. But it felt like more, and the things he'd said, if they were true, then Kazi felt there was more between them.

He'd fucked around in high school but had never really entertained loving a man. Did that make him gay? But he had an ex-wife and a kid, so...

He was getting ahead of himself. There was more to worry about than how much Felix liked dick. He chuckled at his own idiocy and stretched.

Kazi's dark pupils widened, drinking him in. Felix liked that expression on him, as though he were about to pounce. "It feels like a dream, like none of this is real. Not like we're in a barn in Maine."

"We're in Maine?" Kazi asked.

"Yeah. I took a look around while you were out. There's a gas station nearby. We're near Eagle Lake."

Kazi stiffened, took his arm back and leaned forward, clasping his hands together. The wounds on his back had healed, leaving just smears of dried blood. Felix dared to reach out and lay a hand on his warm shoulder. The muscles shifted under his palm, and Kazi glanced at him. For a flicker, his gaze was cold, and the predator glared back, almost forcing Felix to pull his hand away, but then the ice thawed, and he smiled, softening the rest of him.

"I need to make a call." Kazi stood, and rolling out stiff muscles, he stretched and ran his hands through his hair, his body a play of lean muscle, like a panther stretching in the sun. "We should keep moving. Vesna is still out there. And I need to make sure what happened here doesn't leak to the public. Will you show me where the gas station is?"

"You're half naked." He gestured at Kazi's bare chest.

"I don't feel the cold."

"That's not..." Kazi's near-naked state would raise eyebrows, especially in a rural town. "Never mind. Let's go." Felix got to his feet too, surprised to feel pretty damn good considering Kazi had snacked on a vein again. Taken other things too... He'd had his cock down Kazi's throat, had the man on his knees, looking up at him with those pretty eyes, and Felix had come with his dick between Kazi's fangs.

If there was a hell, Felix was clearly heading there at full speed.

He cleared his throat and pushed through the barn door ahead of Kazi, keeping his face hidden. Yeah, okay, so he had a few things to work through. Some shit to figure out about himself, but a whole lot made sense now too. He'd been trying to be a husband in a life he had never felt he belonged in, and now he suspected he knew why.

He could come around to the fact he more than liked men. But Kazi wasn't just any man, and when Felix glanced behind him, the vampire's eyes caught some ambient moonlight and shone in the dark.

Felix liked cock and vampires, apparently.

He laughed at himself. He sure knew how to pick 'em.

CHAPTER 18

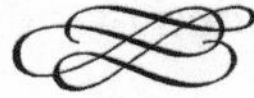

azi

THE GAS STATION attendant glared at Kazi as though he was about to reach for a panic button. Or a shotgun. *Steve*, his badge read.

Kazi leveled his gaze back at Steve, in no mood for his shit.

"Hi, Steve." Felix stepped up to the counter and gave the man his soft smile. "Can we borrow a phone, maybe? My friend here was in a wreck."

"A wreck," the gum-chewing Steve echoed, then checked out Kazi's chest.

He had about three seconds to stop gawking before Kazi cut to the part where he leaped over the counter, muscled him against the wall, stole his phone from his pocket and broke his nose.

"Sure, okay." Steve shrugged. "There's an old phone 'round the back there, behind the photo booth, next to the soup."

"Thank you," Felix said.

Kazi turned away to search for the phone. A camera blinked its small red light from the corner of the store. Kazi ducked his head, probably too late. If the Brotherhood were scanning for him, Atlas's facial recognition software would flag his location within the next hour. The Brotherhood would arrive right after. He could walk out now and keep on walking with Felix at his side. But that wasn't how he did things. He owed the brothers more.

Kazi picked up the wall phone, took a breath and dialed a familiar number.

"Yello," Zaine's drawl sounded down the line.

"It's Kazi—"

"Fuck! You're all right. Wait, let me get Storm—"

"No. Don't. Just... listen." He glanced back at Felix admiring rows of breakfast cereal. Was he really about to walk away from the people he'd given his word he'd serve alongside, walk away from the one man who'd given him a chance to balance the scales? From Mikalis? But he didn't have a choice. He'd made a feeder. He'd taken blood from the vein. He cared. He was in so deep there was no digging his way out of this hole. "I fucked up, Z."

Zaine laughed. The dick. "You? What? *Perfect* Kazimir. Say it again. I wanna put you on speaker."

"Fuck you," he growled, turning his back on Felix when he glanced over. "Can you not be a dick for five fuckin' seconds?"

Zaine's chuckle faded. "C'mon, man. You know I've got your back. What's going on? You all right?"

"Yeah, it's..." This was harder than he'd expected. "Zaine, listen. I'm in Eagle Lake. Nyxians ambushed me. They used my blood to make nyk—"

"What the fuck! Stay right where you are. We'll get a team up to you. Mikalis will burn those fuckers—"

"Zaine, stop talking and listen. I dealt with it. Most of it. There's a woman. Vesna Dragovic. She's their leader. I torched their compound, but she got away. Find her. Bring her in for questioning. I don't think this Nyxian cell is the only one."

"All right. Okay. I hear you. Debrief us when you come in—"

"I'm not coming in."

Zaine's pause stuttered down the line. "What?"

He glanced again at Felix, who had now moved to the soup cans and was studying Campbell's tomato soup as though it were a science textbook. How was he equal parts innocent and hot? How could he look so damn cute in clothes that didn't fit, with his hair all mussed? How had he gotten so completely, and obviously, under Kazi's defenses?

Kazi braced against the wall and sighed. "I'm compromised."

"Kazi, shit." At least Zaine knew what that meant. "It's all right. Come in. We'll fix it."

"There's no fixing this."

"Look, you'll get a few decades in a box to work it out of your system."

A few decades? Felix would be middle-aged when Kazi got out. He'd have moved on, providing he'd be able to get his head clear of the venom. Venom fucked feeders up, especially when they were taken from their masters. Throwing Kazi in isolation for a few decades could tip Felix over the edge. Mikalis would use that. Frame it like a suicide. "Shit..." Kazi snarled. "Z, I'm going dark. Don't look for me."

"It doesn't work like that, Kazi, and you know it. Whatever happened, you gotta come in."

Felix dropped the soup can. It clattered on the floor. He scooped it up, noticed the giant dent in its side and discreetly slid it back onto the shelf, hiding it behind other soups. He plunged his hands into his pockets, as guilty as sin, then spotted Kazi watching and smiled like an idiot.

Kazi's heart swelled. "I understand now, and I'm sorry I didn't get it before."

"Get what? Kazi, just come in. It's the only way to get through this. Nobody *leaves*."

"What you have with Eric, I'm sorry I dismissed it."

"Oh shit." Zaine paused again, his mind working. "It's Quaid, isn't it? Is he alive?"

"Nobody touches Quaid." The growl came out louder than he'd planned.

"Okay, I hear that, but... you still gotta come in."

"Mikalis will kill him," Kazi whispered, making sure Felix didn't hear.

"No, maybe... He's mellowed lately. Look at Eric."

"Zaine, you caught lightning in the bottle. You got your happy ever after. That doesn't happen in the Brotherhood. We never get involved. We never take from the vein. We never create feeders. We never care."

"Is that what he is, your feeder? Because if that's what you've done, you fucker, you need to put him down and get your skinny ass back to Atlas right fucking now or Mikalis will hunt you down like the nyk you are, and you can bet he won't go easy."

Kazi thumped his forehead against the cold wall. It hurt, hearing Zaine talk like that about him, but he was right. Kazi was a nyk. "I can't lose him."

"Kazi, if you go rogue—"

"Goodbye, Zaine."

"Wait, don't hang up. I can help—"

He replaced the phone in its cradle. It was over. He was no longer a member of the Brotherhood. And if he wasn't one of them, he was their enemy.

"All right?" Felix asked.

"Yeah, let's get out of here."

Felix thanked Steve as they left but fell silent as they walked south, leaving the gas station's bright lights behind them.

CHAPTER 19

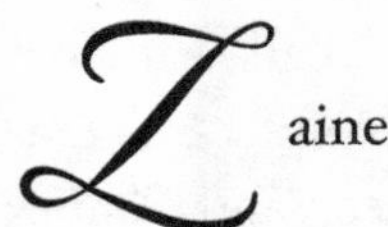aine

ZAINE CLIMBED into the back of the black helicopter, alongside Storm, Aiko and Raiden. Aiko already dozed with his butterfly knives cradled in his lap. He appeared vulnerable, but he could kill with his eyes closed. He was quick with those knives, some said quicker than Storm.

Storm sat like a slab of man-meat and glowered a hole into the chopper's bulkhead, as furious as Zaine had ever seen him. Raiden tapped into a laptop perched on his knees, immune to most things unless it was scientifically significant. He'd opted to come along to study whatever remained of the Nyxian compound and their twisted practice of force-turning a bunch of humans into nyks using Kazi's blood.

This would be Zaine's first brush with Nyxians, although he'd read the reports from previous Brotherhood scuffles. They hadn't been much of a challenge before, but if they'd caught Kazi, then they'd be changing. He checked his twin pistols in their holsters and peered through the glass at Atlas shrinking beneath them.

Octavius piloted them into the starlit skies over New York's suburbs, pointing the helicopter's nose north toward Maine.

He'd told them about Kazi's call, about the cult and the woman Kazi had named as the Nyxian leader. But he hadn't told them everything. Such as the fact Quaid was alive and *with* Kazi in more ways than one.

Kazi was walking a thin line, a line Zaine had walked with Eric. But they'd survived, and Kazi could too. Maybe.

If Kazi had turned nyk and Mikalis gave the word, Zaine *would* put him down. Hating every goddamn second of it. And himself.

Before Mikalis condemned Kazi, Zaine was going to find him, see for himself what he'd done, try to help him. He owed the prick that much for having had his back throughout the years and for helping him and Eric. Kazi wasn't good though. None of them were. He'd stabbed Zaine in the back a few times, and Zaine wouldn't hesitate to do the same in return, if Kazi had gone rogue.

Mikalis was already at the scene of the burned-out compound by the time they'd raced through the forest, following an old railway branch. How he'd gotten there so fast, Zaine preferred not to think too hard on. There was a great deal about Mikalis that didn't add up, hints of old secrets. Eric had noticed it too. Sebastien, Eric's sick fuck of a master, had revealed a few things about the Brotherhood leader. Things Mikalis hadn't wanted shared.

But Mikalis was what he was and their leader. Nobody questioned that. Ever.

Except for that one time Zaine had mentioned a few things, turned the screws a little, and made sure Eric was safe among their number. Mikalis couldn't hurt Eric, not if he didn't want the rest of the Brotherhood to know he wasn't like them. Mikalis was something else entirely.

"Nyxians," Mikalis snarled, rising from his crouch among the debris while brushing dust from his hands.

"It's been a few centuries since we crossed paths with them," Storm grumbled, stopping next to the Brotherhood leader.

Kazi had fucked up the Nyxians pretty good. And considering the amount of nyk dust blackening the ground like filthy snow, he'd torn through their little experiment too. Kazi was a hard son of a bitch, harder than his pretty-boy looks. He'd survived shit Zaine still only knew the half of. But a raid like this one would have tested his control. He couldn't be blamed for tasting some of Quaid to help heal. Zaine had done the same with Eric. A little blood went a long way in a tough situation.

But from Kazi's call, it sounded as though he'd taken a lot more than a few sips.

"Anything we can use? Any clues for where to look next?" Zaine asked.

Mikalis narrowed his eyes at the swathes of dark forest surrounding the compound. "That way... There's a barn. Storm." He jerked his head, and Storm started heading that way.

"The gas station from where he made the call is a mile north of here," Aiko said. He turned soft Asian eyes on Zaine. "You said he got cut off. If the Nyxians have him, there may be witnesses."

"I'll er... I'll go check it out." The last thing he wanted was some witnesses reporting he'd seen Kazi walking off into the sunset with Quaid.

For now, the Brotherhood only needed to know Kazi was missing.

"Any sign of Felix Quaid?" Mikalis asked.

Zaine studied a piece of bent metal bar. Kazi owed him for this. If Mikalis discovered Zaine had been withholding information, Zaine could book a stay in a glass prison for a few weeks.

"There's this." Octavius emerged from the ruins and handed Mikalis a tattered, half-burned notebook. Mikalis scanned its pages. His expression darkened almost to a snarl.

"Looks as though Quaid has been planning more than just

exposing Kazi," Octavius added. "The man's clearly obsessed. Probably unhinged. That makes him more dangerous than Kazi likely planned for."

Zaine pursed his lips. He didn't want to come off as too keen, but he needed to get a look at that notebook. What if Quaid *had* somehow ambushed Kazi? Kazi's confidence in his own perfection could easily have had him underestimating Felix Quaid's passion for revenge.

Mikalis tucked the notebook into his back pocket and circled a finger in the air. "Let's wrap this up. Zaine, take the gas station. Kazi will be found, and this Quaid, if not already dead—bring him to me."

"What about Dragovic?" Zaine asked. "She's still out there."

"Atlas is working on it," Mikalis called, then vanished into the dark.

Nyxians creating nyks and bleeding a Brotherhood member was the perfect storm of chaos, not to mention fuckin' torture. It was no wonder Mikalis had radiated the kind of pissed-off vibes that meant someone somewhere was going to suffer a whole world of hurt.

Zaine could only hope that someone wasn't Kazi.

CHAPTER 20

Felix

IT HAD SEEMED like a good idea, coming home. But now that he stood outside his old house, his heart pounded and a hundred different instincts told him to run. Leaves had fallen in the yard, smothering the grass. Rosa's bike lay on its side by the porch steps.

"Is this your home?" Kazi asked, buttoning his shirt. He'd stolen it from a house down the street. They'd forgotten to take their washing in for the night.

The dark blue cotton complemented his eyes, and fuck... Felix should never have brought him here.

"You need to give me your word, right now, that you won't hurt them." God, what had he been thinking? Kazi was *dangerous*. They'd needed somewhere to go, just for a few nights, while Kazi retrieved a stash of cash and documents he'd left in Portland, so he'd said, for emergencies like this. As they were already in Maine, it had made sense to go home, but...

Kazi frowned. His pretty face hardened. "I gave you my word already. They're safe."

"I need to hear it again."

"They're your family. I understand—" Kazi reached for his hand.

Felix stepped back, and the brief flicker of hurt in Kazi's eyes cut him to the bone. But his wife—ex-wife—Julia couldn't see *that*. She didn't know he was... maybe... could be gay, and she definitely did not need to know about all the vampire shit. "You know what, I can't. You and me, it's fine, but you and them? No. We can't. We can't be here. I can't do this—"

"Daddy?"

They both turned toward the house. Rosa stood on the porch, wearing Hello Kitty PJs.

She rubbed her eyes. "What yah doin' out here?"

Julia burst through the front door and scooped Rosa into her arms. "Rosa! You can't—*Felix?*"

Damn it, it was too late. Now he had to stay and somehow explain everything. "Hi, honey." He started forward, up the driveway.

"You can't show up like this, Felix." Julia turned and scooted Rosa back inside, then glowered from the porch. Slim and blonde, full of fire and flare, she was the perfect woman, the perfect mother, and he knew he was bad for them.

He stopped at the bottom step. "She's gotten so big."

"It's the middle of the night, Felix. What are you wearing? Are those pajamas?"

He'd forgotten he was dressed like an escaped mental patient. He frowned at himself, then back at Kazi standing on the sidewalk, hip cocked, somehow all dramatic with his windswept hair, perfect face, stolen shirt and creased trousers.

"Who's he?" Julia asked. She tilted her head, eyes narrowing. "Wait, is that..."

How did he even begin to explain?

"He's er... He's..." He winced, falling at the first hurdle. A friend, a boyfriend, a blood-sucking vampire from medieval Europe?

Julia sighed. "Where's your car?"

"We took a bus," he answered in a rush, glad he could answer *something*.

"Well, you can't stand out there all night. You and your friend had better come in."

Felix stepped into the warm, comfortable surroundings of a house he'd once belonged in. He'd painted the hallway when they'd been pregnant. The bottom step of the stairs always creaked. When Rosa had been small, and a light sleeper, they'd known to avoid that step. Through the hall, into the kitchen/dining room, was where they'd thrown parties, had Christmases, drunk wine, laughed and once made love over the table.

He'd been gone two years.

"There's coffee if you want some. You look like you need it." Now that they'd all made it to the kitchen light, Julia eyed Kazi's sauntering entrance and arched a questioning eyebrow at Felix.

"Thank you, Mrs. Quaid," Kazi said. He wasn't physically threatening, but in their home, in all the soft furnishings and shiny surfaces, a hint of *other* set him apart.

Having him here was so goddamn surreal that Felix couldn't find his voice.

"It's Somerville now," Julia said. "I... went back to my maiden name."

Kazi smiled and nodded. "Thank you, Miss Somerville, for your help. As you can see, we're in need of it."

Rosa flew in and flung her arms around Felix's leg. "Daddy! Daddy! Read me a story!"

"Oh, Rosa, Daddy can't stay," Julia said.

He'd have snapped at her for that before, but now he knew she was right. He couldn't stay. He shouldn't even have come.

Rosa pouted. "But he just got here?"

His heart swelled to bursting. He stroked Rosa's golden hair, his whole chest aching. Julia hadn't forbidden him from seeing Rosa, but he'd taken himself away all the same. "I can read her a story."

"Yay!" She tugged on his hand. "C'mon..."

"Why don't you go get a book, Rosa? Let me talk to Daddy for a little while, okay?"

"Okay!" She bounded past Kazi. He turned and watched her leave, his expression soft.

"I don't know what shit you two are into, but you do not drag it into my house, understand?" Julia warned through a thin smile. "You can read a story, and get yourselves cleaned up, and that's it."

"Ma'am," Kazi said, perfectly behaved. "I'll go do that, if that's all right? Leave you both to catch up."

"Good idea. You do that," Julia said. "There're fresh towels in the closet at the top of the stairs."

Kazi left, having been thoroughly dismissed. Not even a thousand-year-old vampire was going to argue with Julia.

Felix swallowed, then tried to clear his throat. "Thank you—"

"What's *he* doing here?" she hissed, keeping her voice down.

She knew of Kazi—knew his obsession to get answers had begun around the Kazimir Skokan story. "Look, it's... complicated. We'll be gone tomorrow. I'm sorry. I didn't plan this, okay?"

"No, yes, it's okay..." She sighed. "I just... It's a surprise, that's all."

She was too nice, too good. Even now, after all the shit he'd put her through, she wouldn't turn them away. "How are you?"

"I'm fine. Rosa's fine."

"That's... good."

"We haven't heard from you in six months, not even a call. I don't care, but Rosa... She misses you."

God, he was a terrible father. "I know. I'm sorry." He slumped against the kitchen island and had to fight to keep the choking knot from rising back up his throat.

"*Are* you okay, Felix?"

He couldn't reply, not without breaking down, so he nodded and smiled, and wished he hadn't disappointed her in so many ways.

Julia's sympathetic expression screwed the guilt down even worse.

"I'll make that coffee," she said. "When your *friend* is done in the shower, you can get cleaned up too. I still have some of your old clothes in the spare room."

He dragged a hand down his face, scratching through an emerging beard. "Thank you. I mean it."

"Yeah, I know. Just don't tell my ex-husband, okay?"

CHAPTER 21

azi

As he passed a bedroom, a montage of framed photographs hanging on the wall caught his eye. Downstairs, the Quaids talked in hushed tones, and clearly, Felix needed it. They wouldn't notice if Kazi took a look. He stepped into the room, lit by just the landing light, and scanned the array of pictures and awards. *Felix Quaid Investigative Reporter of the Year, New York Times. 2017, 2018, 2019.* Next to those awards were a few pictures of Felix in a blue PRESS flak jacket, hard hat on, standing among a group of people in front of war-torn ruins. He dropped his gaze to photos of Felix in the yard outside, lifting baby Rosa into the air, Felix in his high school football gear, Felix and Julia on their wedding day.

Atlas had shown him some of the same pictures, but standing in the man's house, meeting his wife and daughter, had struck a sensitive chord with Kazi that he hadn't known existed.

He'd have killed Quaid in that parking lot if the Nyxians hadn't stopped him. And an amazing, brilliant, sometimes funny, often slow-to-catch-on man would have vanished from the world, like a star blinking out of the night sky. Few people would notice it gone. But that star would never return.

Kazi closed his eyes. The Brotherhood never got involved, and they never cared, because it made their lives easier, not because it made a difference.

"Hey, mister. Mama says it's wrong to snoop. You snoopin'?"

He opened his eyes and frowned at the Quaids' little girl. She had Felix's humor-filled eyes and her mother's golden hair. But Felix's soft eyes hid the man's occasionally shrewd mind, and she'd be like him. "Maybe? Are you gonna tell?"

Rosa shrugged and held out a picture book. "Maybe. Unless you read this to me. Daddy and Mama are talking, and they never talk anymore, so I think we should let them."

Kazi folded his arms and peered down at her. "Is it a good book?"

"It's about a horse and blackberries."

"Hmm, does the horse eat the blackberries?"

"No, silly, it's scared of them!"

"And I'm the silly one?" He chuckled. "All right. Fine. You and me, let's find out what's so scary about blackberries."

He sat on the floor at the end of the bed, and Rosa settled next to him. Kazi and kids... He couldn't remember the last time he'd talked with one. They didn't feature much in his life. But this one, she seemed worth the time to converse with. He read aloud the story of the horse and the scary blackberries. When that book ended, Rosa found another and another, until her mother leaned against the doorframe. She waited until Kazi was done reading and said, "Rosa, it's a long ways past your bedtime."

"Mama! Really? Just one more?"

"No. Kazimir needs his sleep too, you know." Julia beckoned her daughter from Kazi's side and gifted Kazi a smile.

With the girl gone and the room quiet, he heard the sounds of a shower and assumed Felix was using it. The radiators hummed, Rosa still chatted away, and a phone somewhere pinged a notification. All normal family sounds in a soft, family world—an alien world to Kazi.

"I don't know what you did to my husband, but if you hurt him, don't think I won't come for you." Julia smiled, reappearing back in the doorway.

"Duly noted. And I won't... hurt him."

She narrowed her eyes. "Man like you, you take what you want and throw it away when you're done. Is that who you are?"

She knew of him, knew of Felix's battle with his career and how it was Kazi who had begun her husband's downfall. "It was," he admitted. "But not anymore."

"Good. See to it you stick to that path, Mister Skokan." She left and Kazi stayed at the foot of the bed, on the floor, listening to the homely noises, feeling more at peace in Quaid's house than he had in centuries.

He liked Julia. Felix had liked her too. They had a lovely daughter, a fine house, a normal life.

Kazi and the Brotherhood would poison it all.

"Hey." Hair wet, towel around his waist, Felix arrived and dropped a pile of clothes onto the bed. Warm, soapy scents wafted around him. "Julia found some clothes that'll fit you, if you want to, you know... give that shirt back to our neighbor?" His gaze skipped to the wall of frame photos, saving Kazi from answering. "She kept them up..."

"She loves you." He'd said it because it was true, even as jealousy twisted a knife in his heart. Kazi would never have this life or anything like it. He couldn't give this to Quaid. All he could do was take it from him.

"Yeah." Felix's expression turned complicated. "I love her. Just... maybe... not like she deserves."

"Tomorrow, stay." Kazi got to his feet, putting Felix close, too close for *friends*. "I'll go back to the Brotherhood. Tell them to stop looking for you."

"And that'll work?"

He nodded. "But you have to promise to let it all go."

Felix's jaw clamped, making a muscle jump in his cheek. He looked at the photos of his career, his life, and what he'd had. "I can't do that."

"Felix..."

"Everything I've seen, it's just the surface. I can't just forget it. I can't go back to my life and not *know*."

"Felix." Kazi hooked a finger under his chin and threatened to kiss his mouth. Warmth thrummed between them, and the pull Felix had on him was undeniable. "Don't do it for you. Do it for them."

He swept his lips over Felix's mouth, seeking more. Felix moaned, helpless in Kazi's thrall. Kazi ended the kiss, stroking Felix's clean-shaven cheek. He'd never have a man like him again, but it was for the best, because he'd never deserved him to begin with. "Every time I bite you, I poison you."

Felix blinked. "What?"

"The venom I inject targets the part of your brain that produces endorphins, triggering a dopamine hit. Every bite takes you deeper until you begin to crave me, like an addict chasing a high. None of it is real."

Felix recoiled and shoved at Kazi's chest, rocking him back. "You asshole," he hissed, still coherent enough to keep his voice down. "You've been drugging me this whole time!"

It was true. It had to be. That was how feeders and masters worked, even if it did feel different with Felix, as though their connection was hinged on so much more. "Yes."

His top lip curled in a snarl. "Then this is... what? Nothing?"

"It's something, but not what you think. It's a relationship based on you submitting and me fucking you every way I can." The words cut him like knives. He'd never known a nyktelios to fall so heavily for a feeder, but he had, and he'd fallen hard.

Felix backed away again. "You stay the night, and tomorrow, you can fuck off back to your fake fuckin' life, Kazimir. Your millions of fans can stroke your ego." He left, and Kazi was alone in the quiet room, listening to all the soft noises, hating himself all over again.

CHAPTER 22

elix

KAZI WAS GONE BEFORE DAWN. Despite the ache in his chest trying to tell him he missed him, it was probably a good thing he'd gone so Felix didn't punch him through a wall.

He'd *cared* for him. Or thought he had. Now he didn't know if any part of it had been real. Even now, he sat at the breakfast table, Julia and Rosa chatting, and half of him pined for Kazi. Maybe that was the poison too.

He felt... disgusted, violated. He'd been used. Kazi had bled him. Then he'd kissed him, wanted him, fucked his mouth... rubbed him off. He'd thought he was fuckin' gay! Now he didn't even know if *that* was real.

"Am I gay?"

Julia dropped her spoon.

"What's gay?" Rosa asked, stabbing at the halved strawberries in her bowl.

He blinked, clearing his head. "Shit, sorry, I—"

"Shit." Rosa grinned. "Where's Mister Kazi?"

"Oh my god, Felix!"

"Fuck, I mean—"

Julia scooped Rosa up and glared daggers in Felix's direction before taking his daughter upstairs.

He buried his face in his hands. Why did he have to be like this?

"What has gotten into you?" she snapped, returning to the kitchen in a whirl of fury to scoop up the dishes and almost throw them onto the counter. She grabbed a cloth and began cleaning aggressively.

"Kazi. He... did. It was him. He got into me. It's all been about him!"

"Not this again." Julia threw the dishcloth down. "When will you let your obsession with that man go!"

"I can't!" He could feel him inside him now, inside his veins, hot and slippery. "Something is wrong with me."

"Felix, for goodness' sake. You need help. I told you that years ago. I can't make you see someone. But you *need* to."

But the problem wasn't him; it was Kazimir. It wasn't Felix's fault he'd been drugged and tricked into caring for a vampire! "Julia... when we were together... was I... Did I... you know...?"

"Are you gay?" she asked, sounding cruel. She huffed and folded her arms. "I don't know. Maybe."

"What?" He'd expected a simple no. Not a maybe. What the hell was maybe?

"Felix..." She sighed. Tears shone in her eyes. Felix shot to his feet to go to her, but she shook her head and hugged herself. "You were with me but never *with* me." A tear slipped down her cheek. She swept it away. "Some things you said, about your time abroad... with the guys."

He had fooled around once when he'd had too much to drink. "That was just guy stuff."

"Felix..." She spread her hands, almost begging him. "You told me you kissed a man somewhere in Afghanistan or something. You said it like it was nothing, but it wasn't nothing, honey. Because I saw it in your eyes. You were asking me if it was okay. Didn't you know?"

"No... I... Maybe. I mean, yeah." So then that wasn't all Kazi's venom or poison he'd stuck in Felix's veins. Because it had happened before he'd met him. So that was Felix's feelings, all on his own. He was gay. Did you feel gay once you knew? He just felt the same as he always had.

She laughed even as she cried. "I love you, honey, but you're such an idiot sometimes."

He leaned back in the chair, numb, as though her words had knocked the confusion out of him. "I'm so sorry. I should have talked to you about this before now."

"Yeah!" She gripped the counter on either side of her and smiled, giving him the I-told-you-so look. "Did you and Kazimir...?"

He swallowed. "Was it obvious?"

"Just a little... He's super intense and you're all... you. You've been acting weird since you got here. More weird. But I thought you hated him."

"Yeah, I do. It's just... everything's really fuckin' confusing right now."

"Look, you always have a home here with us. I don't care whether you're gay or bisexual, or whatever. I just want you to be a father. I just want Felix back, for Rosa."

He nodded, and that damn knot in his throat tried to choke him again. "I can er..." He cleared it with a cough. "I can do that."

Maybe Kazi was right, and his leaving had been for the best. The venom would wear off. And he'd try not to go looking for trouble to keep Rosa safe. If Kazi could stop the Brotherhood from coming after him, then Felix really did have another chance at making this work.

But what would Kazi's efforts to save Felix cost him?

He didn't know much about them, but from the snippets Kazi had revealed, the Brotherhood didn't seem like the forgiving type.

~

He spent the day with Rosa, playing in the yard, raking leaves, drinking hot chocolate on the porch and staring out over the sun-dappled neighborhood he'd once taken for granted. The evening drew in fast, and the temperature dropped, forcing him and Rosa back inside, where Julia had prepared lasagna. He watched her for a while, and now he knew he loved her, but loved her in a different way than the one he'd tried to shoehorn into his life. It all began to make sense.

Rosa summoned him to the living area, where she'd built a tower of picture books. "We're going to read this one first. It's about a horse and blackberries."

"All right." He sat on the couch, tucked her close and began to read.

"Not like that, Daddy," she scolded. "You have to do the voices."

He chuckled. "'Voices'? Okay..." So he began again, making an effort to put some acting into the narration.

"Mister Kazi did a funny voice for the horse."

"He what?" When had Kazi read to Rosa?

"For the horse, he did a silly voice, because horses can't talk. That's what he said."

Something fragile cracked around Felix's heart. Kazi had read to Rosa? Why the fuck that mattered, he couldn't imagine, but it did.

"He doesn't like blackberries either."

"Who doesn't?" he mumbled, heart thumping.

"He said they're full of worms." She giggled.

"Kazi told you blackberries are full of worms?"

"Yeah. He's so silly."

"Dinner!" Julia called.

Rosa bolted, leaving Felix staring after her, the book about horses and blackberries open in his lap. Rosa had *liked* Kazi. Either Kazi was a damn good liar, or he'd liked her too. In all the madness, all the blood and chaos, the sex and insanity, he'd forgotten Kazi had feelings. He'd become this thing in Felix's life, a fantasy, a nightmare, and a dream all at once. But he'd never really looked at him and seen someone who hurt, someone who suffered, and somehow someone who maybe cared like Felix did.

He'd left *because* he cared.

What had it cost him to leave? Did the venom work both ways? And he'd vowed to protect Felix from the Brotherhood, knowing the cost, even if Felix didn't.

Shit. What if under all those shallow grins and photogenic poses Kazi had an actual heart?

"Felix?" Julia called from the kitchen.

"Coming..." He set the book aside.

Outside, through the window, a figure stood on the sidewalk, looking right back at Felix.

Felix leaned over the couch, trying to fix the guy in his sights. Tall, built well, and despite the cold, he only wore a red V-neck T-shirt, as though winter didn't touch him. He had the kind of sandy-blond hair normal men couldn't get away with and startling blue eyes.

His heart skipped.

He knew that man; he'd seen him with Kazi when he'd been photographing him for the *New York Times* exposé. And now he knew what he was. Brotherhood.

"Julia..." He pushed from the couch, backing toward the kitchen. "Do you still have that Beretta?"

"What, honey?"

He bolted. "The gun! Do you still have the gun!"

She blinked, lasagna pan in hand. "Top of the cupboard."

Felix climbed the counter, grabbed the case from above the wall cupboards, threw it open, plucked the small handgun and clip, rammed both together and flicked off the safety. He dashed back into the living room.

The vampire was gone.

A knock sounded at the door.

"Shit." He braced the gun in his palm and aimed at the closed front door. "Julia, keep Rosa back there. Don't come out."

Another knock. "Open the door, Mister Quaid," a muffled male voice said.

Felix kept the gun raised, grabbed the handle, took a breath, and flung open the door. He pointed the gun at the stranger's face. A *different* man from the one who had been standing across the street. This guy was dressed in jeans and a thick winter jacket. He had dark hair, not blond.

He raised his hands. "Mister Quaid, my name is Eric Sharpe. I'm a detective with the NYPD." He reached for the badge on a thin chain around his neck.

Felix glanced at it. It sure looked like an NYPD badge, although it could equally be a fake one bought off eBay.

"Lower the gun or—"

He didn't see the wrecking ball coming. His shoulder hit the wall, his body rocked as though he'd been hit by a silent explosion.

The guy with blond hair slammed Felix's hand holding the gun to the wall, once—twice. Pain snapped through his wrist. He yelped, dropped the weapon, and tried to shove him off, to fight, but the man's hold was as hard as iron. His blue eyes blazed, so like Kazi's.

They'd sent this one to kill him.

"Zaine…" the detective said, adding his own bite to his voice. "He wasn't going to shoot."

"You can bet he wasn't going to shoot, not with me here. *Were you, Quaid?*"

"Felix!" Julia screamed. She stopped in the kitchen doorway, hands at her mouth. Behind her legs, Rosa bawled.

"You goin' to kill me in front of my kid?" Felix snarled.

"Ma'am! Stay there!" Eric barked. "This situation is under control." He showed her his badge. "Everyone needs to calm the fuck down." Eric picked up the fallen gun. "Zaine, let him go."

Something ancient and vicious flashed in Zaine's eyes. He gave Felix one last long stare, then dropped him and backed up.

"I apologize for my partner," the detective said with a sigh. "He gets protective."

Felix kept himself plastered to the wall and eyed the pair. Were they both vampires? Or just the blue-eyed one? If they were here to kill him, they'd proven exactly how little chance he had at stopping them, but he'd try. "Julia, take Rosa upstairs."

"That won't be necessary. We're not here to hurt you," Detective Sharpe said. He kept saying things as though all of this was routine, but there was nothing normal about having a six-foot blond guy throw Felix against a wall.

Felix jerked his chin at Zaine but faced Eric. "I know what he is."

"Yes, we'd assumed you did." Eric was the calmer of the two. The other one still looked as though he'd like nothing more than to throw Felix around like a doll and then snap his neck over his knee. "Look, we can do this here, or you can come with us and we can talk somewhere else."

If he left with them, they'd make it so he'd never come back. "Go where?"

"Just a café. Maybe you know somewhere in town? You pick the location." Sharpe raised his hands. "I'm not arresting you. This is just a chat. We're here to talk. You have my word. And Zaine won't touch you."

Zaine narrowed his eyes.

"Is this about Kazi?"

The blond vampire started forward again. "It's about a lot of things, Quaid. It's also probably the only chance for you to tell your side. We can talk here but..." He nodded toward Julia and the still-crying Rosa. "The more who know, the more complicated it gets. You understand, right?"

"No, not here." He had to get these people away from his family. "I'll go with you."

He kissed Julia on the forehead, then hugged Rosa. "It's okay. I'm going to be okay. I'll come right back." She sniffed and nodded. He smiled and ruffled her hair, and heading for the door, he didn't dare look back. "Let's go."

The detective drove while Zaine simmered in the back seat.

Felix directed them to a diner that opened late in town. He picked one on the busy main street, bustling with early evening shoppers.

Inside, red leather booths cushioned the conversations. Felix picked a booth at the back, with a little privacy but not too much. He needed to be seen. The three of them sat, and Zaine ordered coffee and cake, making the cop smile. They were comfortable around each other, like two men who had worked together for years.

"You're a long way from New York, Detective," Felix said.

"I'm not here on *official* business."

Zaine sprawled in the corner of the booth, one arm draped on the table, the other over the back of the seat, with his body angled toward the detective. He was West Coast handsome. All warm skin and honeyed hair. But there was a sharpness to him too, the same kind of sharpness Kazi had. As though all those smiles could turn deadly at the click of his fingers.

"I didn't think they let vampires have badges," Felix said, checking Zaine's dazzling eyes for a reaction.

"Funny man, huh?" Zaine smirked. "I'm not a cop."

No, he didn't look like one either. But he probably knew a thousand ways to kill someone, and another thousand to cover it up. "You said partner, so I thought—"

"We're a couple," Detective Sharpe said. "Although we do work together."

"A couple? Like... in a relationship?"

"That a problem?" The way Zaine asked suggested he'd make it a problem if Felix wanted to.

"No, I... No." The similarities between them and his situation with Kazi swirled in Felix's head. Vampire and man. A *couple*.

Their slices of cake and coffee arrived, and the pair busied themselves with sugar and cutting bits of cake. They shared a few secret smiles and glances. He saw it now, how they fit so comfortably together.

"So you're his feeder?" Felix asked.

The detective spluttered, choked on cake, coughed into his

hand and then took several gulps of hot coffee. "No," he croaked.

"I don't understand."

Zaine's eyes held silent laughter now, as well as a murderous gleam. "How much do you know, Mister Quaid?"

"Are you going to kill me?" Felix asked, ignoring his question.

Zaine doubled down on the bad-ass glare. "Who told you we would?"

How much was he supposed to say about Kazi? Would anything he said here hurt Kazi somehow? He didn't want that, even if he did hate him for filling his veins full of poison. "Kazi and me, we had a deal." Felix lowered his voice. "I gave him blood, and he protected me. He's gone now, so it's over. It's all over. I don't want any trouble with your people. I won't tell anyone about any of this."

Zaine folded his arms on the table and sighed. "They all say that. They'll never tell... And you won't for a week, a month, a few years. But it'll eat at you. You'll always wonder. And a curious man like you, an investigative reporter, you won't be able to resist picking at the scar until it bleeds. Enough time will pass that you'll think we won't notice if you upload a few podcast episodes about missing people, about how vampires might be real and you have the evidence to back it up. You have documents, articles, photos. Right now, besides the nyks and the Nyxians, you're our highest level threat, Mister Quaid."

When he laid it out like that, he could see their point.

"But that's not why we're here," the detective added, prompting Zaine to sit back in the booth.

"Have you been hearing voices, Mister Quaid?" Sharpe asked.

"No."

"Cold sweats, withdrawal-like symptoms?"

"What? No. Nothing like that."

"When was the last time you and Kazimir engaged in blood-sharing?"

"I er..." He peered into his coffee's foamy top. It had been a while since the old barn, since he'd let Kazi bite him, and then... had the best blow job of his life. "A few days, I guess."

"And you haven't experienced any ill effects?"

"I said no. Apart from, you know..."

"What do we know?" the detective pushed. He was clever, this one. Sharp with his questions as well as his name. Felix could see how he'd make a damn good cop.

"I er..." He sniffed, picked up his coffee and, without meeting anyone's gaze, said, "I miss him."

"That's not a bad thing, Felix."

The gentle tone in Detective Sharpe's voice almost choked him up. "Isn't it, Detective?" He sipped his coffee and chanced a look at the man's face. They probably thought he was a loved-up idiot drugged by a vampire. A feeder or whatever. "Because it feels pretty wrong."

"Call me Eric. Like I said, I'm not here as a cop. I want to help."

Okay, so they wanted to help. Why? "So what is this, then? You're here to see if I'm addicted to nyktelios blood, and if I am, then you put me down like a dog?"

"That's about it, yeah," Zaine replied. "Are you?"

Eric rolled his eyes. "Z, maybe you could go watch the door?"

"He needs to know the shit he's in. And we need to know how far Kazi has fallen."

"He knows the shit he's in, kaerasti."

Zaine huffed and scooted out, then sauntered to the front of the diner, drawing attention with every step.

"That word, 'kaerasti'?" Felix muttered.

"It means *loved one*," Eric said, shaking his head. A slight blush touched his face.

"You love him? A... *vampire?*" Felix whispered.

"I know. Crazy, right?" Eric didn't look insane or like a blood-crazed feeder. So was his love real? And if his was real, then why weren't Felix's feelings real? Why did it have to be about venom with him and Kazi?

"I know it's a lot," Eric said, probably seeing the panic in Felix's eyes. He dug into his pocket and brought out a small white thumb-sized device. "Will you consent to a blood sample?"

"Why?"

"Just a theory me and Zaine are working on."

"What theory? C'mon, you have to give me more than that."

Eric teased the small white box between his fingers and glanced toward the big windows where Zaine stood like a bodyguard. "There's a lot I shouldn't say, but keeping you in the dark is bullshit too. I'm not a feeder, but I should be. Zaine and me... we're intimate, like you and Kazi—"

"Not anymore we're not." Felix snorted a bitter laugh. "The prick poisoned me."

"With venom, right? Okay, but there's another explanation. So, technically, you and I should be half-mad feeders, blood addicts feeding on our masters for the high. But I'm not, and Zaine suspects you're different too."

"Different how?"

"If you're like me, then our blood is different. It means we're immune to their venom. And if we're intimate with a nyktelios, we get benefits."

"'Benefits'?"

He hunched forward, keeping his voice low. "Like quicker healing, feeling stronger."

Holy shit. "Really?" Felix had felt different lately. Not right after he'd let Kazi feed off him—that had mostly left him exhausted—but a few hours later, yeah... there'd been that sudden sense of recovering fast and coming back stronger.

"It's just a theory, and we've hit some resistance from the Brotherhood in trying to figure it out, so we're here, checking it out for ourselves, off the books."

Hmm, this *was* interesting. So not everyone at the Brotherhood wanted Felix gone. And there was a chance Felix hadn't been drugged. "The Brotherhood doesn't know you're here?"

"They know we're here, checking on your house. But we didn't find you because you're not an idiot who'd go back to the most obvious place we'd look, putting you and your family in danger." Eric blinked pointedly.

"Yeah, shit..." Felix rubbed the back of his neck. "I did that."

"Be grateful it's us here and not Mikalis." He held out the small blood testing device.

"This Mikalis is bad?"

"Only if you like breathing."

Felix took the device, tucked his forefinger inside and jabbed the button. A sharp nip of pain signaled the sample had been taken. He handed it back, and Eric put it down next to his phone. "It'll take a while, around twenty minutes. Then we'll know if you have the same quirk in your blood as I do."

"And if I do..."

"That's above my pay grade."

Felix sipped his coffee and eyed the big blond vampire by the window. If his blood was different, like Eric's, and Eric was alive, that suggested Felix might get to escape this Mikalis's judgment too. And if his blood made him immune to venom, then he might need to have a whole new conversation with Kazi. "How old is he?"

"Zaine? A few centuries." Eric smiled at his lover. "He's the youngest."

He'd expected him to be older. "Kazimir is over a thousand years old."

"Yeah, so I've heard."

"I can't even begin to imagine what it's like to live that long," Felix thought aloud.

"Painful, I assume," Eric replied.

Felix hadn't considered it like that. Kazi had lived a lot and lost it all. Yeah, that would be painful.

"I don't know too much about the rest of them," Eric said. "They're pretty secretive. And most of them don't like to talk about the past, especially around me."

"Shame. They must have a whole lot to talk about."

He nodded. "I get the impression they've all made a lot of mistakes, and they're trying to make up for them."

"Yeah... Kazi... he did some bad shit."

"Who told you? Not him?"

"No, the Nyxian leader. Nasty piece of work. She made sure I knew all about Kazi's vicious past."

Eric's eyebrows lifted. "But you don't buy into it?"

"Maybe I do, or did... I don't know, honestly. He told me he'd been manipulating me... turned me into a feeder, so... It's hard to know what to believe."

"Well, if the results come back that you're different, then whatever you feel, and whatever he feels, it's real. And knowing Kazimir like I think I do, he doesn't just *go nyk* after a thousand years of control... Do you know where he is?"

"If I did, I wouldn't tell you. No offense. You seem nice. It's that one I don't trust."

Eric smiled. "Kazimir helped Zaine and me, although ask Kazi and he'll deny it. He's not as cold and vicious as he appears to be. Some of the others are a whole lot worse."

"Yeah, I'm beginning to see that."

Eric's phone pinged. He checked the screen, then looked over at Zaine, also on his phone. "We've got company. We have to move."

"Huh?"

Eric scooped up the device and urged Felix from the booth. "Out the back. Go."

Felix caught sight of a man-mountain walking by the window—shaved head, muscles like barrels—and shoved through the back door, passing the toilets toward the fire exit. He opened the door and checked behind him to see if Eric was following.

"Go," the detective said. "But don't go home. Give it twenty-four hours before you go back. We'll have moved on by then."

"You're not coming?"

"No, I have to be here, for Zaine. You'll be fine, Quaid... I've got a good feeling about this. About you."

"What about the blood test?"

"I'll figure out a way to get the result to you. Just go before you're caught."

"And Kazi?"

Eric shook his head. "Kazi's on his own."

CHAPTER 23

azi

THREE DAYS AGO, he'd left Quaid's house, collected an emergency stash of cash, bank cards, and new IDs outside Portland, and left an electronic trail all the way down the New England coast to New York. Away from Quaid.

A few hours ago, he'd posted a picture of himself outside one of his favorite bars. *Sorry for the hiatus. Back on the scene and looking fine.* The likes and comments spilled in. He turned off notifications and waited.

The Brotherhood would come. They didn't have a choice.

He ordered a few drinks. He might as well enjoy his last night of freedom for decades. If he was lucky, Mikalis would put him away for twenty or thirty years—a life sentence in human terms. For him, a drop in the ocean. Enough to kick the desire for blood from the vein, to get Felix Quaid out of his system.

Felix would be gone when he got out.

Kazi gulped his drink, wincing at its burn.

This was for the best. Quaid got to live, hopefully. Kazimir Skokan, the internet sensation, would vanish from the public eye. Mikalis would cook up some kind of story, maybe even kill Kazi's persona off. The story would be he'd died in some hotel room somewhere, probably drugs, maybe suicide, depending on Mikalis's mood for the dramatic. The Brotherhood leader had never much agreed with the attention Kazi garnered.

A girl across the bar, trying hard not to be noticed, caught his eye. Early twenties, dark hair. He wouldn't have given her a second glance if he hadn't seen the tattoo of a dagger and eye on her neck.

She wasn't the only acolyte he'd seen lurking in his peripheral vision over the past few days. A man on the last bus he'd taken had been watching Kazi with too much interest. He'd shrugged him off as a fan. Now he wasn't so sure.

They'd found him *before* the post on Insta. Either they had someone inside the Brotherhood, a ludicrous thought, or the Nyxians were tracking him. Somehow.

He finished his drink and ordered another.

He'd cut out the inhibitor chip. But what if there had been two chips? A second microchip somewhere under his skin?

"What are you doing, Kazimir?" Mikalis slid onto the stool beside Kazi.

The music and the crowd had overstimulated Kazi's senses some, but not that much. The Brotherhood leader had a talent for appearing and disappearing in a blink. And for blending in. As he was doing now. A shark in a pool of minnows. And nobody had a clue as they danced, and chatted, and went about their lives with no idea how close they'd come to a real-life nightmare.

Mikalis raised his hand and ordered a bourbon, then gave Kazi the unsettling weight of his glare. Mikalis wasn't a friend. He'd throw each and every one of them under a bus to protect the Brotherhood. At least, that was how Kazi had always known him to be, but there were hints that there was a heart beneath the ancient and terrifying creature his subtly Greek appearance disguised.

"I had a whole speech prepared," Kazi said. "A hundred reasons why you shouldn't confine me."

Mikalis snorted. "Am I not going to hear them?"

"No, because they're all excuses."

Mikalis accepted his drink from the bartender and twisted on the stool to face Kazi. "What happened?"

There was too much to explain, much of it he probably already knew from speaking with Zaine. "Before we get to that, you should know the Nyxians are here."

He lifted the drink to his lips, eyes sparkling. "I'm aware."

Of course he was.

"I fear I am compromised in more ways than one. They implanted an inhibitor chip in my spine. I was able to remove that one, but I hadn't considered a second tracker."

Mikalis wet his lips, casually tasting his drink. "What was done to you at Eagle Lake is abhorrent and unacceptable."

Kazi's gut flipped, fearing he'd disappointed him. "I killed the nyks—"

"Not that. Although that would have been enough for the Nyxians to earn my ire. No... Nobody bleeds my Brotherhood and lives." An ancient earth-shattering predator slithered through the man's blue-eyed gaze. What would happen if Mikalis ever lost control?

Kazi cleared his throat, and a little trill of fear almost had his fangs dropping in response, either to back off Mikalis's threat of violence or run from it.

Vesna's words about Kazi never being Mikalis's crossed his mind. He blinked them away, dismissing the woman's ranting. She had no idea what the Brotherhood meant, the good work it did. If she did, she never would have kidnapped him. All she cared about was resurrecting Nyx, an insane idea. Although creating nyks—the very creatures she should hate—went against her story about her ancestors. Perhaps she'd never cared for those people, just revenge on him, personally.

He had no doubt Mikalis would stop her. He'd wipe her and her cult from existence, leaving nothing behind. He'd do the same to Felix too.

"In all my centuries, I've only once asked you for something," Kazi said.

"A request I denied," Mikalis said without hesitating, remembering that day, long ago, when Kazi had begged him to kill him. He took a few gulps of his bourbon. "What are you asking, Kazimir?"

"Let Quaid live."

Mikalis's smile was all perfect teeth without a trace of humor. "The Brotherhood comes first. He is a threat."

"He's one man—"

"Don't assume a single man cannot bring down a civilization." He laughed, the sound sharp and hollow. "Don't underestimate them."

"He has a wife and a child."

Mikalis shook his head and tilted his face toward the lights above the bar. "We do not care, Kazimir. Or have you forgotten?"

"He won't pursue us. You have my word."

"Time erodes the most stalwart of promises."

"Quaid will be old or dead by then. No threat."

Mikalis's sudden glance accused Kazi of things he knew he shouldn't have been feeling but couldn't stop. "First Zaine and now you?" the leader mused. "There must be something in the blood bags." He finished his drink in one long gulp.

"Lock me up for however long you want, but leave him—"

Mikalis *moved* quicker than Kazi could track. Suddenly, Kazi was bent backward over the bar, with a steel-like hand clamped around his neck and Mikalis leaning over him. The music, the chatter, it had all vanished, and when Kazi looked, the people were frozen, motionless like statues. Enormous dark shadows bubbled up behind Mikalis, two heaving clouds, but as Kazi watched, the shadows unfurled, turning from smoke to jagged, featherless *wings*.

"*Quaid dies,*" the leader growled.

Kazi gripped his arm, trying to pry him off, but Kazi's strength was nothing compared to his. "I will... protect him..." He forced the words through clenched teeth.

Mikalis withdrew. The noise from the crowd washed back into the bar. People danced and chatted, and among them, Mikalis stood, as normal as any man. He righted his jacket and smiled—but Kazi had seen the terrifying being inside him.

"Then perhaps I will be forced to agree to your first request from all those years ago."

Kazi snarled, careful to keep his fangs hidden. He meant to kill Kazi. "Perhaps you will."

"Stand against me, Kazimir, and it will be the last thing you do."

Kazi blinked, and Mikalis vanished in a storm of static, as though he'd never been there. Nobody saw it, just him.

He straightened off the bar and shuddered a sigh. By Nyx, Mikalis was one scary bastard. The Nyxian woman had vanished too. Had Mikalis somehow taken her, or had she slipped out while Kazi had been distracted?

Shit... He'd failed. Mikalis was going to kill Quaid no matter what happened, and Kazi couldn't stop him.

He headed for the exit.

He had to get to Quaid.

He'd been wrong. He'd go back there, take Quaid away, and run... keep on running.

He pushed through the club door, straight into a group of people screaming his name. "Kazimir! You're back. We missed you."

He fought to push them away, but more surged in. "Kazi! We love you!" Granted, most of them were young women. But a few men beamed at him too.

And he did not have time for this.

Something cool, hard and sharp dug into his back. "Tell them you're taking me on a date," Vesna purred, her lips soft against his cheek.

Kazi recoiled, but the knife pressed through his shirt into his skin.

"Careful now. We don't want your beloved fans to see how you might not be entirely human."

Where was Mikalis? Probably nearby, but he wouldn't strike in public. He'd wait, tail Vesna, and attack when they were alone.

He just had to get her somewhere private.

"All right." He threw a flimsy smile at the crowd and hooked Vesna into his side. Someone thrust a phone at them, snapping the camera flash. Vesna beamed, playing the part, and then slid with Kazi into the back of a waiting car. As soon as the driver pulled away from the curb, he dropped the human act and snarled. "Wherever you're taking me, you won't arrive."

She laughed. "From what I hear, Mikalis isn't happy with you, prince. You should join us. We'll worship your blood, worship you, while you build us an army of chaos."

He dropped the fangs, letting her see how he was in no mood for games. "An army of insane nyks won't bring Nyx back."

"No, but they will protect Her from you and your Brotherhood."

"They don't protect anything. They're rabid monsters. How can you not know this when a nyk killed your tribe?"

"Fuck you, suka. You did that!" She huffed and sat back, regaining her cool. "I'm doing this for our sons and daughters! Nyx will reign again—we will be her acolytes! And the Brotherhood will be gone."

He was done with her and the rest of her insane group of followers. Their beliefs were madness. He could lunge now and rip her throat out. He wanted little else, but he also knew that wherever they were taking him, it could be a compound like the one he'd destroyed. And once inside, he'd destroy it and every piece of their insane plan with it.

But what about Felix? Mikalis could have already given the word to have him killed.

Damn it. Protect countless thousands by stopping the Nyxians or save one man?

How could he choose?

CHAPTER 24

elix

He LASTED three days before Googling the goddess Nyx. It wouldn't hurt to look. It wasn't as though he was searching for Zaine or Eric Sharpe, or even Mikalis. As long as he avoided keywords like the *Blackrose Brotherhood*, they weren't going to know.

Nyx was the primordial goddess of night, according to Greek mythology. Some information said she wasn't a goddess, but more of a *Being*... There were no mentions of nyktelios creatures, but the Brotherhood could have erased that, he supposed, as well as themselves.

The information was scarce. Nyx didn't appear in the vast Greek God dramas. According to the lore, she was the beginning of everything—she'd birthed time and order, without which the world would still be in chaos. She was far more intangible than he'd thought gods to be.

She probably didn't exist at all. But the nyktelios did. And so did the Brotherhood. So some part of her was real.

He made a few notes, swung back in his office chair, stretched out—and absently clicked over to Instagram. Kazi's smiling face was the third image.

Sorry for the hiatus. Back on the scene and looking fine.

He was in a New York club, as though nothing had happened.

The date posted was two days ago.

"You should call him," Julia said, appearing in the doorway.

He almost fell out of his chair. "Shit, I was just..." What *was* he doing? Rubbing salt in the wound?

"It's fine, you know. But if you want something with him, I'd suggest calling him. Guys like that, they look smart, but they're not. They need to be told. I don't know how you left it with him or why, but if you're not ready to let him go, then do something about it and stop pining."

"I'm not pining," he said, then winced, hearing the whine in his voice. "And I can't. I don't have his number."

"Just message him on IG."

"No, it's... He left. We agreed not to go there."

She snorted. "Either you want to be with him or you don't. Don't torture yourself over it, okay."

It wasn't that simple, with the whole poisoning thing. Or maybe it was simple if he was immune like Eric had suggested. He still hadn't heard from him, so maybe the news was bad.

"Come downstairs. There's a storm blowing in. I've put *Moana* on for Rosa. We have popcorn."

"Yeah, sure." He glanced out of the window behind his computer screen. The sky had turned dark, and a bunch of amber leaves were being tossed around the backyard. He glanced again at Kazi's picture. The woman behind him, at the back of the room. Most of her was an out-of-focus blur, but there was something familiar about her face. He'd seen her before... wearing a hood.

She'd been at the compound.

She was Nyxian.

Shit, who was he supposed to call about this? He typed out a message to Kazi's IG account, asking if he'd seen the woman, and hit send. But his message would disappear into Kazi's inbox, full of a thousand other messages. Plus, the photo had been taken days ago.

He was probably fine.

Felix flopped back down in the chair.

The Brotherhood would be all over it.

They'd been all over it for centuries.

The storm flung leaves at the window.

But this had been different. This time, the Nyxians had caught Kazi. And Felix got the impression *that* had never happened. They'd never bagged themselves a Brotherhood member before. They'd never made nyks... Something had changed. Something that had helped them grow, given them the confidence to get bold, something with resources.

They'd had help.

He Googled Vesna Dragovic and used some old press hacks to dig around forgotten bits of the internet, trawling through the dark web. Vesna Dragovic, the twenty-four-year-old daughter of an Eastern European millionaire and diplomat, owned several companies that had been buying up properties all over the East Coast. One of which had been in Eagle Lake.

These were the compound locations.

But she'd been expanding. She had sites in Poland, the Middle East, Russia. Were they all labs, like Eagle Lake? And was this all her, or were there others involved?

He had to get this information to Kazi. Although... again, if the Brotherhood were so damn on top of this, they'd know already and didn't need Felix. If he contacted them, they'd know he'd been poking around where he'd been told not to.

The lightbulb died. The computer plinked and went dark.

"Honey, the power's out!" Julia called upstairs from the living room.

"Yeah, I know." Now? There had to be an outage *now*?

A blast of wind rattled the windows.

Lightning split the sky and briefly filled the room with white light. Thunder rumbled.

"I'll get the candles!" Julia said.

"Daddy...?" Rosa's little voice quivered.

"It's okay, sweetie..." he called.

Damn, the storm had come in fast. He pushed from the chair. More lightning flashed, and this time, the thunder slammed over their house. Outside, the wind rocked the trees. Leaves raced away. Felix took a step toward the window.

Someone stood in the yard.

"What the..." Felix pressed a hand to the glass.

Lightning forked above the trees, bleaching the yard white. He'd gone.

He staggered and fell against the desk. Was this what Zaine had meant by hallucinations? Was venom withdrawal finally catching up with him? He'd hoped he was different, like Eric. Hoped it was all real. But he'd seen someone, he'd been sure... a man with eyes of ice.

A deep growl of a voice boomed over his thoughts. *"Come to me."*

He clamped his hands over his ears. *Come to me,* the voice rolled over and over like an echo.

He knew what this was—knew *who* it was.

Mikalis.

"My family..."

"They'll live—if you do as I request."

It wasn't a request. Mikalis had power in his voice, more power than just reaching into Felix's mind. The need to obey tugged on his body, demanding he walk right on outside and drop to his knees in front of whatever monster that man was.

Kazi hadn't kept his word. The Brotherhood was here and they wouldn't let Felix live. He wasn't surviving this. Well, damn them, damn them all to whatever hell existed for them. He threw open the office cupboards, rummaged through an old box and dug up his old PRESS flak jacket. Tugging it on, he fled the office and dashed downstairs in the darkness, his steps lit by sporadic lightning.

Rosa helped Julia gather candles in the kitchen.

He grabbed the gun from on top of the cupboards, still loaded from before. "Julia, take Rosa. Get in the car and drive."

"Wait, Felix—what?"

"There's a man in the yard. No time to explain. Take Rosa now. Go to your mom's, somewhere far away. Just go and don't look back." He kissed Julia on the head, then crouched and did the same to Rosa. Her big eyes brimmed with confusion and fear. Hopefully, this wouldn't be the last memory she had of her daddy. "Go on, now. Do as your mom says."

Julia grabbed her handbag, keys, and coats and was out of the door, sprinting off the porch with Rosa in her arms. A moment later, Felix heard the car engine growl to life.

They'd be okay. They'd be safe. The Brotherhood didn't need to touch them.

He turned toward the kitchen window.

Rain lashed against the glass. Thunder growled and groaned, as though the sky were furious.

Whatever he was about to face, he wasn't going down without a fight. Fear tried to fix his feet to the floor. He shut down that part of him, tightened the straps on his flak jacket and threw open the back door.

Wind howled.

The man in the yard almost looked normal in dark trousers and a dark blue shirt. The wind whipped his hair and fluttered his clothes. And the ice-blue eyes burned, shining like stars in the dark. Felix didn't know him, had never seen him before, which made all of this even more insane.

He raised the gun and took a few confident steps onto the grass. Leaves flew between them.

"You want me?" he yelled. "C'mon, then. I'm not gonna make it easy!"

"You already did," the monster said, his handsome face expressionless.

Maybe Felix had learned a few things from Kazi, because he shouldn't have seen Mikalis coming. He saw how Mikalis tensed a split second before he lunged. Felix pulled the trigger, *one-two-three* times, walking forward as he did. The gun boomed, and the rounds slammed into Mikalis's chest, jerking him back, but he barely missed a step and kept right on coming.

Felix fired again and again. The gun kicked. Mikalis twitched. Lightning turned the world white, and for a flicker of a second, Felix saw... *wings*. But then they were gone, and the vampire pushed forward.

He fired again, backing up. Fired again, finger yanking the trigger. The howling wind tore the sound of gunfire away.

Click.

He was out.

Click, click, click.

"Fuck!" He threw the gun at Mikalis.

Mikalis sidestepped, and the gun sailed by him.

God, he'd emptied fifteen rounds into Mikalis's torso. The rounds had had about as much of an effect on him as foam darts.

Felix stood firm, his back to the house, and raised his fists. "And I thought Kazi was the dick. Stop fuckin' around and kill me!"

Mikalis bared his teeth and lunged.

Felix swung and punched the vampire in the jaw, flinging his head aside. Mikalis staggered, eyes wide.

Holy shit, Felix had managed to *hit him?*

Mikalis's side eyes soon darkened. Blackness washed away the shining blue like oil in an ocean.

Felix flung open the back door and *ran* into the kitchen—for a weapon, anything. He grabbed a pan off the burner and spun, swinging away. Mikalis ducked and tackled Felix around the middle, slamming him against the counter. He hit like a truck, stunning Felix.

Mikalis's jaw widened. Fangs gleamed.

Felix fumbled around the countertop, reaching for anything, caught a knife from the block and plunged it into the vampire's waist.

Mikalis reeled, stepping back. He reached for the knife sticking out of him—

Felix still had the pan. He brandished it—he might actually survive—and then, in a blink, Mikalis was on him. Cool, smooth fangs tore into his neck, and venom spilled ice into Felix's veins. He opened his mouth to scream and tried to shove Mikalis off, but he clutched him instead, his weight as solid as stone.

This was it, then. It was over. He'd given it his all. It was never going to be enough, but he'd tried. He'd fought, and he hadn't given up. In the end, that was all a man could do.

The back door flew open. A blast of wind tore through the house. Felix blinked, seeing blue eyes he recognized, and then Mikalis was gone. The dark blur slammed Mikalis into the wall so hard that the partition collapsed, and the pair of vampires spilled into the living room.

Felix's vision blurred. *Shit, shit.* He couldn't black out now. Blood trickled down his neck, warm and wet. He cupped a hand over the wound and stumbled away from the counter. Through the new hole in the wall, he saw Mikalis at the far side of the living room, and in front of him, Kazi stood firm.

"Kazimir, don't make me do this," Mikalis warned.

"You've left me no choice."

Kazi was here...

Elation swirled, lifting the weight from Felix's chest. Kazi had come back. He could have come back a few minutes earlier... but Felix would take the save. He clung to the island unit. If he could stay on his feet, he'd be okay.

"Don't be a fool. You're worth a thousand men."

"I've followed you for over a millennium. In all that time, I believed you were right. Until now."

"I don't discuss my actions with traitors." Mikalis lunged, flying at Kazi, teeth bared for the killing bite.

Kazi met him, blocking the vampire leader's strike. They danced, locked in a deadly embrace, both at arm's length, and then Kazi ducked, Mikalis swooped in for the bite, and Kazi swirled away, moving like smoke.

Felix couldn't watch, couldn't keep track of their fast blows. The sounds of glass and furniture shattering filled the air. Kazi was fighting for both their lives. But if he didn't hurry up, Felix wasn't sure he'd be conscious to see the winner.

He pulled his hand from his neck. Blood covered his fingers and ran down his wrist. *So much blood...*

And it was all his.

The room tilted sideways, or Felix did, and he was on his knees, blinking at his bloody hands in his lap. He knew he should get up, call for help, do something, but the knowing and the doing were too far apart. He couldn't make his body work.

A car engine roared; he heard that much. Julia wouldn't have come back. She couldn't bring Rosa here to see this.

Although he'd have given anything to see his daughter's face one last time.

CHAPTER 25

azi

He landed blow after blow and took the punches barreling his way. Mikalis was toying with him—he could break his neck and Kazi would never see it coming. But Mikalis wouldn't, because this was a lesson. Mikalis still hoped not to kill him. He didn't believe Kazi would go that far. He was wrong.

This was the hill Kazi had chosen to die on, and it felt right, like nothing had felt right in centuries. Maybe Felix was just one man, but Mikalis had said one man could bring down civilizations.

But Kazi was losing.

Every blow slowed him, and each of his swings landed with less strength.

When he found himself on his back in the front yard, his body ablaze with broken bones, blood in his mouth, he wasn't sure how he'd gotten there. But if this was his end, he was damn well facing it on his feet.

Mikalis hung back. The Brotherhood leader glared from a few

feet away. He wiped a drop of blood from his chin and waited for Kazi to stand.

"You disappoint me, Kazimir. The Brotherhood always comes first. The fact you're here proves you can no longer be relied upon. I had truly hoped not to do this."

Kazi bent and clutched his thighs, trying to breathe around shattered ribs. "You knew those Nyxians were in that bar, and you knew they'd try to take me again." He spat blood onto the grass. Something inside was a mangled mess. His body was trying to heal, but not quickly enough. "You gave me a choice: protect the Brotherhood or Felix."

"And here you are."

"You were going to kill him while I was wiping out those Nyxians. That was how you were going to thank me for my devotion? By killing the man I love?"

"'Love'?" Mikalis's smile pulled thinly over his fangs. "You've fallen far, my old friend."

"You're not a friend. I'm beginning to wonder what the fuck you are, Mikalis."

Twin headlights flashed, belonging to a car racing up the street. Its engine roared as its driver dropped a gear, and then the car mounted the sidewalk and plowed across the yard, coming straight for both Kazi and Mikalis.

Kazi lurched aside and rolled, landing on his side to see Mikalis burst into a cloud of darkness and sparks. The car exploded through, scattering Mikalis's sparks like fireworks.

But even as the car swung sideways, spinning a U in the dirt, the sparks and shadows coalesced back into Mikalis.

Zaine leaped from behind the wheel. "Fuck..." He raised a hand, mostly to Mikalis, but eyed Kazi warily too. "Kazi, stay the fuck down."

"*Zaine!*" Mikalis yelled. "You have three seconds to explain why you just tried to run me down with a car."

Zaine winced and kept his hand raised. "The grass is wet. The tires lost grip. That's not the point—"

Kazi licked the blood from his lips. Eric climbed from the idling car's passenger door, his hand on his side holster. Whatever this was, Eric was scared. Kazi couldn't blame him. Nobody dared to risk getting between Mikalis and a kill. But they had.

"Where's Felix?" Eric called.

Kazi jerked his chin. "Inside..." Mikalis's gaze flicked to the house, as though he were considering returning to Felix and finishing him off.

A growl simmered through Kazi.

"Easy..." Zaine warned them both. "Easy..."

Eric hurried up the porch and disappeared inside the house.

"Just listen, both of you," Zaine began. "Quaid has the same blood defect or quirk or whatever as Eric."

Some of the primordial rage melted from Mikalis. "What?" he demanded, echoing Kazi's thoughts.

"He's immune to our venom. That's worth investigating, right?"

Felix was immune? That meant... Felix had wanted Kazi for real? It hadn't been a lie. The heat, the bond, the connection—it was all real.

"One is a fluke, but two?" Zaine went on.

Mikalis growled, probably preferring Zaine to stop talking.

"Kazi!" Eric yelled from inside the house. "Get in here!"

If Mikalis was going to stop this, he'd do it now. Clutching his healing ribs, Kazi straightened and held Mikalis's damning gaze, waiting for the leader to strike. But he didn't move.

Kazi turned his back, took the porch steps in one leap and dashed inside the house. The place was a mess, as though a tornado had torn through it.

"Here!"

Eric knelt in the kitchen next to Felix on the floor, propped against a counter cupboard. Felix's head lolled. His face was white, in stark contrast to the bloody mess Mikalis had made of his throat.

"Quickly, stop the bleeding," Eric urged.

Kazi dropped to his knees and pulled Felix into his arms, heart and head thudding. He lapped at the neck wound, where Mikalis had torn into him, tasting sweet blood and bitter venom. Distantly, he knew the thunderous growling was his and didn't care. Mikalis had done this... Mikalis had almost killed Felix, might even still if he didn't recover.

He pulled back and looked at Felix's face.

"You came back," Felix croaked, then his heavy eyelids fluttered closed.

He wasn't dead yet, but his heartbeat thumped out of rhythm, clinging to life.

"He'll be all right..." Eric said.

He couldn't know that. None of them could know that. Life was so fragile. So bright one moment, snuffed out the next.

"Kazi...?" Eric was a good man, and he returned Kazi's gaze with an understanding Kazi would have expected from a being far older. "He has the same blood marker I do. That makes him tough. He's going to be okay." He gripped Kazi's shoulder, fingers digging in, anchoring Kazi's thoughts. "So, when he wakes up, you're going to want to be here, yeah?"

Kazi blinked, half hearing the words. A fire churned inside him. He'd given his word to Felix to keep him safe, and he'd failed. Because of Mikalis.

"So what you're *not* going to do is something stupid like attack Mikalis, right?" Eric added. "Right?"

He already had attacked him—his body was a wreck of bruises and broken bones—and he'd do it again. Mikalis had hurt Felix. He'd hurt what belonged to Kazi.

"Kazi..." Eric warned, digging his fingers in. "Nobody wins that fight alone."

Was there more to his words, to the narrowing of his eyes, as though this wasn't a conversation for now? Zaine and Eric had known about the blood. They'd come here, and they'd stopped Mikalis in his tracks with that knowledge.

Kazi nodded, afraid his voice would be more growl than words.

"Good. Now stay with him. Z and I will fix this. You concentrate on keeping Felix alive."

"Eric," Kazi croaked, stopping the man from leaving.

Eric glanced back.

"I owe you."

"No, you don't. Friends don't owe anything."

Eric left, and Kazi caught snippets of their conversation with Mikalis outside. How had the idiot Zaine snared a good man like Eric?

Kazi slumped next to Felix against the counter. "You had better live. I didn't go through all this for you to die on me now."

He wasn't even sure what it was about Felix that had made him turn his back on everything he'd known and trusted for so long. Perhaps it was his tenacity or his strange humor in the most unlikely of places. It was definitely how he tasted, both blood and body, and Kazi would be lying to himself if he didn't admit to wanting to taste him again.

If Felix didn't want him, he'd let him go. He'd have nothing. Mikalis would probably double down and kill Kazi if he continued to think him a traitor. But Felix would live. That was all that mattered.

He wasn't sure there was going to be a happy ending at the end of all this, but he'd fight for one.

Strange to think the man slumped next to him had such a hold over Kazi's choices. Not just strange, but terrifying too. Felix could tell Kazi to fuck off, to never come back, and he would do it. Felix might wake and say he didn't want Kazi, didn't want the chaos and destruction in his life. He wanted to be a father and a husband, and Kazi had no place in that world.

He gently scooped Felix into his arms, carried his limp body up the stairs and laid him on the bed in the spare room, the room with all the photos depicting a life he'd lost. Kazi was sorry for his part in that.

"Kazimir." The Brotherhood leader loomed in the doorway.

The growl Kazi let him hear was all the warning he'd have.

Mikalis raised both hands, took a few steps into the room and cast his gaze over Felix. If he so much as twitched, Kazi was going to throw him through the wall.

"We're not done, you and I," he said to Kazi. "But Zaine is right. Whatever is happening with Quaid's and Eric's blood needs further investigation. Your man there has earned a reprieve."

"And what have I earned? A few decades in confinement or a quick death?"

"My patience. Do not test it."

A heavy silence stretched between them. The storm outside had passed. The house was quiet again.

"He needs medical attention," Kazi said.

"No, he needs you." Mikalis turned away but lingered on the landing. "I'll see to it that this mess is covered up for the sake of security. But I suggest you stay no longer than necessary."

"Then?"

"Then bring Quaid to Atlas. I'll have Raiden run some tests."

Once Quaid saw Atlas, there would be no going back. Although he'd already seen too much to put that genie back in the bottle. Once Felix was in their territory, it would also mean Mikalis could kill him in an instant and nobody would bat an eye.

Mikalis hesitated as though he had more to say, but whatever it was, he chose to stay quiet.

"You should check in with the NYPD on your return to New York," Kazi said. "After I realized you'd left me to manage the Nyxians, hoping I'd be too distracted to save Felix, I escaped their car and tipped off the cops regarding my attempted kidnapping by Vesna Dragovic. She should be in custody by now."

Mikalis narrowed his eyes. "You *did* act for the Brotherhood."

He'd acted, and he'd raced up to Maine, fearing he'd be too late. "And it almost cost me everything."

FELIX SLEPT INTO THE DAY, and Kazi stayed with him, only leaving his bedside to check on a number of trucks that had pulled up outside. Builders erected an eight-foot-high construction fence around the house, creating the ruse that the Quaids were renovating.

Felix grumbled awake near dusk, asking for water and eyeing Kazi warily. By the time Kazi returned with a drink, Felix was up and in the shower. Kazi listened for a while, checking he was moving and hadn't collapsed while in there, then left the glass of water on the bedside table and headed downstairs, giving Felix space.

Kazi had worked through a few things since last night.

He'd tell Felix everything, answer any question. He'd earned it. And if he wanted Kazi out of his life, he'd respect that.

Kazi tidied the mess in the kitchen and fixed a pot of coffee. The workmen had boarded up the broken windows and fixed the doors. But the gaping hole remained in the kitchen/living room wall. The Brotherhood would pay to right the house, making it as though nothing had happened. Kazi would make sure of it.

"Hey," Felix croaked, wandering into the kitchen. He rubbed a towel over his damp hair. Slacks hung low off his hips, so low a small tug was all they'd need to fall. Droplets of water glistened on his chest, around a smattering of small, dark hairs.

Kazi averted his gaze and fought the sudden and violent desire to wrap Felix in his arms. The visceral need rocked him where he stood, banishing any thought that he might be able to resist the man's inexplicable pull. He could no longer blame it on venom.

Kazi poured Felix a mug of coffee and slid it across the counter.

"Thanks."

"How are you feeling?" Sipping his own coffee, he chanced a few glances. He looked good, a little pale. His heartbeat was strong.

Felix picked up his mug and carried it to the counter, then dumped a few spoonfuls of sugar into it. "Better than dead."

The muscles of his naked back shifted in perfect symphony, and it was all Kazi could do not to imagine having the man under him while Kazi licked up his spine and buried his cock between his ass cheeks.

Felix was likely traumatized. He didn't need Kazi coming on to him *hard*. Sex was probably the last thing on his mind. It should have been the last thing on Kazi's mind, but the treat of seeing Felix half-naked was a wicked tease. He wanted the man's legs spread around him, could imagine it so clearly it almost hurt.

"I take it Mikalis no longer wants me dead?"

"For now."

Felix's mouth flirted with a smile. He leaned against the counter and resumed sipping his hot drink, relaxed, comfortable. "I almost had him. He was goin' down, one punch away from lights out, so..."

Kazi couldn't stop his own smile. "I'm sorry I missed it."

"I'm pretty sure I hit him with a frying pan. Probably a first for both of us."

Kazi chuckled. He was certain nobody had *ever* hit Mikalis with a frying pan. "You did good, and there's a reason for that. Zaine and Eric saved both our asses last night. They had information. Your blood is... unusual. That's why Mikalis has spared us. It also means you'll likely have some benefits from our... relationship. Such as increased strength, reflexes and accelerated healing."

"Okay."

That was it? Okay?

"The detective, Eric, he said as much," Felix added.

He was taking this well. "So er..." Kazi needed to say he'd been wrong but had no idea how to say it. Wrong about everything. He wasn't often wrong. It was a new sensation for him. Everything to do with Felix was new, including caring. It had been easier before. He'd had an excuse. Now he had to admit to wanting this man in his life, knowing the best thing for Felix was for Kazi to walk away.

"You didn't poison me," Felix said, filling the extended quiet.

"Apparently not."

"And when we..." Felix rolled his hand, sipped his coffee and peered over the rim of the mug. "What we did was... real."

"When I sucked your dick?"

"Yeah, that," he croaked, glancing away with a shy smile that almost pulled Kazi over there. "It was genuine and not some fucked-up addiction thing you vampires do to your victims. Am I getting this right so far?"

"Precisely."

"So, the fact I hate your ass and love it at the same time is all me and not vampire voodoo."

"Yes?" He loved his ass? This wasn't how he'd imagined this morning-after conversation to go. He'd expected Felix to be furious, scared, distraught. He'd almost died. Again. He should have been a mess. But Kazi was more of a mess than Felix appeared to be.

"What?"

"You're taking all this well."

"When I know the facts, I can work with them."

That was the reporter in him showing. A fact finder. He rooted out truths. Kazi liked that about him, liked a lot of things he was only now beginning to allow himself to feel.

Felix set down his coffee. "I need to call Julia... Let her know I'm okay." He left the kitchen, probably searching for a phone.

Calling his wife was a natural thing to do, tell her to come home with little Rosa. Kazi didn't fit in that life, though, and never would. He sipped his coffee and listened to Felix's murmuring voice from the other room.

Felix returned later, having finished the call, his face troubled. "So what happens now?"

"I take you back to New York. They run some tests, try to figure out why you and Eric are unique."

"You haven't encountered this glitch in our blood before?"

"Not as far as I know, and considering Mikalis's reaction, I don't believe he has either, which is far more of an indicator that something isn't right. Nothing surprises him, except you."

"And Eric, I guess. I like them... They're good people."

"Yeah, they are." And they were better together. He couldn't help wondering if he and Felix could have that. He almost didn't dare think it, fearing it would lead to dashed hopes.

"I'll get dressed. Let's get this over with." He hurried from the room again.

"Is your wife coming home?" Kazi called, trying to hide the note of strange concern in his voice.

"No," Felix called back. "I told her to stay away for now."

Should Kazi ask him if he was planning on making a future with her again? It felt wrong to ask, as though he had no right to know. But while he wanted Felix to be happy, to survive and live until he was an old man, watching Rosa grow up... it also made his heart ache to think he'd do all that without Kazi.

He'd never cared enough about anyone before to be baffled by such thoughts. Should he climb the stairs and go to Felix, tell him how he felt, or just withdraw now and save them both the heartache?

CHAPTER 26

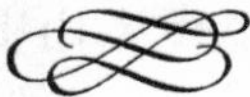

elix

Kazi was too quiet. He obviously had a lot on his mind. The Brotherhood, the blood revelation, defying Mikalis. None of that was going to be easy to deal with. Maybe he'd open up later, or maybe he'd decided to back off for good?

Felix's own emotions were a tangled mess. He wasn't thinking about how he'd almost bled out on his kitchen floor. That shit was done, and he was somehow alive, and that was all there was to it.

However, the blood issue might be his only saving grace. Figuring out why his blood was different meant more tests, so now they were going to New York—into the lion's den where all the Brotherhood vampires lived. If nothing else came of it, at least he'd see the truth of them. The reporter in him needed to know all of it. Maybe then he'd be able to complete the pieces of the picture of the Brotherhood in his head and what they meant to the world—good or bad.

"I er..." Kazi stood in the doorway, shoulders low, his expression more troubled than Felix had ever seen. "I need to say some things, and once they're said, it's done. You can decide what happens. It's your choice. No venom, no threat from me because of what I am. Understand?"

Felix continued to button his shirt. "Okay... sure." Was this the reason he'd been so quiet? Was Kazi about to tell Felix it was over before it had even begun? It made sense, he supposed. What did a thousand-year-old vampire want with Felix anyway? Some blood, a hand job, and he was lucky to be breathing at the end of it.

"You understand I'm not good, right?" Kazi lifted his eyes, managing to look wounded and vulnerable while strong and defiant.

He almost laughed. "Yeah, I got that."

"My past is... It's a lot. I'm trying to balance the scales some, to save more lives than I stole. Back then, I was...." He sighed and flung his gaze at the ceiling. "There are no words. I was uncontrollable, more beast than man. I was a nyk. Mikalis saved me. I suspect because I begged him to kill me. He's been making me pay ever since, and he's not wrong."

Kazi combed his fingers through his loose hair, raking it back from his face. In the shadows of the bedroom, and without his constant smile, his flashy poses and snarky comments, he briefly seemed... lost.

"What I'm saying is... you er..." He swallowed, then laughed softly. "This is more difficult than I—"

He had to end the torture now. For the both of them. Julia had said a man like Kazi needed to be told. So to hell with it. He was gonna tell him in the best way he knew.

Felix crossed the floor, cupped his face and thrust a bruising kiss onto his lips. He didn't know what the fuck he was doing or how he was supposed to do it. He just knew that he could stop Kazi's pain with a kiss.

Kazi's mouth opened, accepting, and his hand slid down Felix's back, hauling him tight to his chest. The kiss turned breathless and messy, sparkling into something brighter, like a match to an already burning flame.

It was Kazi who pulled away, but he bumped his forehead against Felix's. "I want you, Felix. I don't deserve you, but I want you more than I can bear. I thought I could walk away, tell myself I'd let you live your life. I could still do that, if I must. Just tell me you truly hate me, tell me you don't care, tell me you want me to go. And I'll go. You'll never see or hear from me again."

Felix searched his eyes, tinted with a hint of silver around their fierce blue. He didn't know what made him special to Kazi, or why Kazi felt the way he did, but he wasn't going to push him away for it. "Kazi..." He tucked Kazi's hair behind an ear, then skimmed his knuckles down the fine line of his jaw. "I don't hate you, and I'm not telling you to go." His heart hurt, his body thrummed, his veins burned, and his dick, well... if he didn't stop this here, there would be no hiding how much he wanted Kazi. "I'm not going to lie. It's a lot. And I don't know half of what's going on around you, but... I think I know you, under all the thin veneer you show the world. I know you in here." He poked Kazi's firm chest, over his heart. Kazi looked down, and Felix tipped his chin up again with a finger, although that meant Felix had to stand on his toes to meet his gaze. "I'm not telling you to leave, because I want you to stay. I'm not sure I ever hated you. I didn't *know* you. I hated the idea of you and blamed you for all the shit in my life... my shit, not yours."

It was true. No lies. No poison.

He scooped Kazi's free hand into his and twined Kazi's slim, precise fingers with his. "I want to know more of you. And this is all new to me, okay, but... I want to know what makes you really laugh. I want to see your real smile all the time. I wanna know what your favorite food is, and you know... what you like to do for fun, when we're not being chased by blood-raving monsters. I just kinda wanna know *you*, the man, I guess."

Kazi's kiss struck so fast it staggered Felix almost off his feet. He reeled, clutched Kazi's arm, and thrust his tongue between Kazi's lips, sweeping and tasting.

His back hit the wall, holding him up as Kazi leaned in, his knee clamping Felix's thigh so close there was no escaping the hard warmth of his whole body pushing in.

Suddenly and desperately, he needed to feel more of him, to have his hands on his skin. He pulled Kazi's shirt from his trousers and swept his hands up his back, reveling in his shudder and how his muscles tensed under his fingers. It wasn't enough though. He needed so much more. He shoved into the kiss, demanding with his body. He needed to feel Kazi against his skin, under his mouth, between his teeth.

And it was all them. No poison. No vampire voodoo. Felix owned these desires, and damn, now that he knew his own mind, he ached to explore those desires with a man who was equal parts vulnerable and monstrous.

Felix dropped his hand, cupping Kazi's erection through his trousers. Kazi gave an animal grunt, then growled, "You sure you want this?"

"Yes..." Felix grabbed Kazi's hand on his thigh and shoved it to where his own dick jutted, as hard as it had ever been, at least since the last time Kazi had had his fingers and mouth on it. He wasn't sure how this worked—his high school escapades had been a long time ago and the rest had been fantasies in his head. He hadn't even dared to watch porn, fearing it would answer too much about what he suspected about himself.

Did he fuck Kazi? Would Kazi fuck him? He kissed him again, rocking them together, grinding his dick against his thigh. Someone was going to have to take control, and he wasn't sure he could.

Then Kazi's quick, confident hand found its way inside his trousers, and Kazi's fingers encircled his dick, and it was all he could do not to whimper. He dropped his head back, moaning his pleasure, easing his length through Kazi's grip, and then Kazi's hot mouth was on his neck, his tongue firm and wet. Maybe he should have been afraid. He'd healed from Mikalis's vicious attack, but it had only been a few hours since he'd almost died. He trusted Kazi not to hurt him. He'd been there when he'd needed him. Nobody had ever done that for Felix.

"What do you like?" Kazi purred, nuzzling his chin. "Hard and fast? Soft and slow?"

Just the fact he'd asked brought a strange whine to Felix's voice. "I wish I knew."

"Hmm, then we'll find out."

Kazi's grip vanished from his dick, and Felix almost whined at that too, but then both wrists were suddenly pinched above his head. Kazi's silvery-blue eyes filled his vision, and his hot, hard body pressed over him in all the right ways.

"Fuck..." Felix spluttered, unsure. He couldn't bring his hands down, couldn't move. He squirmed, driving the rod in Kazi's trousers over his own hip.

"Too much, baby?" Kazi purred, mouth on his cheek.

"Ugh, God."

"Not anymore." Kazi kissed him, then drew his bottom lip between his teeth and bit—fast and sharp. Blood bloomed over Felix's tongue. That was bad, wasn't it? Or was it good? It felt good, like having his wrists pinned felt good, and Kazi's dick rubbing him felt good.

Kazi kept one hand on Felix's pinched wrists, but the other he used to grab Felix's chin. "If it feels good, don't fight it."

But he'd been fighting it all his life.

"I've got you, baby," Kazi whispered, skimming his mouth over Felix's, teasing a kiss and more.

He might combust into a pile of ash if Kazi kept this up. He'd never been worshipped like this, never been shamelessly fucked by a man like he knew Kazi could do to him. He wanted to be, though. That was his secret, one he'd never let himself think, let alone fantasize over. He wasn't sure he was ready for that. Not yet.

"Your mouth," he moaned.

Kazi's smirk promised wicked sex. "You like my mouth?"

His dick twitched, trapped between them. Kazi must have felt it too.

"Baby, you can fuck my mouth any time you like." He pushed the words into the corner of Felix's mouth and cheek.

Kazi dropped to his knees and freed Felix's dick.

Felix found his wrists were free and plunged his hands into Kazi's hair. He grabbed his head and slid his cock into Kazi's smart mouth. Fuck yes, this was where he wanted to be, buried balls deep in warm, wet, tight muscle. Kazi's tongue hugged his girth. Felix's dick stroked the back of his throat. It was almost too much. He didn't want to come so soon. He pulled free, panting, and dropped to his knees, mirroring Kazi.

Kazi's eyes shone with wicked delight. He was fucking loving this too.

"Hmm," Kazi purred. He licked at Felix's lip, making the earlier cut tingle as it healed. Fingers dug into Felix's hips, and Kazi began to grind himself against Felix's exposed dick—his own still inside his pants. He clearly knew what he was doing. He'd probably had so many partners he'd lost count.

"Should we er... use protection?"

"Only if you want. My blood destroys anything that doesn't belong."

"Okay. It's just..." He looked down between them, at Kazi's dick tenting his pants. His erection ached, and his mouth watered at the thought of wrapping his lips around him. He wanted that, but... "This is maybe not the time, but... if I suck you off, is it safe? I won't... y'know... grow fangs?"

Kazi peered through his lashes and smirked like a bastard. "Wanna fuck around and find out?"

"I'm serious!"

He chuckled, and Felix's dick leaked to hear that delicious sound. "No, you won't turn. You'd need to ingest my blood multiple times and even then it's unlikely."

"I have—I've done that."

"Not enough." He freed Felix's hips, undid his own trouser fly, grabbed Felix's hand and placed it on his cock. "You feel how hard I am for you?" Felix could hardly miss it. Kazi was well proportioned, long in more than just height. Felix closed his fingers around half of it, unsure if he could manage to swallow it all.

"Stop overthinking, baby," Kazi purred. "And suck me like you hate me."

Felix's grin slipped sideways. "I don't think you want that."

"Don't I?" He stood suddenly, giving Felix an eyeful of his long, veined, taut cock in front of his face. Kazi gave his dick a quivering twitch and smirked down at him.

Fuck him. Felix pulled Kazi's cock down, slipped the head through his lips and opened wider, taking him in as deep as he dared. Which turned out not to be all that deep, but a quick glance up revealed Kazi's glare burning down on Felix, his pupils shot with silver, his fangs extending into place. And he looked a whole lot as though he needed this.

"I love seeing you like this," Kazi snarled. "On your knees for me."

Felix liked it too, more than he'd dreamed. He might have been the one on his knees, but he had Kazi exactly where he wanted him.

Felix had one hand on his hip, one on his dick, keeping it angled just right, and he worked his tongue up and down its length. When Kazi tried to pump, Felix pushed at his hip, holding him back, and found his own rhythm of sucking, head bobbing. He'd sucked dick in high school, if not much else. This he knew how to do.

Kazi's fingers dug into his hair. He pinched his lip between his teeth, avoiding his fangs. In the light flooding into the spare room from the landing, Kazi stood silhouetted, his eyes shining, and he was like something untouchable, as though he might vanish from Felix's life and it would all be a dream.

Before that happened, Felix was going to make him come, to have it so he couldn't hold back, make him lose himself in the best way, and he wanted to see his face when that happened.

"Oh baby, yes... Your mouth is so tight and wet. It makes me want to fuck your every hole, Felix."

Felix moaned around his thick cock. His own neglected dick wept. He ached to pump himself, but he also needed to keep Kazi back, keep him from ramming his cock down Felix's throat. Kazi shuddered. His hips jerked, his body trying to thrust.

Maybe there was a way...

Felix pulled off, earning a dangerous glare from Kazi. "You do hate me, huh?" He smirked.

"I'm not done. Sit on the bed there." He wiped his mouth and jerked his chin at the bed behind Kazi.

Intrigued, Kazi sat, his dick a jutting, erect rod.

Felix kicked off his own pants and sauntered over. Kazi's gaze tracked the bounce of his dick, and a thrill danced down Felix's spine.

He straddled Kazi's legs, kneeling on either side of him, lowered himself to his lap, and laid his arms over Kazi's shoulders. His dick nudged Kazi's. This was better, fairer... He rolled his hips, sliding his erection along Kazi's. The thrilling tease tingled low in his balls. It was fascinating, and gorgeous, and hot as fuck to see his dick rub against another man's, even more heart-racing to know that the other man was Kazimir Skokan.

Kazi's smirk was all real. "You gonna come on me, baby?"

He opened his mouth to deny it, but Kazi dropped his hand, encircled both cocks and pumped them together. Felix stopped rocking, threw his head back and rode the rising wave.

CHAPTER 27

azi

Heat flushed Felix's face and neck. Kazi wanted to rip Felix's shirt off and bite him all over, but to do that, he'd have to stop working both their cocks, and that wasn't possible. Wet with pre-cum, his fingers glided, building glorious friction. And to know it was Felix's cock sliding right up his own—that was the best part. Sex had always been just sex to Kazi—methodical, routine, dull.

But not with Felix.

Felix panted. He was so close to coming. He shuddered and twitched, teetering on the edge, probably trying to delay the inevitable.

There, on his face, how his mouth pulled at a smile, then his lips parted. He threw open his eyes, gripped Kazi's shoulder and fixed him in a devastating stare.

"Gah... Fuck... *Fuck*!"

His hips bucked, and his dick jerked. Hot cum slickened Kazi's fingers, and if he hadn't already been a few strokes away from coming, he was now. He pumped with Felix's still unloading, and blind pleasure snapped through Kazi. He came with a ragged shout, shuddering and twitching, trying to bury himself in his own hand, or Felix's dick, or any part of him, to claim him, own him, make him Kazi's in a way that perhaps wasn't all man and was instead some ancient part of the beast inside trying to feed and fuck and possess Felix as its own.

They trembled and panted together, and before Felix could begin to doubt himself, or them, Kazi flung his arms around him and pulled him down onto the bed, trapping him against his chest. They weren't naked enough. Kazi hadn't licked or sucked enough of Felix—he definitely hadn't made the man gasp enough—but there would be time for that.

He hoped.

If the Brotherhood didn't scare him away.

Which they would.

Dread took some of the shine off his postcoital afterglow.

Soon, Felix would have to meet Storm and Octavius. Aiko wasn't so bad, as long as he didn't think Felix was a threat. Raiden—shit, nobody knew with Raiden. Too quiet, too obedient, too intelligent.

"What are you thinking?" Felix asked. His finger circled one of Kazi's shirt buttons, tickling his chest.

"How not to fuck this up."

"Can it get more fucked up?" Felix asked.

Kazi pressed his lips together, opting to remain quiet. Things could definitely get more fucked up. There was knowing about the Brotherhood and then seeing it. They were two very different things.

"What's your favorite food?" Felix asked.

"Hmm?" He rolled onto his side, sliding Felix into the valley beside him, still keeping him close, but now, when he propped his head on a hand, he looked down at the man who just might be the end of him. "My what?"

"Your favorite food? You've been around for a few years. You must have tried everything. I wanna know what you like."

He swallowed, pretty sure Felix was trying to distract him from thinking of their return to New York. He'd tried many an exotic dish. Food, when he'd been mortal, had consisted of broth and bread. But there was one thing he couldn't resist. "Apple."

Felix snorted. "No, it's not."

"It is."

"An apple?" He arched an eyebrow.

"A Papirovka, to be precise."

"Is it amazing, this apple?" His tone definitely mocked.

Kazi laughed. "You asked."

"Okay, so why this Pavlova apple, then?"

"Papirovka. My father had several trees imported from Rome, and before I was... Before I became what I am, I'd walk through the orchard in the morning, alone, before the servants arose, and I'd take an apple from one of his trees. It's resistant to the cold, and my land was always cold." He remembered it so clearly. He could smell the wet grass and the tinge of apple in the air.

Felix's expression had lost all of its humor, turning intense. "Where is your land?"

"The Carpathian foothills. A wild, rugged place. Cruel and unforgiving, but also rich with magic and soul. Well, it was. Now I fear it's more of a tourist attraction."

"Does it hurt, going back?"

"I haven't been back." He smiled sadly. "I can't, not after what I did."

Felix fell quiet, and they both lay in silence, listening to a ticking clock somewhere in the house. "It's easy to forget... what you are sometimes."

"If only that were true for me."

"You weren't always a nyktelios? You got turned, right?"

"I was a prince, set to inherit the crown of my father's rich and prosperous kingdom. To this day, I do not know if the nyks' attack was random or if they knew who I was. We would hunt wolves, a great party of us, for days, deep in endless wilderness. The hunt that time was like any other, except the wolves had proven so elusive that I'd pushed us deeper into distant valleys. I didn't know it, but the wolves weren't there to be found. A nyk had driven them out."

"Are they able to plan like that? Aren't they all rabid monsters?"

"The youngest are ravenous and mad with it. The oldest... They behave like you or me, able to blend in perfectly and adapt. Their madness is restrained. Instead of killing indiscriminately, they create feeders, and they procreate."

Felix fell silent for a little while, his fingers still teasing over Kazi's skin. "One of those found you?"

"She attacked our camp and took me. I thought her a demon, tried to escape, but it was fruitless. And when she was done, she let me go. Most of the rest is a blur. Nyks rarely recall their first few years. It's carnage until they are killed or until they gradually control their hunger."

"Did you control your hunger?"

"No."

"So... what stopped you?"

"Mikalis. I learned later how word had reached him of a monster terrorizing the Carpathians. The beast would drain its victims of blood and hang their carcasses from trees. Rumors swirled of worse acts. It had been years since I'd been turned. I was the lost prince, and then later, I became the blood prince, a myth and legend told to frighten children and travelers from the forest."

"Doesn't the whole vampire myth originate out of Central Europe? Wait..." Felix sat up. "You're not telling me that was you?"

Kazi smiled. It was a nice thought. He'd have liked to be so infamous. "No, there's a word for vampire in almost every ancient language. The legend began long before me."

"Okay, good. So you weren't, you know... Dracula."

"Dracula is fictitious, baby," Kazi purred, but Felix shot him a sidelong glance that made it clear he wasn't buying it. "What do you want me to say? A nobleman who was known for his madness and viciousness became the Dracula of Bram Stoker's legend? Besides, Vlad was born in Hungary, not Poland."

"I'm just sayin'... it's the right time period, the right area. If it walks like a duck and quacks like a duck—"

"It's Dracula?"

Felix laughed and lay back down, tucking himself close. Kazi had no idea what he'd done to deserve Felix in his life, but he'd do everything in his power to keep him.

"I should er... probably shower again." Felix lifted his head.

Kazi kissed him before he could escape. It would be too easy to fall into more than kissing Felix. There was so much more he wanted to show him, so many ways to make him come. He never wanted to let him go.

But Felix was already gently easing out of his arms. "Or we'll never leave this bed," he said after buttoning up his trousers and heading for the shower.

Kazi laced his hands behind his head and stretched out on the bed. The soft warmth in his chest soon turned cold. There were some in the Brotherhood who would hate Felix just for being mortal and for putting the Brotherhood at risk. Eric Sharpe had gotten away with somehow blending in with their numbers, but it hadn't been without friction. How they'd react to a second mortal man was anyone's guess, but it was unlikely to be good.

The day was coming when Mikalis would make him choose again, and this time, he might not escape the consequences.

The Blackrose Brotherhood always came first.

And that was one rule none of them dared to break.

CHAPTER 28

elix

NOW THAT THEY no longer had to hide their tracks, Kazi hired a car and drove through the night, stopping in the daylight hours to rest up in a motel and remind Felix exactly how much he loved Kazi's mouth. The daylight hours seemed to drain Kazi of more energy than he'd admit to, so Felix was content to watch him sleep, wondering about all the things he'd seen and done and what would happen to him after Felix died of old age.

Even if the Brotherhood didn't get to him, he maybe had another fifty good years left. He'd be an old man, but Kazi would remain unchanged.

That didn't seem fair, but Felix was getting way ahead of himself. They probably wouldn't even get that far.

Near midnight the next day, Kazi rolled the rental up to a set of security gates and spoke his name into a receiver. The gates jolted, then rattled open. They passed a glossy, backlit sign—*Welcome to Atlas – where technology meets science*—and then cruised down a neat asphalt road lined with clipped lawns around mature trees. It looked like a university campus. All low-level, ultra-modern, shiny buildings and green spaces sparkling at night.

Kazi hadn't said much about the Brotherhood on the journey, and now that they'd arrived, he glared out of the windshield, cheek twitching as though he were a second away from turning the car around.

"I've met the worst of them, right?" Felix asked, nerves beginning to rattle.

"You've met Mikalis. He's... powerful, but you know where you stand with him."

"Okay, so tell me about the others."

Kazi pulled the car to a halt outside a glass-fronted single-level building and cut the headlights. "It's best just to assume they'll all kill you, and it's only Mikalis who's stopping them."

"Mikalis, the vampire who wants me dead, is the only one keeping me alive."

"He doesn't want you dead right now, and that's your best defense. If anyone gets frisky, remind them of that—and of me."

Kazi opened his door and climbed out. The main doors of the building swept open, and Eric strode out. The one friendly face he knew. Thank fuck for that. If Eric could survive them, then so could Felix.

Kazi shook Eric's hand and had said a few words by the time Felix joined them.

Eric smiled. "Hey, man... You look better than the last time I saw you."

"Eric is the one who found you out cold in your kitchen," Kazi explained tightly, glancing toward the building. His body language had stilled, making him seem harder, more distant. He caught Felix watching and flashed him a grin. "You've got this."

Did he have this? He thrust his hands into his pockets. "I feel like I'm about to meet the parents, but they're mass-murdering psychopaths with itchy trigger fingers."

Eric laughed. "Accurate. But they're not all bad once you get to know them. C'mon." Eric waved him on. "Best rip off the Band-Aid."

The foyer was a sprawling space with an unmanned desk along one side. Potted plants and leather chairs gave the place a bland, corporate feel. Nothing like Felix had expected.

Then the man-mountain he'd seen briefly before running out of the back of his town's café sauntered around a corner. A white tank top stretched over his barrel chest, spray-painted over every muscle. He wore a black knit cap over his shaved head, black jeans and heavy black boots and probably wrestled bears for fun.

Eric stopped, which meant Felix stopped, and then the mountain offered his hand. "Name's Storm." His voice growled like thunder.

Felix took his hand, wondering if he was about to lose it, but Storm shook once and let go. "I'm here to take you straight to the lab. Kazi, you're with us too."

Kazi nodded, and that was where they left Eric, who threw Felix a half-hearted wave. Eric frowned, clearly worried, which was not a good sign.

Storm led them into an elevator and then down several floors, deep underground.

"Storm looks and sounds as though he throws busses for fun, but he's actually an all right kinda guy," Kazi said.

Storm arched an eyebrow.

"He will also fuck you up without batting an eye," Kazi added. "But you'll see it coming."

"Noted." Felix swallowed.

Storm side-eyed him, and when the doors opened, he didn't move. Felix stayed rooted to the spot too, sensing this was some kind of test. Then Storm slid his gaze back to Kazi behind Felix. The doors began to close, and he shot out a hand, blocking them.

This was definitely a test.

"Storm," Kazi grumbled. "None of us are getting any younger standing here."

"I've known Kazimir a long time," Storm said. "He hasn't once defied Mikalis, until he met you, Mister Quaid."

Felix shifted from one foot to the other. What was he supposed to say? "I understand."

"I don't think you do," he growled. "But you will." He stepped from the elevator car.

Kazi gripped Felix's shoulder and urged him forward.

"Are they all this intense?" Felix whispered.

"No. The others are worse."

They walked glossy corridors to the sounds of their footfalls and the whirr of a ventilation system and Felix's heart trying to thump its way out of his chest. The only reason he hadn't turned on his heel and bolted was Kazi's firm, protective presence beside him.

Storm entered a side room. The lights flooded on, illuminating several empty hospital beds with dark monitoring screens slung over them. All right, he'd known they were technologically advanced—they had to be to do what they did without being exposed—but exactly how large an operation it all was had only now begun to sink in.

"You're not the only Brotherhood, are you? There's more of you in other places?"

"Sit on the bed," Storm said, flicking on the machines and various screens. "Kazi, get over there and strip to your waist. Mikalis made it clear you have a tracker on you. I'm removing that before anything else."

"Aren't you concerned the Nyxians know he's here now?"

Storm side-eyed him. "In all likelihood, they've known exactly where we are for years."

Felix sat on the edge of the bed. "That doesn't concern you?"

"Roll up your sleeve. I'm going to draw blood and test it to make sure Eric's assessment was correct."

"If it wasn't?"

"Then we'll have ourselves a problem."

Felix rolled up his sleeve, flexed his forearm and watched as

Storm pierced a needle into his vein and drew blood into the syringe.

"Not even the Nyxians are foolish enough to try to infiltrate Atlas," Storm said, answering his earlier question. He withdrew the needle, pressed a cotton pad to Felix's wrist to stop the bleeding and fussed about depositing the blood sample into a test tube. For a big guy, he had a gentle touch.

"What is Atlas, exactly?" Felix asked.

"Full of questions, aren't you?"

"Quaid's a reporter," Kazi said after stripping off his shirt.

"Yeah, I read his file after we thought he'd abducted you."

Kazi snorted. "I had it under control."

"Hmm," Storm grumbled, sounding unconvinced. "It sounds to me as though the Nyxians got the drop on you while you were distracted by Mister Quaid here."

That was exactly what had happened. Kazi rolled his eyes. "They stuck me with three highly illegal, over-powered Tasers."

"Just three?" Storm asked. "That must have ruined your hair."

"Dick," Kazi grumbled, standing shirtless, hip cocked, arms crossed. "Do you know what they did to me after?"

"No, but I bet you're about to tell me all about it." Storm's dark eyes caught Felix's gaze and sparkled with a dry, hidden humor. "Turn around." He approached Kazi. "I'm gonna scan you for a signal. Hold still."

Storm grabbed a small, slim device and waved it over Kazi's back. It beeped at his right shoulder. "There we go... Don't move." Working fast, he grabbed a scalpel, cut out the small metal square and plinked it into a petri dish. Kazi's cut sealed back up in seconds.

"Because we heal so quickly, it's surprisingly easy to hide devices under our skin." Storm handed the dish to Felix. "What do you make of that?"

He wasn't sure what he was supposed to be looking at. The device was a small rectangular computer chip made of black plastic and silver wires. "I er... I'm not sure."

"It looks like the Nyxians have help, is what it looks like," Storm grumbled.

"Shit, right..." He handed the dish back. "I meant to tell you, but with everything happening... I was researching Vesna and—"

"You were, huh?" Storm glanced at Kazi, and Kazi frowned, buttoning his shirt back up. "You know what curiosity does, Mister Quaid?"

"Yeah, but listen... She has properties all over the US and Europe, including that compound at Eagle Lake. That wasn't her only base of operations. There are more, which suggests she's going to pick up more nyks or more Brotherhood. Kazi wasn't her only play."

Kazi sauntered over, his expression troubled. Storm was more difficult to read. "We know this, right?" Kazi asked him.

The big guy nodded. "Probably. I'm not up to speed. Mikalis has called a meeting. You can ask him."

"They won't let Quaid in the Ops Room until the blood results are in."

"No." Storm folded his cable-like arms. "Eric's going to babysit."

Felix rolled his sleeve back down. "I'll be fine. I don't need babysitting."

"It's for your protection," Storm said. "You'll live longer if you don't argue." He started for the door. "Kazi..."

Kazi swooped in and kissed Felix quickly on the lips. "I'll be right back."

"I can help, you know. Vesna talked to me."

"She did, huh?" Storm opened the lab door. "Then maybe you two can catch up later, as she's in our custody."

They left, and Felix stayed on the bed, feeling like the spare piece of LEGO left at the bottom of the box. *He could help?* Idiot. All the state-of-the-art equipment made it obvious they didn't need his help. And this was just the kit he'd seen in one room. On the ride down in the elevator, he'd counted several floors. They probably had resources that would blow his mind.

He hopped off the bed and wandered around the room. Storm

had left the screens and equipment running. The box he'd locked the blood sample in was lit from the inside with a clear plastic lid. An automated pipet took drops of blood and deposited them onto different slides, then fed them into some kind of scanner. Beside it, numbers danced on a screen, and graphics rippled. It was all very fancy, and Felix had no idea what any of it meant.

He headed for the door. Would they have locked it? And if they had, did that mean he was a prisoner? He tried the handle, and the door popped open. "Okay, not a prisoner..."

"I wouldn't wander about alone," Eric said, striding down the corridor. "That's how you find trouble, trust me."

"Did you find trouble?"

"Let's just say, if you want to go off alone, don't let any of them corner you."

"Are they *that* bad?"

He laughed. "Yeah. Let's get a coffee."

They took the elevator up and walked to a comfortable kitchen/dining room that was the size of Felix's New York apartment. A large dining table at one end provided for "family" meals, he figured, and at the other, a comfortable couch and cushion area helped soften the whole prison vibe.

"All right." Eric poured the coffees. "Here's what I know and what you should know. If your blood is confirmed as being like mine, then we're new and Mikalis isn't keen on surprises. He didn't like my getting on board, and he's not going to like your arrival either. But he's not your problem. Kazi turned out not to be as much of a hard case as he pretended to be, but the rest? The Brotherhood comes first to them, and if you're seen as a threat, they will eliminate you."

"How'd you survive?"

"By being useful, and... a few other tricks that maybe you'll get to know. One to watch for is Octavius. He's vicious and cold. He will not take your arrival well and will, at some point, make sure you know it."

Avoid Octavius. "Okay."

"Aiko comes across as relaxed, as though he doesn't care, but he'll stab you in the back the second he has any doubts, and you won't see it coming."

Aiko was the stabby one. Right. "Jesus..."

"You've met Storm. If he wants you gone, he won't dance around it. Like Mikalis, he'll just get it done. Raiden is... quiet. I haven't had much interaction with him. He's the science guy and doesn't do much fieldwork. Thebeus is away in Asia. And then there's Zaine, the youngest and my other half."

"Okay," he said again, absorbing it all. "There're others, though?"

"There are... in other countries. And..."

"And?"

"There's someone else. He's in one of the confinement cells they use to contain nyks and their own, if they become a risk. Nobody talks about him, and if you ask, they'll claim they don't know. Just Mikalis knows, and I like my life enough not to ask."

"No name?"

"I'm not sure... Zaine *doesn't* know, but he said Kazi let slip the name Saint once."

"Huh."

"Right."

So Kazi knew who the mysterious prisoner was. Felix would ask when all the drama was over. "Why are you telling me all this?"

"It's nice to talk to someone who doesn't think I'm nuts, and not long ago, I was in your shoes. The Brotherhood can be fuckin' terrifying. I wouldn't wanna be among them without a friend."

"Well, thanks. I appreciate it. These last few days have been... tough."

"Yeah, I bet. *Surprise*. Vampires are real. Joke's on us, huh?"

He laughed. "Yeah, something like that." Eric seemed like an easy guy to like, but if he was mixed up with the Brotherhood, then he couldn't have had it easy either. Given how hostile they all were, he must have done something impressive to earn their trust. Felix didn't have that. Storm's warning about not understanding what it meant that Kazi had defied Mikalis came back to him now.

They drank coffee and chatted idly about life outside the Brotherhood, and then Eric produced a torn notebook from his pocket. "I almost forgot. This was found at Eagle Lake..."

His notes on Kazimir. He winced. "You read it?"

"Yeah, and not just me either. Mikalis, Octavius... probably all of them, honestly."

"Great." There were things he'd written in there that should never have seen the light of day, like his thoughts about Kazi when he'd blamed him for everything.

Eric handed it over. "I'm not going to judge you, but they will. Do you still hate him?"

He sighed. "It's not like that." He didn't want to get into the whole heap of issues he'd had, not now, not with Eric. "I made a mistake. And this..." He spotted a trash can and got to his feet. "This doesn't mean anything." He dropped it into the trash. "Kazi is... He's shown me things about myself, some of it bad, but a whole lot of it good too. I don't wanna hurt him."

"Good, but those words you wrote, some might take that as evidence that you'll do anything to bring him down, making you a threat."

He would have, back then. "Yeah, I know how it looks. Kazi and I kinda worked through it, I think."

"You and him, you're... close?" When Eric asked if they were close, it meant more than just *close*.

"Yeah." Felix rubbed at his chin, suddenly self-conscious under the detective's glare. "Which is kinda new, honestly."

Eric smiled, clearly relieved, and sipped his coffee. "Well, if you tame Kazi, good for you."

"Did you *tame* Zaine?"

"No, he didn't fuckin' tame me." Zaine waltzed in, went straight for Eric and claimed him with a kiss on the lips. The kiss grew so heated that Felix looked away and cleared his throat. Felix was still trying to figure out how it all worked, while these two had no such trouble. They seemed happy, despite their differences, and that gave him hope.

Their kiss ended, leaving Eric flushed. "Your results are in," Zaine said to Felix. "You're definitely a person of interest. Your blood has the same quirk as Eric's."

"What does that mean?" Eric asked before Felix could.

"I'm not sure anyone knows. It does, however, mean Mikalis is pissed off. I get the impression he had hoped to brush your differences under his rug and never mention it again."

"Now he has to do something about it," Eric said.

"Do what?" Felix asked.

"I guess we'll find out." Zaine freed Eric from his embrace. "Kazi is waiting for you in the Ops Room. With the others." He and Eric shared a glance that did not suggest Felix would be getting a warm welcome.

This was going to be a baptism of fire. It couldn't be any worse than reporting from a war zone. "Time to meet the family."

CHAPTER 29

azi

Tension simmered in the silence. Nobody said a damn word as they waited for Felix's arrival.

They'd been briefed. Mikalis had stood at the end of the operations table, where he was now, Storm beside him, and told them how Felix's bloodwork was unusual enough to keep the man alive to study.

He'd told the room that Felix Quaid was under his protection until such a time that Raiden could decipher what Felix's and Eric's immunity and heightened abilities meant. Raiden had nodded and taken himself off to begin that work. Zaine had then left to retrieve Felix, leaving only Aiko and Octavius at the table. Aiko sat cross-legged at the far end, flicking butterfly knives between his fingers. Octavius hadn't moved or breathed in ten minutes.

So, this was it.

He was dragging Felix into his dysfunctional... family. Although, they hadn't been given a choice.

The door opened. Zaine entered first, Felix behind him, and Eric at the rear.

Kazi's heart kicked him in the ribs. Felix looked tough, but he'd walked into a room full of hungry lions. Every instinct screamed at Kazi to get him out.

The trio stopped at the table.

Felix skipped his gaze over each of them, keeping his face neutral. "Hey."

Nobody replied.

"You okay?" Kazi asked.

"Yeah. Good. Fine."

Kazi just had to take a few steps to his right, grab Felix's hand and drag him from the room. It wouldn't solve a damn thing though, and this had to happen. So he stayed still.

"Onto the issue of Vesna Dragovic," Mikalis began. "She's been resistant to questioning, but Mister Quaid has a rapport with her, or so I'm told." His gaze fixed on Felix. "Are you willing to speak with her on our behalf?"

"Sure." Felix brightened. "I was also able to discover the Eagle Lake compound was one of many. She has properties all over."

Kazi listened to him talk as he explained what he'd discovered about Vesna. Nobody appeared to be dismissing him. If anything, it was going too well.

"Her influence ends in America," Octavius said abruptly, stating a fact.

Felix hesitated, then licked his lips. "Look, I know you have all this super-tech and I'm just some outsider, but you need to look into her holdings abroad—"

"That's right, you are an outsider." Octavius's tone was cool and sharp. This wasn't a discussion.

"I know what I discovered, and she—"

"You are one man doing a desktop search. We have Atlas, an AI with countless eyes in a thousand cities with access to every official database there is. Vesna Dragovic was working alone. The sites she's linked with on US soil are about to be raided. Human law enforcement will incarcerate her, with our subtle help. We have her." Octavius looked to Mikalis. "We don't need him."

"Be that as it may," Mikalis replied, "I'd like to hear Quaid speak."

"It's a waste of our time."

"Do you have somewhere else to be, Octavius?" Mikalis asked. Nothing in his voice had changed, but the temperature in the room dropped a few degrees. "Mister Quaid, go on."

Felix dipped his chin, and as he spoke, he found his stride. "As I was saying, she has connections abroad, and considering the lab we found at Eagle Lake, I'd recommend you have your people investigate each site as a matter of urgency. If there's more than one nyk factory, don't you want to know for sure?"

"Why are we listening to a feeder when all he wants to do is fuck Kazimir?" Octavius said. "That's the only reason he's here. He's Kazi's bitch, like Eric is Zaine's."

Anywhere else, with anyone else, Kazi would have already launched across the table and pummeled Octavius through the wall.

"They weaken us," Octavius went on. "They're a threat."

"Back off, Octavius," Kazi warned, blood simmering.

"You know it, Kazimir. Whatever quirk is in their blood has you all tied up in knots. It's their poison in you. That's what Raiden is going to find, and the fact we're even standing here discussing our ways, our lives, with two Brotherhood traitors among us—"

"That's enough!" Mikalis barked. "When did you become leader, Octavius?"

Octavius snarled, "Maybe someone should be."

"Octavius, choose your next words carefully," came Storm's rumble.

Felix—of all people—snorted a laugh. "We could continue to stand around and measure each other's dicks, or we could, you know, be interviewing the woman who got the drop on Kazimir, which none of you seem to be taking seriously. But you didn't fuckin' see what I saw. You didn't see them chain him down and bleed him—"

"Felix," Kazi said. He appreciated the support, but now was not the time to yell at a room full of vampires.

"You didn't see the pods in their basement, clearly made to keep people inside and turn them into those nyktelios monsters—"

"You've been here for ten minutes and you think you know us!" Octavius snapped, teeth displayed. "We are eternal. You are nothing." He lunged.

Kazi tensed, about to defend Felix, but Mikalis tore Octavius out of the air and slammed him against the wall, pinning him by the throat. "Touch Felix Quaid while he's under my protection and you will feel my bite. Whether you agree or not, my word is law. That means something. It means *everything*. Remember who we are, Octavius. Remember what you stand for, or by Nyx, I will take you down myself if you don't get yourself under control."

A warning growl rumbled through Octavius. He pushed uselessly at Mikalis's arm.

Mikalis's growl trembled through the floor and walls. "Do you understand?"

Octavius stopped trying to fight free, taking too long to realize that moving Mikalis was like moving a mountain. "Yes."

"Good." Mikalis dropped him.

Octavius righted his clothes and regarded everyone watching him. He sniffed, then lifted his chin. "I'll look into Quaid's claims."

Octavius left, taking the tension with him.

"Does anyone else want to test me?" Mikalis asked. "No? Good. Quaid, please speak with Dragovic. I'm interested to see what you can get from her."

"Yes, sir. And er… thanks, for that…" Felix said.

Mikalis at least smiled. "It's always in your interest to align with me rather than against me." He headed for the door too. "Although some of the Brotherhood occasionally like to test that theory."

The others trickled out. Eric told Felix where to find him in the Atlas compound and then left with Zaine, leaving just Kazi and Felix alone.

"Holy hell," Felix sighed. "Is it always like this?"

"The Brotherhood does not like change." Kazi pulled him close, and when he folded into Kazi's arms as though he'd always belonged, he inhaled the warm scent of him.

"Do you think any of what Octavius said is right? Is my blood somehow bad for you?"

Kazi leaned against the edge of the table and pulled Felix between his knees. "Baby, if your blood is bad for me, then let it poison me, because I can't say no." He bowed his head, planting a kiss on Felix's neck that had his fangs throbbing and his dick more than interested. He hadn't taken any of Felix's blood since the barn—it was still forbidden, still a slippery slope to losing control. Did Zaine drink from Eric? Would he tell him even if he did?

Felix leaned back in Kazi's arms, his eyes sly with want. "I'm half terrified and half aroused right now."

"Hmm." He kissed him long and slow, leaving him breathless. "I can hear your heart racing, your blood pumping—" Felix dropped his hand, claiming Kazi's dick, and it was all he could do not to throw him down onto the shiny, smooth ops table and fuck him raw. But not even Kazi could get away with that if they were seen. With great effort, he pushed Felix's hand aside. "Hold that thought until after the interview."

"Oh really?" Felix teased a kiss on his lips. "Is it a date?"

"Do you want it to be?"

"Yeah, I do."

"You want to have dinner with me?"

Felix laughed. "You say that like it's the worst thing in the world. Yes, I want to have dinner with you." His fading laugh still played on his lips. "Why is that so hard to believe?"

By Nyx, he loved that brilliant, carefree laugh. It hinted at the joy in Felix—and there was joy in him; he'd just lost it of late.

"I want to be with you, Kazi. The Brotherhood can't scare me off." He smiled, revealing a hint of shyness. "Can we do that? Go on a date like two normal people? I'm not... a prisoner here?"

"No, you're not a prisoner," Kazi kissed him back, light and quick. "You can do what you like, baby. Including me."

~

KAZI WATCHED FROM ANOTHER ROOM, behind a one-way mirror. Felix sat across a small metal table from Vesna. Storm had tried to pry answers out of her, but she'd remained quiet and too full of smiles for his liking.

She knew what to expect from the Brotherhood. But Felix was different. And according to him, she'd been keen to recruit him to her cause.

This should be interesting.

The two of them asked how the other was, full of polite smiles and simple small talk. It was... strange, seeing them so familiar. Vesna had been responsible for a significant amount of pain and had almost killed Kazi and Felix. But Felix spoke to her as though they were old friends.

A reporter had to remain neutral, Kazi supposed. Felix performed the role well.

"I like him," Storm grumbled.

"Yeah." Kazi danced his gaze over the man he couldn't get enough of. "He's made some mistakes. He's been trying to put them right for a while."

"Like someone else I know." He not so subtly side-eyed Kazi.

Kazi folded his arms and leaned against the wall, keeping the adjacent room in his sights. "Some mistakes can't ever be put right."

Storm huffed and watched Felix and Vesna discuss Maine as though she hadn't drugged him, thrown his ass in with a predator and used him to feed it over and over.

"The longer we live, the more mistakes we make," Storm added.

"Felix isn't a mistake. Storm... have you ever... loved someone not of your clan? Someone you've met? Not family..." What was he trying to say? "Have you experienced a love that grew naturally, not from any bond?"

Storm arched an eyebrow. "Is that what you think you have with him?"

"I don't know what it is I feel, but it's fierce," he admitted. "I've lived a long time and never loved, never cared. I was turned young, and before that lived a closeted life. Then there was the Brotherhood, and that's all there's ever been. Until now."

Storm had stilled, but his cheek twitched as he stared through the one-way glass. Perhaps he had loved but didn't want to speak of it. None of the Brotherhood ever seemed to. But they had all been human, once.

"Whatever love is, and whatever I feel for that man, I know I'll kill for him, stand against Mikalis for him. I'd die for him. But it's more than even that. I'd walk away from him too if he asked it of me. If that is not love, then love does not exist."

Storm turned his head, and Kazi feared he might be about to claim he cared too much, that it was wrong and the Brotherhood should take that place in his heart that Felix had slotted into. But he didn't say any of that.

He swallowed and said, "You deserve some happiness. You've paid a high price for your place among the Brotherhood."

Kazi dipped his chin, acknowledging Storm's words, silently thanking him for not judging. He wasn't yet sure if Felix was going to stick around like Eric had. The brothers hadn't scared him off—yet. But there was plenty of time for that.

Shifting his stands, he took a breath, clearing his head. "You think it's a coincidence that it's two mortal men who have this blood anomaly? Not women?"

"Too few data points to know for certain. There could be a hundred thousand people out there with the same genetic defect and we just haven't met them yet." He fell quiet for a while, listening to Felix ask Vesna about her father's money and the family's reach. "I should have Raiden look into the US population's medical records, see if this anomaly has shown up elsewhere and we just haven't been looking for it."

The lights flickered, then blinked off and back on.

Storm frowned and pulled his phone from his pocket. "Atlas has been glitchy lately."

"Yeah, I heard."

"We never did find out how the footage of your kidnapping was erased." He tapped out a message on his phone.

"—Octavius..." Vesna was saying.

Kazi faced the glass. "Why is she asking after Octavius?"

"Hmm." Storm's eyes narrowed. "She said she wants to talk with him."

Nobody wanted to talk with Octavius. Ever. He didn't exist outside the Brotherhood. He was a ghost, more than any of them. She shouldn't have known his name. Kazi fixed his glare on the woman whose family had a personal vendetta with Kazi. How much did she really know and how? On the outside, she had no links to the Brotherhood, just her crazy Nyx-worshipping acolytes. But she'd talked as though she knew them well.

Storm growled at his phone. "Raiden says something is drawing a shit-ton of power from the grid, and it's not Atlas." He shook his head and headed for the door. "You've got this?"

"Yeah, sure."

"Why do you want to talk to Octavius, Vesna?" Felix asked, his voice filtering through the interview room's internal speakers. "What's he to you?"

She smiled and flicked her gaze over Felix's shoulder, through the one-way glass as though she could see Kazi. "They think they're all so indestructible." Her laugh dismissed the idea. *"The Brotherhood is all."* Shifting sideways on her chair, she smirked, so damn confident. "*Memento mori.* Except they don't die, do they? Because Nyx made them all with a piece of herself. Traitors, all of them. They should worship her, not kill her children."

"Why Octavius?" Felix asked again, keeping her on track.

Kazi wanted to know the answer to that question too.

She smiled. "You threw your lot in with the wrong side, Quaid." Tilting her head back, she blinked at the ceiling. "But it's not too late. She can save you."

Felix slumped back in the chair. "Your goddess has been dead since before time began, Vesna. She's not coming back just because you made a few nyktelios."

"No, not her..." Vesna shrugged. "Kazimir knows who." She peered through the mirror again. "An old friend of his."

Kazi frowned again. Something about Vesna had never sat right with him. She'd always been too confident, too calm. She looked at him now, and she smiled without fear. Nobody did that in Atlas. Anyone who got this far was usually a quivering mess.

Vesna leaned forward. "What if everything you've seen so far, Quaid, is all a lie?"

"How so?" Felix asked.

Kazi didn't like this.

Something was wrong.

Vesna raised a shoulder, playing coy. "We could have taken any nyk, but we tracked and kidnapped Kazimir."

"You have a history with him."

"Hmm, yes. But do you really think that's all it is, Felix?"

"No, actually. So tell me what I'm missing."

Her slippery smile grew. "Do you know how hard it is to get *inside* the Brotherhood? Although, apparently, in your case, you can suck dick to get in. But for me, no... I couldn't just walk in. Nobody just *walks in.* This place is like Fort Knox and Alcatraz all in one with a shiny exterior. Yet, here I am..." She spread her hands, then walked her fingers across the tabletop. "Right where I want to be."

Kazi narrowed his eyes at the sly woman. Why would she want to be *inside* Atlas?

She knew something, had something on them. She had a wild card, one she was about to play.

The lights flickered again.

Vesna noticed and sat back in the chair. "Nyx doesn't need to rise from the dead. She's in all her children. She's in the nyktelios who captured a prince so long ago and turned him into a monster."

Kazi's sire? Was the witch alive? He had to know. He had to go in there and demand she answer him.

"She promised me I'd have my revenge," Vesna continued. "While she got hers on the Brotherhood that stole her son, her blood prince."

Felix leaned forward now. "Are you telling me you're working with a nyk, Vesna? And she's the one who turned Kazimir?"

Vesna grinned. "All this?" She waved a hand at the room. "Poof. And when the dust settles, there will only be us, disciples of chaos."

Felix swore under his breath. "Where's this nyk you work for?"

Vesna laughed. "And you're supposed to be the smart ones. It's like taking candy from a baby."

That was enough. Kazi had to get him out of there, away from her—

The lights went out, plunging both rooms into darkness.

Kazi blinked, his sight adjusting in milliseconds, in time to see Vesna jerk to her feet and lunge across the table, reaching for Felix.

CHAPTER 30

elix

THE LIGHTS WENT OUT, and complete darkness rolled in, rendering him blind. Did the Brotherhood have power blackouts?

A chair scraped.

Gloom and shadows swirled, gradually forming shapes. One of them being Vesna—standing. She lunged.

He spilled out of his chair and swung wildly, not even sure what he was swinging at, anything but shadows. His fist clipped something, Vesna grunted, and then the sound of glass exploding filled his ears, and broken bits of glass rained over the back of his head and shoulders.

It was so damn dark, but he heard a wet grunt, heard a body hit the floor, and then the grisly crack of breaking bone.

The lights blinked back on with startling ferocity.

Kazi stood over Vesna's motionless body. Her head was cricked at an odd angle. Her open eyes stared without blinking.

"Fuck!" He'd just been talking with her seconds ago. A blink and she was dead.

Kazi whirled, eyes silver.

"Fuck!" Felix shoved away. "Just..." He thrust out a hand, holding Kazi back. "Stay there... Shit, you killed her."

"She was about to kill you."

"No... No, we were talking—"

"Felix... she was going to kill you."

Someone's phone pinged, then pinged again. Then rang. Kazi's, in his pocket, although he ignored it, instead staring at Felix.

Vesna was dead.

Kazi had killed her in a split second. And he didn't care.

"Just... shit..." He braced against his thighs. "We could have gotten more from her..."

Zaine flung open the interview room door and took in the scene full of broken glass and Vesna's dead body. "We have a fuckin' bigger problem happening than this."

"So deal with it," Kazi snarled.

"Atlas went down."

Kazi's phone stopped ringing.

"Deal with it, Z. I'm busy," Kazi said, dismissing his concerns.

"Yeah, but... Fuck, you know that room we don't talk about?" Zaine said. "Saint...?"

Felix caught Kazi's flicker of concern. He knew of Saint all right, the Brotherhood member nobody talked about.

"Yeah, him," Zaine said. "A second, that was all it took. We lost power, and... he's out. I don't know how bad that shit is, but I'm betting you do."

"Find Mikalis—now." Kazi reached for Felix. "We all need to leave."

Felix rubbed his face and straightened. Clearly, there was a whole lot more happening here than Kazi killing Vesna. She'd had a plan; that much was obvious. Maybe this chaos was it. She'd been pretty confident. She maybe hadn't expected her own death.

Kazi's and Zaine's phones pinged at the same time. Whatever

the message said, both Brotherhood members froze upon reading it.

"What is it?"

"Code Black," Kazi said, as though that explained everything.

"What?"

Zaine swore, then said, "Take Felix. I'll find you later." He vanished in a blur of speed that Felix had no hope of tracking.

"What's a Code Black? What the fuck is going on?"

Kazi reached for him.

Fear, adrenaline or shock had Felix flinching away. "I just… I'm good. Give me some room. I'm good, okay?" He knew he needed Kazi close and wanted to wrap his arms around him, but he also knew Kazi had broken a woman's neck as though she were nothing. He'd seen Kazi plow into the cultists, but that had been different. He hadn't killed them. And that had been survival.

As much as he'd disliked the woman, he hadn't expected to see her murdered in front of him.

"You and I need to leave right now," Kazi said, crowding too close.

"Leave the building?"

"Leave the whole fucking state."

Felix straightened. This was clearly not the time to lose his shit. "What's a Code Black?"

"It's a nuke-it-from-orbit situation. We need to leave." This time, Kazi offered his hand. "We have approximately eight minutes."

"Until what?"

"Just… trust me. Please. Whatever you think of me right now, trust that I will always keep you safe."

"Okay. All right." He took Kazi's hand, relieved by the warm touch of his fingers.

Kazi hauled him from the room. They'd made it two steps when the lighting switched from glaring white to dull red, then a low drone of an alarm sounded throughout the building.

"Keep moving," Kazi urged.

Felix hurried along. Was Vesna behind this? Had she somehow orchestrated the attack? She'd hinted at it, saying she was right where she wanted to be. But how could she do this?

"It was the chip," Kazi said, jogging ahead. "It had to be. I brought it in. I can't think of any other way she'd have gotten anything through security that could do this."

"You know, when you say shit like that, I start wondering if you can read my mind..."

Kazi threw him a sly smile, and now Felix had more questions.

They rounded a corner into a corridor, and Kazi jolted to a stop. He threw back his hand, holding Felix still. "Do. Not. Move."

A man stood at the far end of the corridor. An emergency light flickered on and off above him. He was angled away, as though he'd been caught running. He turned his head. Silver eyes marked him as Brotherhood, but he hadn't been in the Ops Room with the others.

He wore a well-fitted black suit, the jacket open and the shirt gaping at the collar, as though he'd returned from a formal night out. He wasn't big like Storm, nor slim like Kazi. Apart from the clothes, he almost looked *unremarkable*. Short hair, a little scruffy. The red lighting made its color difficult to define.

Kazi slowly raised his hand toward him and hunkered down, making himself appear less of a threat.

The suit-wearing vampire lifted his chin and sniffed.

"Don't... fuckin'... breathe," Kazi whispered.

Felix had already held his breath, sensing that whatever this was, if Kazi was scared, then so was he.

The stranger sniffed again, then vanished so fast that Felix missed his direction.

"Fuck..." Kazi sighed, then moved on. "Not the elevator." He pushed through the fire exit doors and started up the steps, quickening his pace so Felix had to run to keep pace. They emerged in a dimly lit underground parking lot. Several bays were empty. Two other cars screeched away too fast to see who drove them.

"Who was that back there?" Felix glanced behind them, checking they weren't about to be jumped by the stranger.

Kazi plucked a set of keys from a rack and ran to his black Jaguar. He leaped the hood and unlocked the doors, then dropped behind the wheel. Felix flung the passenger door open and fell in as the engine roared, and the car lurched from the bay.

"You just survived meeting Saint." Kazi swung the sports car in a J turn, then rammed it into gear and launched it forward, speeding up the ramp fast enough to leap all four wheels off the asphalt.

Was it necessary to drive as though they were both immortal? Felix grappled with his belt. "Put your belt on."

Kazi glanced over. "Huh?"

"Your belt."

Kazi swung the car down the neat but narrow compound roads. "I'm immortal. If we wreck, I'm just gonna get right back up."

"Put the damn belt on!" Felix snapped.

Kazi grabbed his belt and clicked it into place.

"You're not immortal, though, are you! Just really hard to kill. But you can die. And I can definitely die." Yeah, okay, so maybe it wasn't the belt that was pissing him off, just *everything else*. "Jesus, slow down!" The gates were coming up fast. There wouldn't be enough time to slow and open them—but it didn't matter. Someone else had already plowed them down.

Why were they all running like rats from a sinking ship? Was it really that bad?

Felix twisted in the seat and peered out of the rear window. It all seemed a bit... dramatic for no—

A blast tore the night sky. The car's back window shattered, dashing Felix's face with safety glass. The car lurched, sliding sideways. Fire barreled out of Atlas in a huge, hungry wave. The Jag bounced and screeched, then Kazi spun the wheel, found some grip again and shifted gears down, racing from the flames boiling in the mirrors.

"Jesus Christ..." Felix pushed himself into the seat.

Kazi flung the car onto a country road and broke a whole lot of traffic laws before eventually slowing along a dark, winding road.

"I didn't know you literally meant nuke it from orbit!"

"Well, not *literally*. The explosives were built into the foundations."

He gaped, at a loss for words. He'd been in the Brotherhood's compound for less than a day and now it was gone. All that tech, those buildings, everything. "How long... How long has the Brotherhood been based there?"

"A few decades."

"Did everyone get out?"

"Probably."

"'Probably'?" Felix flung his head back and squeezed his eyes closed. Okay, he needed a minute. It was all good. "If you'd told me it was all going to blow up, I'd have run faster."

Kazi snorted. "Baby, if I'd thought we weren't going to make it, I'd have slung you over my shoulder and carried you out of there."

A little laugh slipped free. Yeah, okay, he could do this. They were out, together, and *probably* everyone else had survived. "Nuke it from orbit," he muttered, still not sure what had happened or if he was dreaming.

"Well, you certainly left your mark on the Brotherhood," Kazi said.

"I didn't do this." He didn't think he had. Had he?

"Was one hell of a coincidence. You show up and boom, Brotherhood's gone." Dry humor sparkled in Kazi's eyes.

He groaned. "Mikalis is going to kill me again, isn't he?"

"No," Kazi chuckled. "He'll know this wasn't you. It wasn't even Vesna."

"Was it about that guy back there... Saint?"

"No." Kazi's smile twitched. "Saint is what happens when a Brotherhood member goes full-nyk. Mikalis will deal with him. He's not our problem right now." He shifted up a gear and cruised the car at a more respectable speed that wouldn't catch the eye of any local traffic cops. "I know who did this. And I have to fix it."

Yeah, now that Felix could think again, he had a good idea who

Kazi was going after: his creator, the woman who had made him what he was now—a nyktelios. Felix just didn't know her name. Kazi had killed Vesna before he could ask.

"Her name's Jadwiga. At least, that's what she had me call her while she turned me," Kazi said, fixing his stare on the road. "I believed her long dead." His grip flexed on the wheel, making it groan. "She got her claws in Vesna, and Vesna got to us... somehow."

"Do you know where she is?"

Kazi glanced over. The glow from the instrument panel made all his sharp angles dramatic. "You ever been to the Carpathian Mountains?"

"No. That's somewhere in Europe, right?"

"The range stretches from Poland in the north to Serbia in the south. It's a vast, wild and sprawling wilderness... or it was a long time ago." He hesitated, as though lost in thought. "I have to go back... Will you come with me?"

Concern and maybe doubt made Kazi's face severe. He didn't want to go home—he'd admitted as much to Felix—but now he had to. A thousand years of avoiding somewhere, only to be forced back to fix a mistake. It wouldn't be easy for him.

"Never mind." Kazi swallowed and peered ahead at the dark, winding road. "I've already asked too much of you. With Atlas gone, the Brotherhood will be flying blind for a while. It's the perfect time to disappear, if you want that. A chance to get your life back, if you want that too."

"Tempting." It wasn't an option, not really. He couldn't forget any of this. And there was still the matter of his blood and the mystery surrounding its differences. "But I kinda like you, so I'll stick around, if you'll have me."

Kazi's flashy smile sprang onto his lips. "You *kinda* like me?"

"It's a step up from hating you."

Kazi sighed through his nose. "I do not deserve you, Felix Quaid."

"I dunno. I'm not exactly perfect either."

"You are to me... I said that out loud, didn't I?"

Felix laughed. And there was no fucking way he was leaving Kazi to go back to Poland without him. They were in this together. Good or bad. Right or wrong. The more he considered it, the more he knew everything he felt for Kazi was real. He'd stick with Kazimir, because somehow, with him, Felix could be a better version of himself, a truer man than he'd been in a long time. Kazimir was the anchor Felix had sorely needed. And maybe a life with Kazi beside him would be a life worth fighting for.

KAZI HAD them board a private jet from a quiet, non-commercial airport. They didn't have any bags so didn't have to wait, and there weren't any security checks.

Kazimir later confessed the privacy was more to do with the fact they'd be traveling during daylight, which made him cranky and liable to snap at members of the public.

He fell asleep almost as soon as the jet breached the clouds and the sun peeked around the window blinds. Felix tried to do the same, but his thoughts whirred.

It wasn't long ago that his only purpose in life had been to destroy Kazimir Skokan. Since then, his whole world had been tipped on its head. It should have been terrible. He'd learned monsters were real. He'd been attacked, bled, threatened, beaten. He'd spent half the time terrified for his life or his family's life. And to top it all off, he'd told his wife he was gay.

He should have felt wretched.

But when he admired the sleeping Kazimir, none of that mattered. He was exactly where he was supposed to be, sitting on a plane next to a man who'd lived countless lifetimes and seen civilizations rise and fall. It was all kinda huge, and he fucking loved it. All of it. The insanity, the breathlessness, the fact magic was real—a kind of magic anyway. He had to be insane to be happy, didn't he?

He was about to step into a country he'd never been to with a man who wasn't a man to find the monster who—by all accounts—was probably as vicious as Mikalis. And he'd never felt freer in all his life.

Felix slotted himself on the curved couch next to Kazi. The vampire grumbled in his sleep, then opened one eye.

"Go back to sleep," Felix whispered, then brazenly stroked his fingers down Kazi's jaw and kissed his soft lips. "I'm not going anywhere without you."

Kazi's snarky lips ticked, then he closed his eyes and fell back to sleep with a smile on his face. Felix tucked himself close. Yeah, this was good, he told himself. It felt like home.

THEY LANDED in a small airport in Poland's far south and hired a car to Zakopane, a resort town where nobody would think twice about Felix's American accent. The town was nestled in the foothills of the Tatra Mountains, one of the highest peaks in the Carpathians—Felix read on the local tourist information board. They'd arrived in darkness, so he didn't get to witness the dramatic skyline, just billions of stars stretched above, as though someone had spilled glitter across black silk.

Kazi picked up a set of house keys from a ski and outdoor sports store, which also apparently provided vacation rentals, and walked Felix up a steep, winding street. The buildings on either side were all multi-tiered, timber-framed "villas" and cabins.

In snow, the town would look magical, like a European fantasyland. It already did and was so unlike the US that it left Felix speechless.

"Do you ski?" Kazi asked. He'd been quiet since they'd landed, but he'd smiled and swept Felix into the car, so he wasn't angry, perhaps only anxious about being on his home soil.

"I can. Haven't in years though."

"We might catch some snow. It's rare this time of year but does happen. If we miss it, will you come back and ski with me in winter?"

"For sure." That sounded like long-term date plans, as though Kazi was thinking ahead. Felix's heart flopped in the way it did when Kazi said anything soft. He almost reached for his hand, forgetting they weren't in America. "Is it... you know... safe for two men to be seen together here?"

"Safe as in nobody is going to threaten us, but they have some ways to go," Kazi said, turning up a path to a small cabin. "Resort towns like this one are likely to be more relaxed. But we should still be careful." Kazi keyed in a code on the door, twisted a key in the lock and pushed inside. "For their own protection. I do not suffer bigots and small-minded people who believe their beliefs are the law when their beliefs are theirs alone and should not be forced upon others."

The dark tone of his voice shivered down Felix's spine. "Yeah, I encountered some of that at high school."

Kazi swung his dark glare to Felix. "What did they do?"

Felix laughed to soften the murderous tone. "It was a long time ago." He reached for the light switch, assuming Kazi hadn't because he could see in the dark.

"Say the word and I'll track them down."

There was something primal in having Kazimir threaten to track down his school bullies. Dangerous too. Because if Felix gave that word, Kazi would follow it through. "Noted. But I'm past it."

The open-plan cabin was an eclectic mix of old and new, with autumnal-colored drapes and couch cushions but a shiny, all-modern gray and white kitchen. Pine stairs climbed to the second-floor loft bedroom. The view from up there would be stunning.

Felix stood in the main living area and breathed. Even the air tasted better here, like pine and mint.

"There was a time men and women were permitted to do whom and what they liked," Kazi went on, shrugging off his coat and sauntering toward the kitchen. "Without fear of their choices being torn from them."

"Yeah, Ancient Greece, right? A free-for-all, I read."

Kazi's laugh rumbled. "You should ask Mikalis."

"No thank you. I like my balls between my legs."

Kazi leaned against the kitchen counter, folded his arms and arched an eyebrow. His gaze crawled over Felix, trying to undress him. "What a coincidence. I admit to liking them there as well."

"Oh really?" He was beginning to realize he *loved* to flirt. He'd always loved it, just not where it led: to pointless, unsatisfying flings —before he'd married Julia.

He moved toward Kazi, drawn to him.

"We still need to explore exactly what you like, Quaid," Kazi purred, smirking now he knew he'd caught the heat in Felix's gaze.

"Don't you think we should focus on making a plan? Discuss what happened back in New York?" He rested a hip on the island counter, keeping a few strides from Kazi. "Vesna said some—"

Kazi blurred, then suddenly became solid and real and all up against Felix. His firm finger pushed on Felix's lips. "We've just arrived. I deserve some downtime, don't you think?"

"What about me?" Felix mumbled, relishing the electric thrill Kazi's touch delivered.

Kazi smirked. Felix had walked into his trap. "You want to go down. Is that what I heard? By all means, go down, Felix..." He plucked his finger from Felix's mouth and skimmed a kiss across his lips.

If his tongue tried to pry, he'd take him and kiss him as though he wanted to devour him, but Kazi held back, likely sensing how Felix's whole body strummed for more. "You just go straight in for the kill, don't you?"

"This might be abrupt for you." He molded himself close, all hot male and corded muscle, predator and man. The heated dick digging into Felix's thigh was hard enough that he'd been sporting it for a while. "But I've been thinking about having you since we landed." He skimmed the near-kiss down Felix's jaw. "I just haven't decided how we're going to do this." Kazi's almost-kiss hovered over his neck, and Felix turned his head, aching for the contact.

"Don't I get a say in it?"

"Do you want one?"

He wasn't even sure he knew what to ask. So far, they'd mostly jerked off together, and that had been enough, but now... He wanted Kazi naked, wanted to make love, but he'd never been with a man like that, and this was Kazimir. Ignoring the fact he was older than dirt and had probably fucked all the ways possible, he'd also had a new partner warming his bed every night. He must have done everything at least once. Felix didn't want to look like an inexperienced idiot, but he was, in this anyway.

Kazi's ice-blue gaze flicked over his face, reading his every concerned crease. "There are many reasons to fear me, but sex is not one of them."

"I wasn't..." Maybe he'd been a little afraid and a lot overwhelmed.

"You cannot fail. You can do nothing wrong." Kazi's fingers entwined with Felix's. "If it's any consolation, being with someone I care about as much as I do for you... It's new for me. The world lost all color. It's how I survived. But you..." His mouth nudged Felix's, urging him to open. "You have me seeing things anew."

Air rushed from him in a small gasp. When Kazi talked like that, he loved it, but a piece of him hated it too, as though he wasn't worthy. "I don't know if I'm that special."

"You are to me." Kazi's fingers slid across Felix's cheek into his hair, cupping his head. "Perhaps you'll allow me to show you how much?"

His body thrummed, desperate with need, his dick heavy, and all he wanted to do was throw himself at Kazi and let whatever was going to happen, happen. Did other people feel this way when they cared for someone so hard it hurt? Or was it some crazy vampire stuff?

"Say yes," Kazi growled, his mouth a hot, sweet tease. "And I will worship you until you beg me to stop."

"Yes," Felix whispered, a little scared, a lot aroused.

Kazi's top lip twitched, and when Felix lunged to seal the kiss, to thrust his tongue in and begin the whirlwind he knew Kazi would take him on, the vampire's fangs were already exposed. Felix licked one, tasting bitter venom—knowing he was immune—then tangled his tongue with Kazi's. He trusted him. He'd given himself to him, and it felt like freedom.

CHAPTER 31

azi

Felix's fists scrunched in Kazi's shirt. When Felix yanked Kazi deeper into the kiss, he had strength behind his muscles, a new kind of strength, one that hadn't been there before. Kazi could crush a man to dust if he lost control, and he'd been acutely aware of their physical differences before now. But something was changing in Felix, the same something Eric Sharpe had experienced, and it gave Felix a strength no normal man possessed. It also meant Kazi didn't have to hold back for fear of hurting him.

He shoved Felix, bending him over the island counter and worked fast to unbutton his shirt. Felix smirked, his eyes already drunk with lust, his body primed and ready. Kazi dared not touch his cock. He'd want it in his mouth, and then he'd have to make him come because he loved to see that just-fucked look on Felix's face. No, this was going to be different. He was going to make his body sing for sex, make him moan and beg, make him writhe and sweat.

He tore his shirt free. Fabric ripped, and Felix gave a dark little chuckle. That chuckle turned to a gulp when Kazi swept his tongue over Felix's right nipple, then flicked the pert little nub with his right fang. Felix moaned, his hands buried in Kazi's hair.

"Want you... naked," Felix moaned. His words were soft, but his glare demanded he be obeyed.

Kazi's cock throbbed. That glare speared his heart, delivering a shot of lust so cruel his dick leaked and his skin burned.

He stepped back, admired Felix half-sprawled over the countertop and worked his own shirt free, then tossed it aside.

Felix's gaze burned. He smiled and wiped a thumb across his bottom lip. "All of it..."

"You want me naked, baby?" Kazi smirked. "Come here and make it happen."

Felix straightened and stepped up to Kazi as though squaring off for a fight. He undid Kazi's trouser fly and shoved them down off his hips. Warm fingers dug into Kazi's underwear. Felix clearly couldn't resist looking down, needing to see his prize.

Kazi's dick twitched under the weight of Felix's glare. Then Felix wrapped his fingers around Kazi's cock and jerked his underwear away with his free hand.

He gave Kazi a few strokes, just enough to heighten sensation, then let go and returned to the island to admire all of Kazi.

Kazi kicked off his boots, then the trousers and socks, removing everything until he stood in the kitchen, naked from head to toe, and cocked his hip.

Felix inhaled, his chest swelling, and muttered, "Fuck, you're gorgeous." Color warmed his face, as though he were embarrassed to admire a man's body. He turned his face away, licking his lips, trying to deny and resist.

"Put your hands on me, Felix."

Felix half lifted his head and looked over, fighting himself over what he wanted and the old demons telling him he couldn't have it.

Kazi stroked his own dick, drawing Felix's attention. It worked.

Felix sauntered over, then circled him. A thrill spilled down Kazi's back when Felix's gaze roamed his ass.

"I want it all," Felix growled. "But don't know where to start." His hand landed on Kazi's lower back, leaving its brand on his skin. Kazi gasped and stopped stroking. Too much of that with Felix's hands on him and he'd come too soon.

Kazi spun, pinned Felix under his glare and marched forward. Felix backed up. He stumbled into the tall cupboard and laughed the moment Kazi grabbed his wrists. Kazi pinned them together, just like before, and held Felix's arms over his head. With his free hand, he made short work of Felix's trousers, but left them hitched to his hips and checked Felix's eyes first. Those soft eyes begged for more. His little breaths panted out of him, between soft, plump lips.

Kazi pressed his entire body against Felix's—skin on skin, thigh to thigh, hip to hip, chest to chest. Felix rolled his eyes and moaned. Yes, this was what they both wanted: no more barriers, total sexual freedom.

Wetting his hand, Kazi wrapped Felix's cock in his grip and stroked, sliding over its head and down its length, and with each pass, Felix quivered, strung as tight as a bow.

He bit into his bottom lip. "Feels so good..."

Kazi opened his fingers, rubbed downward, his palm pushing Felix's dick against him, and cupped his balls, massaging. Felix writhed and moaned. Pre-cum slickened Kazi's forearm. He gathered some of the wetness between his fingers and massaged lower, seeking the tight path behind Felix's scrotum.

Felix shuddered. His abs stuttered, muscles bunching, and then he seemed to realize where this was going. He snapped his eyes open. "I er... I don't..."

He wasn't ready.

Kazi withdrew his hand, kissed him hard and fast, banishing any doubt, and rubbed his dick along Felix's—still keeping Felix's wrists pinned above him. "Will you trust me?"

"I do..." Felix puffed. "More than I should."

Kazi nodded. "Turn around."

Felix's throat undulated in a gulp.

"Trust me, baby." Kazi stroked his neck. "I'll never hurt you."

Felix twisted, shuffling around since his trousers were still tangled around his ankles. He faced the cupboard, and now his back was a canvas for Kazi to kiss. He began at his shoulders, sweeping his tongue and dragging his teeth across his skin just enough to indent the flesh but not break it. His fangs throbbed, seeking the bite, ancient and primal urges demanding he bite while fucking him and claiming him.

Kazi dropped Felix's wrists, needing both hands, and swept a trail of kisses and safe bites down Felix's spine. When he got to the taut curves of his ass, he pinched one cheek between his teeth. Felix bucked and swore. But the reaction was a good one. Kazi stroked his tongue over the indents in Felix's skin, slickened his own dick with pre-cum and, as he straightened, pushed himself against Felix's closed thighs, rubbing upward.

Felix shuddered some more. He knew what part of Kazi touched him and where, and as Kazi rocked, sliding through the valley between the backs of Felix's thighs, Felix shifted his stance, opening a space.

He was so damn perfect. He had no idea what he did to Kazi.

Kazi leaned in, smothering Felix's back under his chest, sucked at his shoulder, and slid his dick between Felix's tight, muscular thighs. Felix grunted and moaned and clutched the cupboard. Deeper, Kazi thrust, touching the head of his dick to Felix's balls.

Felix raised his arms, spread open for Kazi. He could fuck his thighs like that, but he wanted to show him more, tease what he could be having.

Kazi grabbed him by the hips and yanked him back two steps, bending him ass-up.

He grunted, bracing his palms on the cupboard, and glanced over his shoulder, his eyes narrowing.

"Trust me?"

Felix nodded. If he didn't know what he was missing, he couldn't know what he wanted?

Kazi leaned over him, kissed his spine and, reaching around, took his erection between his fingers. He pumped until Felix shivered and twitched and wetness dripped from Kazi's fingers. Before Felix could climb that pleasure too high, Kazi let go, spread his ass cheeks and flicked his cum-slick fingers over Felix's hole.

"Ugh... fuck. I..."

Kazi stopped. "I'm not going to penetrate—unless you demand it."

He threw a look over his shoulder, half-smiling. "Okay..."

Kazi smiled back. "Close your eyes."

He couldn't see if he obeyed, but he dropped his head and gave himself to Kazi, and that was enough. Clutching his own dick, Kazi pinched one cheek aside and stroked his head over the slick opening, sliding over sensitive skin. A shudder ran through Felix. When Kazi stroked again, Felix gasped.

Kazi quickened the pace, riding his own crackling edge of pleasure and restraint. It was as much torture as it was ecstasy not to bury himself inside Felix. Like fighting his urges to bite, he needed to sink inside him, to feel him clench around him, knowing that Felix would experience a whole new level of pleasure that he didn't know his body could find.

But he wasn't ready, and Kazi respected that.

Even if the restraint almost killed him.

Felix must have sensed his struggle, because he turned his head and grinned, then tilted his hips, adjusting his angle. Kazi's stroking pace dislodged, and he sank his dick between Felix's thighs again, between tight muscle and over slick skin. He thrust hard, almost out of his mind with desire. Felix swore. His right hand vanished, and his shoulder rolled as he touched himself.

Kazi's control slipped. His fangs leaked. He pumped between Felix's legs, fucking the crack behind Felix's balls until he began to spiral toward climaxing, almost hopelessly lost to the man who had undone centuries of control.

"No, don't stop..." Felix begged. "Fuck me."

And that was all the permission he needed. He fucked between Felix's thighs, pumping hard, breathless, his skin and veins ablaze. Felix let out a garbled cry, and his body stuttered beneath Kazi. That was the final trigger, tipping Kazi over the edge. He spilled between Felix's legs, his dick tight to the back of Felix's balls.

Part of him screamed a madness in his head, viciously demanding he feed and spear his climax to a whole new level.

He shook that desperate desire off with a growl and shuddered a ragged sigh. This was enough. This was fucking *everything*. He fell forward, wrapped Felix in his arms and drew him upright, hauling his back against his chest. The new upright angle meant that when Kazi dropped his hand, Felix's dick was within easy reach.

Felix choked on a gasp. "Easy... I'm still coming down."

"Baby," Kazi whispered in his ear. "We're just getting started."

WAKING up with Felix sprawled alongside him in bed was one of the finest moments of Kazi's long life. He'd learned, long ago, how magic thrived in the little moments. The big moments left their marks too, but small moments, like seeing Felix sleeping, mouth open, snoring lightly, as though he didn't have a care in the world—the little moments were precious and too easily lost or forgotten.

Careful not to wake him, Kazi slipped from the bed and padded downstairs in one of the gowns they'd found in the early hours after their joint shower, where Kazi had welcomed Felix's dick between his lips again. They both liked it there.

He made a pot of coffee, gathered the eggs and bacon the cabin's host had left, and fixed breakfast—at four p.m. in the late afternoon. The sun had dropped behind the mountains an hour ago, bleeding the valley red as it had died.

As the bacon sizzled in the kitchen, he stood at the window, sipped his coffee and admired the view outside. Late autumn and the peaks were already snow-capped. That snow would soon crawl down into the valleys. He remembered its bite on the coldest days, remembered the crackle from the castle fireplaces, the smell of warm furs and tallow candles.

He was home.

Everything looked different, even the mountains, but his bones, and his blood too, knew the land.

She'd be close. Jadwiga. His sire.

The witch who had stolen him from his life as a king's son and turned him into a monster.

He hadn't known what she was or what she'd made him. The knowing had come much later, when Mikalis had tracked him deep into the Carpathians to end his reign of blood.

Vesna had hinted that Jadwiga was behind everything—the rise of the Nyxians and perhaps more than that. The Brotherhood's recent altercation with another ancient nyktelios, Sebastien, had kicked over a few long-buried secrets. Rumors had swirled of Sebastien hinting that more misfortune was coming for the Brotherhood, and now their New York base had fallen.

That was one hell of a coincidence.

"What's the catch?" Felix said, emerging from the bedroom, half-dressed in trousers and an open shirt, his hair sleep-tousled and his eyes still heavy.

"Catch?"

"Sexy vampire fucks me unconscious and then makes breakfast? There must be a catch, right?" He circled an arm around Kazi's waist and kissed him on the neck. "G'morning, Kazimir." He laughed at Kazi's rapid blink and withdrew, heading for the kitchen.

The little things, Kazi thought. A kiss in the morning, given so freely as though it were nothing, but that quick sweep of the lips on Kazi's neck and the little laugh right after had summoned a single, devastating thought into Kazi's head.

He loved Felix. It was true.

He knew it was love in the same way he knew he was home, in his blood and body. It had snuck up on him. He couldn't say when it had happened; rather, it had grown, probably from the first time he'd seen him trying to stalk Kazi in the shadows. It had begun there, as a tiny spark. But it wasn't small now. Kazi loved him so fiercely. It was violent and devastating. He'd killed Vesna because she'd been about to hurt Felix. Snapped her neck because he'd lost control. He'd do the same again in an instant.

What did it mean?

There were fine lines between the Brotherhood and the nyktelios they hunted. Lines like not caring, not drinking from the vein. Lines like making sure the Brotherhood came first.

Kazi had crossed all of them.

If the Atlas building had been standing, Mikalis would have locked him away by now. For his own safety and the safety of the Brotherhood.

"What's our first move?" Felix asked, spilling the bacon onto a plate, unaware of Kazi's silent crisis.

Was Kazi nyktelios?

But he didn't have feeders. He wasn't gorging on blood. He didn't kill indiscriminately. He had control. That meant he was still Brotherhood, didn't it?

"Hey... you okay?"

Kazi blinked. "What?"

"What's wrong?"

"Nothing. I'm just... thinking."

Felix arched an eyebrow but didn't press. He carried the food to the table, poured a coffee and sat, waiting. "Want to join me?"

"Yes..." Kazi pushed the unsettling thoughts aside. Now was not the time to be distracted.

"I've been going over Vesna's last words."

"I'm sorry."

"What?" Felix asked.

Kazi winced. What had gotten into him? "Vesna Dragovic did not deserve to die."

Felix slumped back in his chair. He studied Kazi's face and narrowed his eyes. "You're not sorry though."

Kazi plucked some bacon from the dish and dropped it onto his plate. "All right, no, I'm not sorry. She was going to hurt you, probably kill you. I killed her because you are mine, and if anyone dares to hurt you, they will suffer the same fate."

"I'm yours?"

"That's right."

Felix smiled, but it wasn't his typical easy and soft smile. "Maybe I should have a say in who I belong to, huh?"

"Yes, of course." He bit down on a piece of bacon, but Felix was staring, not eating or drinking, just... staring. Kazi had the urge to apologize again but had no idea what for.

"I forget sometimes how you're from a different time. All of you are real good at blending in—and then you say *I belong to you*, and yeah, there it is. A thousand years is between us."

"It's true."

Felix snorted. "Way to double down on the entitlement, asshole. I don't belong to you. You know that, right? This isn't the Middle Ages. I'm not a peasant you can summon to your princely chambers and fuck when you feel like it."

"That's not—"

"Whatever. Let's focus on the reason we're here, okay?"

He could either apologize again, which would probably enrage Felix further, or agree and move on. "Fine. Once the sun has fully set, I'm venturing into the valley and foothills, then deeper into the wilderness in search of any sign of Jadwiga."

"*You* are?" Felix picked up his coffee. "I'm not coming with you?"

"I'll cover more ground without you."

"Right, because I'm a slow-ass mortal who's only good for fucking?"

"I thought we weren't talking about that."

He huffed. "Ugh... you know, if you look up your name in the urban dictionary, Kazi is a man who is a massive dick."

A thread of humor tickled him. He'd seen the webpage Felix referred to. His fans had pointed it out, and he may have played up to its meaning. "Actually, *Kazi* is slang for a man who has a huge dick. There's a difference."

"Ugh." Felix rolled his eyes. "What's happening here? Why are you suddenly *being* a dick?"

He wasn't sure, just that Felix's prickly attitude had him fearing the shine on their relationship might be fading. And that thought scared him more than his sire. "I've always been a dick."

"Yeah... you have."

They ate breakfast in silence, apart from Felix clattering cutlery and clearing away the plates as though trying to break them.

The sun had set, and darkness absorbed all the warmth from the valley. But Kazi couldn't leave with Felix fuming. Knowing him, he'd try to follow Kazi into the night to prove him wrong, then get eaten by a wolf.

"Are there wolves here?" Felix asked, staring at his own ghostly reflection looking back at him in the living room's large window.

And again, their thoughts were aligned. "Yes."

"Bears?"

"Brown bears, yes, although they're rarer now than they used to be." He couldn't leave him like this. He approached his side so his reflection joined Felix's in the glass.

"Not to mention vampires, huh?"

"Hopefully, just me."

"And her..."

"If she's still here."

"Is she likely to be?" Felix asked.

Kazi wanted to reach out to him, to fold him inside his embrace, breathe him in, but he held back. He'd upset him—although unsure how. It had to be Felix who reached for Kazi. "She's here, but she won't be easy to find. Ancient nyktelios like her, they burrow deep into the fabric of the world. She'll be controlling a network of feeders who make sure she's cared for. Her every need will be met. Blood, sex, power."

"Like slaves?"

"Yes. She'll be hidden, likely high in the mountains, undisturbed."

Felix folded his arms and sighed through his nose. "Is that what I am to you? A slave?"

"No." Unable to stand it any longer, Kazi stepped in front of him, between him and the view, making Felix look up. "I am not nyktelios, and you are not a feeder." He wanted to tell him he loved him—the words were right there on his lips—but this moment was fragile. If he pushed too much in either direction, Kazi might lose him. "I'm Brotherhood, and that means something. And you're... whatever you want to be. I was wrong. You're not mine. Although I wish you were, because I'm afraid to lose you, like I haven't been afraid in a very long time."

He smiled, and although fleeting, it had been genuine. "Okay... we need to talk about the Brotherhood."

"Why?"

"Aren't you worried about them?"

"No." He'd barely thought about any of the others since they'd left American soil.

Felix pressed his hands to Kazi's chest. "Don't you care that your home is gone?"

"It's not gone. The Brotherhood doesn't exist in bricks and mortar. It's in the members, in Mikalis. He keeps the Brotherhood alive."

"If *he's* alive."

Kazi grinned. Felix's concern was adorable, but unnecessary. "This isn't the first time we've had to burn it all down. We've begun again eight times over in my lifetime. There are multiple Brotherhoods worldwide. One falls, and the others rise. Besides, Mikalis plans for every eventuality. He would have planned for exactly this scenario. He's likely bringing that plan all online now, as we speak."

"How do we find him? How do you know when it's time to go back?"

"Nobody finds Mikalis. He finds us."

"Just be careful out there, okay?" He grabbed Kazi's shirt and shifted onto his toes. "I don't wanna have to come and save you."

"Baby, you already did." The words were worth it to see his

muddled face. Kazi kissed him, then pulled away before he surrendered to wanting more. It was all too easy to lose himself in Felix's touch. "I'll be back before dawn."

"And I'll just sit here, I guess." He flopped onto the couch and grabbed the TV remote. "Have a good night, darling. I'll be sure to have breakfast ready for when you get back." He spread his legs and dropped his chin, peering through his lashes.

Hmm, breakfast looked delicious. Kazi considered heading right back over there, straddling him and kissing that smirk from his lips. "Be sure that you do, baby. I'll be ravenous." He added a growl and caught Felix's laugh as he stepped out into the bitter night, already wishing it was over so he could devour Felix all over again.

CHAPTER 32

Felix

He waited fifteen minutes, long enough for Kazi to travel a good distance away, then threw on his coat, grabbed a scarf he'd found on a coat hook, and headed outside. He hadn't promised he'd stay indoors, and this was a whole new town to explore in a whole new country. No way was he sitting on the couch and watching the minutes tick by until dawn, as Kazi had probably assumed.

If there was a nyktelios holed up nearby, then there would be clues, missing people, unexplained deaths, some hint of something out of the ordinary. Plus, it would make a damn fine podcast episode. *Unexplained in Zakopane.* It worked. Yeah, he was doing this.

He couldn't mention vampires on the podcast or Mikalis would appear and try to peel his skin from his bones. Shame, as this was vampire country. Zakopane was as close to Dracula country as Maine was to New York. He'd Googled it. His podcast listeners would love the vampire stuff. But vamps were off-limits.

Either way, he was too curious to hole up in the cabin like a kept man.

There was nothing *kept* about him, despite what Kazi appeared to think.

He blew into his cupped hands, shoved them into his jacket pockets and strolled down the lit street, mingling with other tourists heading for the local restaurants and nightlife.

He might have overreacted to the ownership comment, but Kazi's admission about why he'd killed Vesna had shifted the blame to Felix—because Kazi cared so much about him, he'd killed Vesna, and while that was sort of a good thing, it was also terrifying and a reminder that Kazi wasn't human. A reminder that tripped Felix's emotions, sending them swirling around his head.

Kazi made it easy to forget what he was. They all did. But forgetting they were killers made any reminders like Vesna's sudden death land like a slap to the face.

If they were going to do this, if they were going to be a permanent thing, then Felix needed to get his head around it all, and he needed time.

The short walk into town brought him to an area with multiple bars, a few clubs, and some restaurants. It was busy enough that he didn't stand out. The size of the place suggested it got much busier, probably heading into winter and the skiing season.

He ordered a drink at the bar, grateful the menus were in English as well as Polish. The young bartender was full of smiles, and Felix struck up a clunky conversation in choppy English. He learned *dziękuję* was thank you, then settled in for some people-watching.

There were German accents among the crowd and some Russian among the more obvious Polish and Romanian. Most were speaking English.

He left that bar after an hour and ventured into the next, chatting with tourists and locals alike. And while it was work, he also enjoyed it. The people part of reporting was the key to it. It always came down to the people.

After midnight, he stepped off the bustling main streets and sought the quieter bars, places the locals would prefer to visit. He found one where Polish was spoken exclusively, pointed awkwardly at a drink on the menu, and tucked himself into a corner to pick up the general mood of the place. The fact he didn't speak or read Polish was proving to be a hurdle, and one he couldn't climb over without Kazi to translate.

He returned to the cabin at 3 a.m. And while he hadn't seen anything out of the ordinary, he had gotten a feel for the place. Maybe Kazi would join him the next night?

After throwing off the scarf and coat, he dropped onto the couch and watched the window for the first signs of dawn.

CHAPTER 33

azi

He traveled fast, covering vast swathes of mountainside and valley. The land had changed, shifted, buckled around the flow of a river, and swelled with aging forests, but while different, it was familiar too. Wolves howled in the distance—a good sign. It meant a hunting nyktelios wasn't close. Although it also meant his search tonight would probably prove fruitless.

When the ground turned rocky and treacherous, he took to the trees. The deeper into the wildlands he traveled, the more it rewarded him with the scurry of small mammals, the hoot of owls, and the screech marking their kills.

The nyktelios had adapted to towns and cities, and so had the Brotherhood. But they'd begun as chaos among the wild things. And as Kazi ran and leaped so fast he almost flew, his face frozen and the breath in his lungs like ice, he remembered what it had been like... the freedom of being at the top of the food chain, the predator all others knelt too. He remembered what it was like to *hunt*.

~

THE CABIN'S LIGHTS GLOWED. Felix was up. Good.

Kazi opened the door.

His prey lay sprawled on his side on the couch, vulnerable... unsuspecting.

The smell of cigarette smoke and beer swirled around him. He'd been with others...

A snarl rippled from Kazi. He braced over Felix and ran his gaze down his face to the beat of the vein at his throat. Life pulsed through him, hot and powerful.

Felix's eyes fluttered open. He turned his head, blinked and froze. "Kazi..." he croaked.

Kazi smiled. "Want to play a game?" he asked, his voice gruff.

"Er..." Felix twisted, angling his body toward Kazi. "Are you okay?"

Was he okay? He'd been running for hours, racing through the world, freer than he'd felt in centuries.

Felix reached up and plucked a leaf from Kazi's hair. "You have a—"

Kazi gripped his wrist and brought it to his mouth. He must have moved too quickly, because fear laced Felix's gasp. Kazi locked his gaze on his and licked up his wrist, relishing the thumping heat beneath his tongue.

"Kazi... you're..."

Kazi grazed his fangs down Felix's skin, delicious resistance pulling pleasure tight inside him. "I need to fuck you." If he didn't fuck him, he'd bite him, and it wouldn't stop there. "Say yes..."

Felix's gaze flicked over Kazi's face. Already on his back beneath Kazi, all he had to do was give permission.

"What are you asking, exactly?"

"I need you." He bowed his head, hovering close, and when

Felix turned his head, Kazi breathed him in. "You smell like strangers—"

"I er... I went into town."

Didn't matter. Kazi wanted to taste him, to bite and fuck him, to sink his teeth in, to drink him down and spill his seed and make him his. It was dangerous. It walked that line they should never cross. He was close to being the thing he'd hunted, to being the monster he'd left behind in these mountains. "I won't hurt you," he breathed the words, made them his vow.

"It's just... you look kinda wild."

He had no idea how right he was.

"I want to fuck you." He growled the words over Felix's lips. "I'm hungry. I need you, Felix. Need to be in you, to taste you."

"Yeah, but..." Felix licked his lips. Fear tainted his quivering voice, but lust too. "Fuck it... Do it." He grabbed Kazi by the back of the neck, holding him hard enough to prevent Kazi from escaping. "Fuck me."

Control hung by a thin, woven thread fraying at the edges. Kazi tore Felix's trousers and underwear from his legs. His hard cock bounced against his lower belly, already leaking. Kazi took it between his lips and fangs, pumped ruthlessly, and then let go and slickened his grip with Felix's pre-cum.

"Ugh... damn, slow down or I won't fuckin' last..."

"You're going to come for me, and then come again."

Felix bared his blunt little teeth but didn't question him. There wasn't time to strip off. Kazi needed to be in him *now*. He freed his own dick, swept a glistening bead of pre-cum from its head and stoked it across Felix's hole as a tease of what was to come.

"Fuck..." Felix moaned.

"I plan to, baby."

He took his eager dick and jerked him off. Felix bucked, his back arched, he dug his fingers into the couch, and suddenly, he ejaculated. "Goddamn... Kazi... I... That wasn't..." He panted around broken words.

Kazi gathered the cum in his palm, wiped it over his dick and

Felix's hole, and grabbed his hips, shifting him downward, cradling him a few inches higher than the couch. While Felix still reeled from his climax, Kazi pressed his dick to Felix's hole.

Felix stilled.

Kazi eased in, going as slow as his control allowed.

"Fuck..." Felix choked. "Wait..."

Kazi stopped—it might kill him, but he stopped with his thick erection cinched by Felix's tight ring.

"I don't..."

"Trust me, baby. It'll feel a whole lot better soon."

Felix breathed hard and glared down his body at Kazi, his knees spread, ass up. He nodded, and Kazi had him.

He shifted his angle, lifting Felix a little higher, and pushed deeper. Felix flung his head back. "Oh... fuck... yes."

There it was.

Felix's dick twitched, his body twinging around the new sensation. "Damn it, that feels... *Yes, move!*"

Kazi withdrew enough to make him moan, then slid back in so the tip of his dick rode that sensitive nub inside Felix, spilling shivers up his spine. He kept the pace slow, kept it smooth, stretching him, easing into it, but Kazi was already too close to snapping his own control to draw this out for long.

"Kazi," Felix snarled. "Fuck me."

Kazi thrust balls-deep, Felix moaned, and then Kazi was lost, chasing a high that was coming too fast, yet he didn't want it to stop. His thighs slapped Felix's ass, scorching his skin raw. Felix's dick re-hardened, his body flushed, and demands spilled from his lips—to be fucked harder, faster. His fingers dug into Kazi's arm, nails drawing deep scratches.

Then Felix's glare pinned onto Kazi. Whatever he saw, he liked. Wet with sweat, he shuddered and moaned, as lost as Kazi was, drowning in a river of ecstasy.

So close to coming, Kazi took Felix in his hand again, and with them joined, he pumped with his hand and fucked his hole, turning Felix into a breathless, writhing animal.

Perhaps they weren't so different.

Kazi came hard on his knees, buried balls-deep, spilling in pulses inside Felix, and then Felix's dick spurted hot cum over Kazi's fingers. Kazi brought his fingers to his lips and licked them clean as Felix watched, wide-eyed and panting.

He liked him there, on his back, wrecked.

Felix sighed and flopped his head back. "Damn." He dragged a shaking hand down over his mouth and chin. "Why'd nobody tell me it's that good?"

"Because it's only that good with me." Kazi scooped him up—still buried in his ass—and pulled him onto his lap. Hot, slick, wet... spent and trembling, Kazi kissed his man, relieved when Felix threw his arms around him and returned the kiss, turning it lazy and messy.

Felix was everything Kazi had lost from his life. He was the light, the color, the sensation. He made the world worth fighting for, made Kazi's stone heart beat again. Mikalis was wrong. Love made a man stronger, made him fierce.

Love was a sword and a shield in the battle of life, a battle Kazi had slowly been losing. Until now. Until Felix.

THE NEXT NIGHT, Felix had Kazi take him into town to see if they could learn anything from the locals, but if anything was amiss, nobody was talking. After their return to the cabin, Kazi spent the next hours until dawn scouring the mountainside. When he returned, Felix was awake, waiting on the couch, his gaze hungry. All Kazi had to do was feed his desire.

They fell into a routine. They'd visit the town in the early evening, then Kazi would hunt for his sire for the rest of the night, returning wild and hungry at dawn, when they'd fuck like animals and inevitably sleep the day away after.

Two weeks passed, two weeks of running free in the mountains, two weeks of burying himself in Felix every night until he lost his mind in him.

He got complacent.

He got comfortable.

That was his mistake.

The night was colder than the rest, and fat snowflakes twirled, shifted by a lazy breeze. Kazi stopped in the clearing. Something had called to him, making him pause.

His boots crunched on a thin, frozen layer of snow. There was no other sound, no owls, no wolves. Huge pines reached toward the starlit sky.

He knew this place. The trees had been different over a millennium ago, the land altered, but the stars above were the same. Those never changed.

Memories assaulted him, like thieves rushing from the shadows. He saw how the witch had torn his horse from under him, ripping its throat open. He'd lain in the snow, stunned senseless, and watched the animal choke on its own blood.

This clearing was where she'd attacked. No trees had grown here, as though the mountain knew the ground was tainted in blood.

He straightened and turned, disturbing his own footprints in the snow.

He wasn't alone. "I know you're here."

Nothing.

Silence.

It had been so long, but the memories of this place were so fresh, that the horrors of the ancient past breathed down his neck.

He moved on, moved slow... walking through the trees. A cliff face loomed. He pulled back a veil of brush and ivy, revealing a gaping cave entrance. She'd turned him inside. Methodically, painstakingly bled him and replenished the loss with her own blood, forcing it between his lips. She'd killed him over and over and brought him back each time. With every rebirth, he came back hungrier, madder, more vicious until there was nothing left of his humanity, just the monster she'd poured into his veins, the monster that suckled from her veins like a babe at the breast.

He stumbled back, away from the cave.

The rest were broken dreams, shattered memories. She'd sent him out into the world, and he'd slaughtered and butchered any living thing he could find. Wolf, bear, man, woman, child.

Kazi staggered. He could taste their blood still, feel it wet and warm on his lips.

Half of him demanded he run, go back to the cabin, take Felix and leave.

But he'd returned to stop the madness.

He'd been running long enough.

He pushed through the brush into the cave mouth. The world outside had changed, but the cave was the same. Walls shining and sharp with ice. A cold so deep it gnawed on his bones.

But Jadwiga wasn't here and hadn't been here for a long time.

He stepped outside and scanned the tree line. Someone was out there, watching. But as old as he was, with senses honed by the passage of time, Jadwiga was older. More powerful.

Kazi had seen enough.

She wasn't here, but she was close.

Now all he had to do was lure her out of hiding.

CHAPTER 34

elix

THE BARTENDER RATTLED off a sentence in Polish that Felix was supposed to repeat, but all the consonants had lost him. He laughed. "Not a chance in hell."

"You learn good. You practice," the bartender said. His English was better than Felix's awful attempt at Polish.

"Yeah, yeah."

The bartender served his other customers, the bar busy, although the numbers had dwindled in the past hour. A quick glance at the clock revealed it was gone 2 a.m. Kazi would be back soon.

A tight flutter of lust tried to harden him. He chuckled at himself. Who knew he'd become addicted to cock? Although it was Kazi's cock, which he was pretty sure few people could resist.

At dawn, when Kazi would return, his hair wild and his eyes alight with icy flame, smelling of pine and snow, damn... Felix would be helpless to resist. It wasn't just the anticipation of sex that had him smiling like an idiot, and it wasn't that Kazi happened to be the ancient, enigmatic epitome of a magic few knew existed. It was the man and how he'd told Rosa he hated blackberries, and how fierce he could be one moment and, in the next breath, achingly gentle. His quick smiles and glittering eyes hid a man full of emotion—emotion he kept caged, teasing Felix with hints of more in his long, soft kisses and his smooth, stroking fingers.

No, it wasn't just sex.

Not anymore.

Although he did plan on making up for a lifetime of missing the best sex he'd ever had.

Did it make him a fool if he wanted to save someone who didn't need saving, if he loved someone who'd outlive him? Loving someone who had to watch him grow old and die seemed like a really stupid thing to do, but Felix was good at making mistakes. He'd made enough of them to know some were worth it.

He settled his tab, threw on his jacket and scarf, and headed out.

The side street he'd ventured down his first night beckoned again now. He hadn't been back to the locals' bar since then. He had a little while before Kazi would return, and it wouldn't hurt to take a second look.

He entered the bar, ordered a drink, and found the same corner seat as before. The few Polish words he'd picked up helped him string a few nearby conversations together, but most of it was spoken too fast and too fluently for him to catch its meaning. He listened anyway and watched discreetly.

Two weeks and they hadn't seen a single sign of a nyk. The place was almost too orderly. No bar fights, no drunken accidents, no missing people, no nothing. That just didn't happen in New York, but Zakopane was a long way from the big city in more ways than one.

"You come back, huh, American?" A woman stopped at his table. Her neat bob of bottle-blonde hair framed a soft, round face.

He glanced around to check that a boyfriend wasn't about to lurch over. "I did."

"You alone?"

"I er..." He remembered Kazi's words about the locals not being too relaxed when it came to LGBTQ+ rights. "My friend is outside."

"He should come inside." She laughed and brushed her arms vigorously. "Warmer, yes?"

"I'll ask him."

"Tak tak..." She beamed.

He nodded and smiled, and away she went, happier, he presumed, for speaking with the lonely American.

He hadn't told her his friend was male. She must have assumed it.

Loud and rowdy, the bar continued to bustle, busier than usual. But he wasn't learning anything new and kept checking the clock, counting down the minutes until he could get back to Kazi.

After he'd downed his drink, he stepped outside, leaving the noise and warmth behind. The woman was right about the cold. Snowflakes swirled, blurred by the distant streetlight.

He took a step and his boot landed in slushy snow. The alley swirled, trying to tip him on his ass. He reached for the wall and propped himself up. He hadn't had *that* much to drink, although the Polish were generous with the volume of alcohol in their beers.

He lifted his head, trying to clear his vision.

Two figures loomed, heading for the bar's entrance. He probably looked like an idiot American tourist who couldn't handle his alcohol, which was half right.

"*Jak leci*?" the guy on the left said.

He had no idea what that meant. Felix smiled, hoping to convey he was fine so they'd move on. But thumping darkness spread through his skull and blurred his vision. He was not fine. He had to get back to the cabin—

One of the guys grabbed his arm and barked more foreign words. Felix's thoughts drifted, detached and unsteady. This wasn't right. The men held him; he knew it but didn't feel it, as though it were happening to someone else.

The drink...

The woman...

She'd put something in his drink.

The thoughts came too slow, too late. He swung a fist and tried to pull from the man's grip, but his efforts hastened another wave of unconsciousness. He clung to reality, trying to stay awake. The men marched him away from the bar and the crowds, away from the safety of the bright lights and people. Away from the cabin and Kazi...

CHAPTER 35

azi

THE SENSE of being observed faded after he'd broken into a run. If it was Jadwiga, then she was still out there. But now that he knew where he could circle around, flush her from hiding, and hunt her down. But not tonight. It was too close to dawn, and as much as his sire would be weakened by the sun, so would he.

The cabin lights were on.

Felix would be waiting. He'd taken to saving time by waiting naked, sometimes in their bed, sometimes not. Kazi climbed the porch steps and opened the door. The lights blazed, but the inside was silent.

"Felix?"

He already knew he wasn't home. His scent was old; he hadn't been back in hours.

It wasn't right, it wasn't normal.

Felix was *always* here.

A growl simmered low in his throat.

He turned away from the cabin and eyed the street. Dawn's weak daylight crept down the snow-dusted sidewalks and roads. Heating units hummed from nearby buildings. A dog yapped somewhere. Nobody was out yet. Snow had settled on the cabin steps, with no sign of Felix's footprints.

Kazi dashed too fast to be seen, keeping to the rear of the villas and cabins, using the long, early morning shadows as stepping stones to conceal himself. The town center was quiet too. The nighttime revelries had ended hours ago. Felix's scent was faint, little more than a ghost, and mingled with a thousand others.

Someone had him.

Kazi crouched in the gloom of a large hotel. The sun had broken through retreating snow clouds, but even as weak as it was, it robbed him of strength and sizzled his skin. He could resist its relentless low-level burn, could pretend he was human for a while, but not all day.

Retreating back into the cool shade, he retraced his path to the cabin. Perhaps Felix had returned? He'd gotten lost or held up somewhere...

But he wasn't inside.

His coat and scarf were missing. He'd left willingly. Then he'd been taken from the town, probably from one of the bars.

Damn them. And himself. He should have told him not to leave without him, to stay indoors. He shouldn't have left him.

Kazi sat on the stairs and stared at the door, willing Felix to walk through it. The sun rose higher and higher. Outside, people laughed and went about their day as though nothing had changed. Shadows shifted around the cabin, marking the passing hours.

Nothing in the cabin changed. Felix wasn't chatting as he fried bacon. He wasn't laughing when Kazi swooped in and nuzzled his neck. There was no moan of delight when Kazi put his hands on him.

The world had changed.

And if anyone had hurt Felix—if they'd touched a single hair on his head—Kazi would make sure their world ended in a hail of blood and fury.

~

THE RESORT OFFICIALS could do nothing unless Felix had been missing for over twenty-four hours.

And the *Policja* couldn't have cared less, just enough to tell Kazi a man of Felix's description had not been arrested and there were no John Does in the city morgue.

With the official routes exhausted before dusk, as soon as the sun had set, Kazi tracked Felix's wisp of a scent from bar to bar before the crowds could grow too large and obstructive.

He asked after his *friend* with each bartender and had it confirmed that Felix had been in town, but he'd left after 2 a.m.

Between 2 a.m. and dawn, he'd been taken.

It wouldn't have happened in public. Nobody had seen a fight or a disagreement, nothing suspicious. So Felix had ventured out of sight, off the main street...

The locals' bar.

Kazi kept his pace slow so as not to trigger human instincts into sensing there was a preternatural being among them. Felix's scent drifted outside the bar and in. Much of the snow had melted in the day, but some remained, turned hard again now that night had drawn in. Too many boot marks had trampled any sign of Felix's footprints.

He stepped into the bar. It was still early, and only a few customers sat at the tables.

Speaking in Polish, he asked the bartender if he'd seen an American, and sure enough, Felix had decided to visit the bar after 2 a.m., but he'd left alone, not long after.

A dead end.

Kazi sat on a barstool and scanned the dim room, then the grim faces of the customers. Someone knew something. An American couldn't vanish into thin air, at least not one who wasn't nyktelios.

Dammit, he could have done with the Brotherhood's help. Even Mikalis would have aided him with Felix still under his protection. But there was no way to reach them, and even if he could, they were all likely several hours' flight away.

Unless he could get in touch with the European branch.

They'd had their own troubles with rising nyk numbers, but they'd help if he asked.

It would still be too late.

Felix could be dead in hours. Might already be...

He hunched over the bar and *breathed*, hiding how his fangs tried to extend. The last thing he needed was to draw attention to himself...

Or perhaps that was exactly what he needed.

This was Jadwiga's territory. A nyk like her, in the same place for so long, she'd have exerted her control, stretching it far and wide. She'd have an extensive network of feeders, people who would lie to protect her. Or she'd have been exposed by now and killed by the Brotherhood. No, she'd been clever, quiet, subtle...

She was right here in Zakopane.

The spider in her web.

And all Kazi had to do was entice her into the open. Make her think she'd caught a fly.

He let his fangs drop, and his human pretense dropped with them. His eyesight sharpened, and his senses burned, coming alive.

It was time to shake the web.

CHAPTER 36

elix

MUFFLED VOICES ECHOED AROUND HIM. He should lift his head, should move, *just move.* Didn't matter where, or how... He tried to shift his arms, but a weight pinned them to his sides. His legs were the same, filled with lead and strapped down. Someone held him...

Memories flashed out of the dark. Hands on him, carrying him away.

His heart pounded. Machines blipped, racing with him.

He blinked, clearing his swimming vision. But the blur didn't come from dizziness... It came from the curved glass held inches from his face.

Figures moved, drifting in and out of his field of vision.

What was this...?

He shook his head. Something cool tapped his forehead. He jerked his head, trying to flick the thing off, and looked up.

Plastic tubes dangled from above—tentacles reaching for him. He jolted in the restraints and gasped—or tried to. Something cold and hard was wedged between his teeth, pressing down on his tongue.

No... he couldn't move. Couldn't breathe! Trapped, hidden, crushed... Nothing made any sense. He had to get out, escape—

"Shhhh, there now, my child. It will all soon be over."

At the sight of the woman's face, the cold panic bled from his veins, leaving him numb and hollow. She had the silver-touched eyes of the Brotherhood, but his skin crawled under her gaze. Long black hair flowed in a loose plait over one shoulder. He felt as though he should know her, that everyone should know her.

She ran a finger down the glass between them.

"When you wake, you will be born anew." She smiled. Four fangs gleamed.

No...

He suddenly understood why the glass curved around him, why he couldn't move, what the tubes were. He jerked his head up. The clear plastic tubes turned red with blood that was coming for him...

He bucked. Restraints held him. He thrashed and screamed behind the metal in his mouth.

"Hush now, child."

Her silvery eyes followed him down into darkness.

CHAPTER 37

azi

He picked up the whiskey glass belonging to the customer next to him and flung it across the room. It shattered and splashed whiskey up the wall.

Now he had their attention.

Kazi hopped off the bar stool and faced the room. Ten customers stared back. He smiled, letting the beast within bleed through. One by one, they began to understand. The smell of fear permeated the air.

"Now," he growled, "which one of you fuckers took my lover?"

Predictably, one bolted. Kazi plucked him off his feet and tossed him to the back of the room, knocking two others down.

"Start talking..."

The bartender raised a rifle. Kazi grabbed the barrel quicker than the man could track and smacked it into his face. When he reeled, nose spurting blood, Kazi tore it from his grip. A second man ran for the door. Kazi swung the gun low and knocked his legs out from under him.

The bar door opened inward, and a couple stumbled in.

Kazi swung the gun one-handed, finger on the trigger, and aimed between the male's eyes. "Another night, hmm?"

They backed out, saving themselves the trauma of what came next.

A woman made a break for the back door. Kazi swung the gun—fired. Plaster exploded from the wall in front of her. She yelped and dropped, hugging her head to her knees.

Like shooting fish in a barrel.

Kazi cracked the gun open, shook the rounds free and flung the useless weapon behind the bar, smashing bottles. The bartender averted his gaze and muttered a prayer.

"The American..." Kazi raised his voice. "He was here. Someone took him. Someone knows exactly what happened. Whoever you are, if you don't start talking, this will be the last night on earth for every single one of you. You'll die here in this nothing bar and I will make it so that nobody knows what happened."

Someone sobbed.

Soon, they'd be screaming.

"Stop!" the hunched woman cried. "Please, stop!"

Kazi moved to her side in a blur. She yelped again and tried to scrabble backward, away.

He grabbed her ankle, yanked her back, and crawled over her, teeth bared. "Where is he?"

"I don't know!" Tears streamed from her eyes and saliva from the corner of her mouth. She reeked of fear—and of lies.

"Tell me."

"They... they said to put something in his drink."

Madness rippled through Kazi. His vision sharpened, narrowing to a fine point, and his thoughts funneled. He slammed a fist into the floor beside the woman's head, shattering the boards. "Where is he!"

She shook her head.

"*Where is he?*" He thrust the demand into her, violating her mind.

She screamed, sobbed, drowning in terror.

By Nyx... what was he doing?

He withdrew, crouched back and *breathed* long and slow, calming his heart and his head. He couldn't do this. He couldn't lose control after so long. This wasn't him... not anymore.

"Tell me..." he said again. "... and live."

"Don't move!" A man behind him threatened. "I'll shoot."

Humans. They never learned.

Kazi spun, ripped the revolver from the man's hand and struck him with the butt of the weapon. He dropped, taking Kazi's last thread of patience with him.

"All right... allow me to relay you a story." He caught the shine of a phone's flash—snatched it from the idiot's hand and crushed it to dust in front of him. "The story of a prince and a witch who tore him from his life and turned him into a monster."

A few more sobbed and snuffled and prayed. He'd lost any chance of getting information out of them. In all likelihood, they didn't know what had happened to Felix. They'd been used. Not feeders, just puppets.

Kazi laughed and spread his hands.

He'd already broken the rules. What were a few more? He could slaughter them all, drink them down, and burn the bar. Nobody would know. Not even Mikalis. But it wouldn't find Felix.

"Be grateful I'm not hungry." He flung open the door and strode from the bar, heading down the alley into the brightly lit main street. Mikalis would kill him for this too. But he was out of options and out of time.

Someone had drugged and taken Felix. He knew who...

People milled around. Tourists, families, children, men and women, happy on their vacations.

He strode through them like a storm cloud on a winter day and stopped in the center of the street.

A car with snow chains pulled to a halt in front of him. The horn honked.

Kazi breathed icy air through his lips, his fangs.

A few seconds later, someone screamed, "*Strzyga*!"

History flashed to the forefront of his mind. Zakopane wasn't a collection of huts around a campfire, nor was he mad with rage and hunger; he was, however, terrified. And like any cornered predator, he'd fight with all the weapons at his disposal.

"Jadwiga!" He kicked the car back, spread his arms and invited anyone to stop him, shoot him, do their worst. "I know you're here. You've always been here. You wanted me to notice. Is that what this is? Well, here I am!"

People ran. Doors slammed. Cars sped away, kicking up arcs of snow. Chaos strummed in the air, and the beast inside Kazi thrived on it.

"The blood prince is back." He smirked, watching his prey scurry into their dens.

The flap of leathery wings beat from the darkness above.

She came like the monster from the legends, all twisted, vicious and monstrous, full of fangs and bristling with claws. But as she landed in the street, smoke swirled around her, and the woman who stepped from the shadows was of a beauty that could only be preternatural. Long black hair spilled over her shoulders like silk. Her skin shone, smooth and hard like the ice in her eyes. Too perfect to be real.

She was other. And ancient. In the way that Mikalis was other and ancient.

"Darling child," Jadwiga crooned. "You return at last."

"Where is he?"

"He's being cared for."

If Kazi attacked, she was more than capable of killing him. He'd lived a long life, hadn't done enough to fix his mistakes, but he'd tried every day and night. He'd sworn himself to Mikalis and the Brotherhood and he'd *tried*. That had to even the scales.

"Let him go," Kazi ordered.

She laughed, and the sound wrapped around him, slithering against his skin and then under it, worming inside parts of his mind. When she smiled, her mouth brimmed with needle-like teeth. "And why would I do that?"

Kazi glanced around them. The people were all gone, the windows dark and silent. He didn't know if that was her doing—warping reality around them as Mikalis could do—or if everyone had fled.

"Where is he?" he asked, softer now. "Please..."

"Oh, sweet child." Her image shimmered, flickered, and jumped in front of him.

Instincts pulled him back a step. Her fingers cupped his jaw, tilting his head back. And some part of him wanted this, wanted her close even as an ages-old rage boiled inside him. She was in his veins, in his head. She'd *made* him.

"My blood prince..." She skimmed her lips across his. "Finally home, with me, at the fall of the old age and the beginning of the new."

"Whose age?" Kazi whispered.

"Ours."

His control—already hanging by a thread—threatened to slip free. If he lost himself, he'd never come back. She'd twist him up, make him mad again, make him the monster.

I'm sorry, Felix. I can't do this.

He kissed her and tasted sweet oblivion on the lips of his sire—then punched her in the chest. She flew backward, struck the windshield of the car he'd earlier kicked away, and tore through its metal shell. The vehicle buckled around her, cocooning her in metal. Her beautiful human form burst apart, and the winged demon tore free.

He already knew he was beaten, and he knew he'd lost Felix to whatever horrible fate she'd dealt him. In the end, he hadn't saved him. But he'd loved, even if it had only been for moments. The smallest moments were often the most powerful and the most devastating. He was honored to have shared them with Felix.

"I should have killed you a thousand years ago."

She flung open her wings and laughed. "How *Brotherhood* of you, child." With her wings fanned open, she shot into the sky and spiraled downward. Kazi had nowhere to go, nowhere to hide. He spread his stance and stood his ground, staring down a freight train.

She slammed into him, dragging him along the asphalt. Air rushed by. He grabbed at her wing and yanked. They spun, rolling. The road slammed up and smashed them together. A wall broke the fall and Kazi's bones. The chaos came to a sudden, jarring stop.

He was sprawled among crumbling bricks and bent rebars, blinking grit from his eyes. *Up. Get up...* He inched forward and tried to stand, but something clung to his chest, holding him down.

A bent rebar pinned him like a butterfly to a board. He blinked at it, disbelieving his eyes since there was no pain.

He coughed blood and tried to heave himself off.

She struck like lightning. Teeth plunged into his neck. Claws raked at his chest, burrowing toward his heart. She'd rip it out and devour it. He'd done the same to countless prey. Perhaps this was all he deserved: sweet irony.

But he'd be damned if he'd survived this long, only to lose another chance at life to the monster who had stolen his first.

She ripped her fangs free, dripping blood but no venom, not yet. "I should hang your carcass from a tree for Mikalis to find."

He reached feebly for the ragged wound gaping in his throat. His body already fought to heal, but it would take time and blood he did not have. Unless he took it from *her*.

"He stole you from me, turned you into a weaker, pathetic version of the monster I made in you." Rage twisted her face, made it hideous. "He's wrong. He was always wrong. Perhaps now he will open his eyes to the truth he hides from you all."

"Mikalis..." Kazi wheezed, his voice in shreds.

"A liar, a thief, not one of you, not one of us! He is darkness itself. He is all that is wrong with this world. And he must be stopped!"

Kazi's vision throbbed in and out of focus. He wasn't sure if the figure behind her was a dream or just smoke. "Behind... you."

She laughed. "You insult me with parlor tricks, child."

Kazi squinted at the figure approaching behind her. "Truly..."

A piece of jagged rebar swung toward Jadwiga's head—cracked across Jadwiga's skull. The ancient vampire's screech pierced Kazi's mind, his soul, demanding he fight for her, protect her, his master and sire. And without the Brotherhood in his life, he would have. Instead, he heaved his torso free of the broken beam and struck, sinking his teeth into her throat. Hot, ancient blood poured down his throat and burned like a thousand needles in his veins. Ancient horrors flashed in front of his eyes. Long ago, he'd fed from her, over and over, so hungry for all she gave.

She ripped him free, flung him down, and whirled on Zaine. He swung his metal bat again.

He danced back. "C'mon, then, witch! Have at it!"

Kazi sprang, landed between her wings, and sank his teeth into her shoulder, missing her artery.

She screamed again and launched into the air, taking Kazi with her, higher and higher. With every wingbeat, the ground fell away. Kazi dropped, slammed into the unforgiving asphalt a second time and spluttered blood. Above, the ancient vampire vanished among the blurry stars.

"Damn, Kazimir." Zaine offered his hand. "You left your mark on this place, brother."

Kazi propped himself onto an elbow. His head spun. His body was broken. A jagged scar ran down the main street, where Jadwiga had dragged him. Smoke poured from several cars he had no memory of hitting. And the building behind him crumbled, threatening to collapse on them both.

He took Zaine's hand and stumbled to his feet, bleeding and healing at the same time. "Thank you, Zaine."

"No problem. I owed you one." He gripped Kazi by the shoulder, probably to keep him upright. "But a hundred people saw you lose your shit and filmed it for all of social media." He squeezed and gave Kazi a sympathetic frown. "Not so perfect now, huh?"

"I hate you."

Zaine grinned. "Yeah."

"We have to find Felix." He shrugged Zaine off and stumbled down the street with no fucking idea where to go. His leg gave out. He dropped to a knee. Blood dribbled in the dirty snow. His vision swam again, dislocated from the rest of him. Somehow, he had to move, to keep going and find Felix.

"Where is he?" Zaine asked.

"I have to find him." Kazi dug his feet under him, forced himself upright, and stumbled on.

"Sure, I get that. But Kazi, do you know where you're going?"

"If it was Eric, you wouldn't stop. You'd find him—you'd find him and save him—"

"Kazi." Zaine blocked the way, becoming an obstacle between Kazi and Felix. Kazi could take him down most days, but not today. "Your cover is fucked," Zaine said. "This street looks like a war zone. The cops are inbound. Unless you know exactly where Felix is, we need to leave. Now."

He didn't know where Felix was, didn't know if he was alive. He blinked at the youngest member of the Brotherhood. He was right.

Kazi winced and clutched at his shredded chest. He could barely walk, and if Jadwiga returned, they wouldn't win a second round. He couldn't save Felix like this.

"We'll find him..." Zaine said. "You have my word."

Sirens wailed, and police cars rushed by outside the cabin.

Kazi sat back on the couch, alone in the dark, waiting for his body to fix itself. But it would take time—time he didn't have, time Felix didn't have. They'd come for him soon: people, a mob, human authorities, Mikalis. He didn't care.

Zaine returned, slamming the cabin door behind him, and tossed two blood bags at Kazi. "So you stop looking at me as though I'm your next snack."

Zaine was right, again. Kazi *was* starved. He plunged his teeth into the bags and emptied both in seconds. It wasn't enough—hunger still simmered in his veins—but it would help speed up the healing process.

"Don't say I never get you anything for the holidays." Zaine propped himself against the kitchen counter and folded his arms. His expression was so full of disapproval that it could have been Mikalis standing there. "This is a clusterfuck, Kazi. Even by my standards."

He knew that and didn't have it in him to care. "How'd you find me?"

"Eric and Google, Vesna's land holdings, and your shady-as-shit past, plus a little help from the European Brotherhood, who clocked your jet landing. They're gonna be real pissed at you, by the way. Not to mention what Mikalis is going to do when he hears about all this shit."

He knew what Mikalis would do. If he didn't kill Kazi, he'd throw him into a cell for decades to cool off. And he'd deserve it.

Zaine sauntered around in front of Kazi and crouched, glaring. "I don't blame you." His tone had turned gentle. "You can bet if these assholes had taken Eric, I'd have done all this and worse. So yeah, I get it."

"Where is Mikalis?" They could do with the leader's help, even if the price was high.

"I haven't had any contact with anyone else."

"Eric?"

"Back in New York, keeping an eye on the cover story for why Atlas went up in smoke. There was no way I was bringing him out here to vampire country to track your ass down in the mountains."

Kazi dropped his head back, closed his eyes and focused on fixing the gaping wound in his chest. His neck was sore but no longer bleeding.

More sirens wailed by.

"I love him." Kazi opened his eyes.

Zaine had moved to the windows and stood there now, his back to the room. "Yeah, figured as much. Does he know?"

"No."

"If he's smart, he knows." Zaine muttered a curse. "And that's what nobody else will understand. They see in black and white. Mikalis treats love as though it's a terrible disease. You and I know he's fuckin' wrong. Maybe he was burned a million years ago, so now he takes it out on the rest of us. If he asks, I didn't say that."

He was sorry he hadn't believed Eric was anything more to Zaine than a quick fuck and feed. He should have listened, should have believed him. They'd locked Zaine up, told him Eric was dead and then punished him for losing control. Kazi knew that grief now. It gouged out his heart. They never should have treated Zaine like they had.

But Felix wasn't dead. He had to believe that.

"I didn't plan this," Kazi grumbled. "I didn't even know I was capable of caring like this. By all rights, I should hate Felix. He's turned my carefully controlled life into chaos."

"Creeps up on you, doesn't it?" Zaine tossed him a sympathetic smile.

"I have to find him." He couldn't sit there a moment longer. Kazi shifted forward, resting his elbows on his knees. "It's eating me up. I can't think... I have to know he's alive."

Zaine leaned against the wall beside the window. "What are we up against?"

"My sire... Jadwiga."

"You're old. So that makes her what... BCE old?"

"Unknown. She got inside my head. And she's strong. Not Mikalis-strong, but close."

Zaine folded his arms and huffed through his nose. "We could really do with him on this, huh? Or Storm."

"Yeah..."

Zaine sighed. "I suspect they're both trying to put Saint back in a box."

Kazi knew only snippets of Saint's past, but it was enough. Saint had all the Brotherhood smarts and a nyk's bloodlust. "Indeed." They wouldn't be getting any help from Mikalis anytime soon.

"What *do* we know about your sire?"

"She's close. Wherever she took Felix, it's not far."

"Why'd she take him? Why not just kill him as a message to you? No offense, but if I were going to break you, he'd be an easy target."

Kazi considered it and shook his head. "I don't know what she wants. She's spouting the same nonsense as Vesna... something about a new age."

"Vesna was Nyxian and hell-bent on bringing back the dark goddess. What's your sire's motive?"

"She hates the Brotherhood, like most ancient nyktelios, and despises Mikalis for taking me, but that's not her motive or she'd have acted before now. There's more to it, more we're not seeing. She helped Vesna for years."

"Eric had a look at Vesna's land holdings, the details Felix discovered. She owns land here, like she did at Eagle Lake. There was a Nyxian compound there. Could there be one here?"

"It's possible. But what happened at Eagle Lake wasn't about bringing back the goddess. That was just an excuse. They bled me to spawn an army of nyks..." What if they were doing the same here, in one of Europe's busiest ski resorts? But there were no signs of anything untoward happening in Zakopane. An army of nyks would mean missing people and bloodless carcasses. Unless they'd been looking *too* closely, too close to see the bigger picture.

What if Kazi had been *inside* the trap all along?

"Have you ever heard of a nyk controlling an entire town?"

Zaine's eyes narrowed. "Control how?"

"Feeders, thousands of them." The thought was as hideous as it was genius. "She'd never need to leave and wouldn't need to switch up her identity every hundred years to keep from being exposed. Each new human generation would be taught to serve her." The more he spoke, the more it made perfect sense. Only an older nyk could maintain that level of patience and control for so long. And she'd need thousands of feeders to do it. "She's been here, feeding, manipulating the population for centuries. That's why nothing appears out of the ordinary, because *everyone* belongs to her." Kazi pushed to his feet. Bruised muscles barked in protest, but he had to move. "I knew she'd have her claws in this land, but I was looking in the wrong place. She's hiding in the open, among the general population. The Pied Piper of feeders."

"You'd better be wrong, because if you're right, we've got thousands of nyk-addicted people between us and her."

"I'm not wrong. I know her. Vesna mentioned being worshipped like a god. To Nyxians, Jadwiga *is* a god."

Zaine winced and rubbed at his forehead. "Damn, we need to get more of us on this. We can't take down a whole town."

"There's no time."

She was here, and the entire town was the center of her web, so that was where Felix would be.

Kazi grabbed his phone and brought up a map of the resort. The tourist sections sprawled away from the old town's center. Jadwiga would be at its heart, a queen in her castle. She'd use a building larger than the rest, with several floors, allowing her to take flight if she needed to.

Zaine peered over his shoulder. "You remember Sebastien? Eric's master? His nest was a high-rise in midtown. Old nyks like high places."

"There..." He showed Zaine the screen.

"Artemis Hotel and Spa? I dunno, even nyks prefer to keep it on the down-low. That hotel has hundreds of rooms."

That was it. The enormous building resembled a castle, with its vast, pitched roofs and multiple spires. A castle full of tourists. Easy pickings for a nyk who could feed and fuck and make her prey forget. "She's never needed to hide. This is her world. She controls all of it."

Zaine handed the phone back. "All right, let's assume she's there. How do we get to her without thousands of feeders knowing?"

"Walk right through the front door."

"Suicide. Right." Zaine rubbed his face. "If this doesn't kill me, Eric will."

"I'd do the same for you."

He snorted. "No, you wouldn't."

Kazi considered it. "I might..."

"You son of a bitch, Kazi." Zaine laughed. "He had better be worth it."

"Yeah... he is."

Zaine's laughter faded. "I'm doing this for Felix, you know that. Not you."

"Sure. Whatever, brother."

"Not your brother, asshole." Zaine sauntered toward the door. "Let's go, while everyone is distracted by the mess you made downtown. Maybe we'll get lucky and the place will be abandoned."

Kazi left the cabin and jogged after Zaine. "It's so reckless they'll never see it coming."

"It's the front door. They can't miss us."

CHAPTER 38

azi

The enormous, sprawling hotel sparkled like a Christmas tree. It sold the fairytale of a winter wonderland resort, promising its guests luxury rooms, state-of-the-art gym equipment, a huge indoor heated pool, and five-star dining. On all the advertising in the foyer Kazi strode by, there was no mention of a vampire queen dining on the guests.

Felix was here. He could feel it. He could also feel a thousand eyes on him as he approached the reception desk. Tourists mingled. A concierge eyed their approach with suspicion.

The receptionist greeted them in English. Kazi switched to Polish, throwing in a few charming smiles. They were in town for one night, he told her, then handed over his black card for payment.

With the formalities over with, Zaine fell into step alongside Kazi. "Ready?" Kazi asked him.

"This is a terrible plan. Storm would be embarrassed for you, Kazimir."

It wasn't the best or most thorough of plans. But it *was* a plan.

Zaine nodded. "I'm ready. Catch you on the other side." He veered off, heading for the stairwell beside the elevators.

Splitting up would split Jadwiga's resources too. But she'd soon have more to worry about than tracking where the Brotherhood was. Zaine vanished through the stairwell door.

Kazi strolled on for a few hundred yards, passing conference rooms and a hotel store.

He counted three minutes. And the fire alarms blared.

Zaine was up to mischief.

Guests spilled from side doors, hurrying back toward the main entrance. Kazi sidestepped them, walking around the flow. All he had to do now was find where Jadwiga was keeping Felix. He pushed into a second stairwell, ignoring the people bustling past him, focused on getting out.

Up or down?

Hotels like this one had a curious quirk. Developers skipped floor thirteen for superstitious reasons, and if they sold holiday units, nobody wanted to buy on floor thirteen. Most hotels had numbers skip from twelve to fourteen. But thirteen still existed, numbered fourteen. This hotel's top floor was fourteen. She'd be up there, and she'd keep her most prized possessions close, under her protection.

Kazi casually strode up the stairs until the flow of people ebbed to a trickle. He dashed the last few floors until a numberless door barred his way. The stairs ended here. He tried the door, found it locked, and thrust some muscle behind it, buckling it inward. Reinforced steel, just not enough to keep him out. Someone didn't want strangers to know what was happening on the top floor.

He kicked it all the way open and stepped through into darkness.

No safety lights, no lighting at all. She wouldn't need it.

A woman wearing a familiar gown with the dagger-and-eye

symbol on her left breast emerged from a doorway and stopped in her tracks. "What are you doing up here? Tourists can't be up here—"

He picked her up by the neck and pinned her to the wall. "Do I look like a tourist?"

Her eyes widened.

"Where's Jadwiga?"

She shook her head.

Kazi dipped his chin and inhaled her scent. Human, but with a trace of nyk too. She was a feeder. "You're hers. Don't lie to me. Where is she?"

"She's not here."

"What is here? Hmm...? What is this place?"

She swallowed and glared, doubling down on her foolish bravery. "You're not one of us."

"No, but I am like her. Don't fight me. You won't win."

"She'll protect me." Her fear was fast evaporating, turning into religious zeal. "She protects us all. We are promised. We are her chosen—"

He didn't have time for the sales pitch. Kazi growled and dragged her forward with him. Shoving through a second door revealed everything he'd feared.

Pods.

A dozen of them.

Monitoring equipment.

Exactly as they'd found in Eagle Lake, and just like there, these were empty. The nyks hadn't yet been made.

"She'll stop you!" The woman dug at his fingers still locked around her throat. She kicked and writhed. "She will resurrect me through her blood! A gift from Nyx, the dark queen!"

"She's not Nyx, you fools." He flung her to the floor, dismissing her, but her words drew him back. "Wait... she promised to turn you?"

The woman shuffled backward across the floor. "We are the chosen ones!"

He rolled his eyes. "You know what 'chosen' means? It means she'll rip you from your life and turn you into a rabid, blood-hungry monster. You will murder and butcher and fuck indiscriminately. Is that what you want? To live forever trapped in your own mind while you watch your own hands slaughter innocent people?"

"Hers is the only way!"

Feeders were too far sucked into a nyk's reality to save. Some, like this one, had been drinking the Kool-Aid for too long and didn't know any other way or want to know. The kindest thing for her would be to snap her neck. "The American, have you seen him?"

She blinked.

"Dark hair, scruffy-looking..."

"No, no..."

"Prisoners, where does she keep those?"

"*Darling child, I eat them.*"

Kazi whirled at the voice. Jadwiga approached from the end of the lab, wearing her human guise. She stroked each empty pod. "You could have been my prince. We would have ruled together, as it should have been."

"I've never been too keen on living in the past. Where is he? Where's Felix?"

"Perhaps you'll change your mind when you understand how your battle is pointless."

"There is nothing pointless about stopping nyks, Jadwiga. You'd enslave the entire human race without us to keep your kind in check. Hand over Felix and I'll kill you quickly."

"You will? Who? You and the blond one? You're alone. Mikalis has abandoned you as he abandons all those he claims to love. He's not who you believe him to be. He lies to control you. I have never lied to you, my prince."

"*I was never your prince,*" he snarled, freeing his true nature, letting it bleed into his voice.

"Fight me, and you will fail. Join me, and we'll reign over the new world together." She offered her hand. Blood-red nails glinted.

"There is no choice, Kazimierz. Accept your fate. Accept me as your queen. The end of your world is already in motion. Join me, or die."

"I'll join you." He stepped forward. "If you take me to Felix."

She tilted her hand. "Your word?"

"You have it." He took her hand, sliding her cool, slim fingers against his palm. Long ago, those fingers had held him down and choked him while he'd lain drenched in fear, his life bleeding from his veins. She'd consumed his life, his soul, tearing his mortality away and replacing it with darkness. He'd never forgotten, never forgiven. And Mikalis wasn't the only one who could lie.

CHAPTER 39

elix

Hunger gnawed at him from the inside out. It wasn't a need; it was a living, roaring monster boiling beneath his skin. His fingers itched to sink his nails into his veins and claw it out, cut himself open and rip the heaving, hungry mass from around his soul.

He opened his eyes—the glass was the same, the cage was the same. He was held down, trapped. Arms and legs locked in place. He screamed around the metal bar, thrashed and bucked. Someone was outside, someone shouting. And drums. Thudding, irritating, endless drums. He didn't know what this place was, didn't know what he was—

Escape.

Run.

Fight.

Feed.

A surge of fury erupted through him. He tore his arms free and slammed his fists into the glass, shattering it. Pieces rained, alarms sounded, and the drums—they kept on thudding against his skull, trying to beat him down and down and down.

His legs came next, the restraints no longer able to hold him. He staggered from the wreckage.

Run.

A hot mass of thudding flesh loomed in front of him. A creature of life and blood.

"Don't move," it said. "You're not finished."

He didn't understand what that meant, but he understood the drums had grown louder and louder, beating through his body, and the thing that stood in front of him, it pulsed with the same endless sound. He could make it stop, but more, he could swallow it, and once he did that, the drumming would be silent.

"No, no!"

He plunged his teeth into its neck. Bitter venom spurted. His prey wriggled and moaned. He crushed it close until its bones broke and the drumming had grown distant.

More.

The drumming was still there, still part of him, still beating and hungry.

For a moment, a second, a blink, Felix was himself again. Alarms shrieked. Lights flashed. Machines blipped. And at his feet, a body cooled.

Blood burned his mouth. Fangs throbbed with want.

What had he done?

CHAPTER 40

Kazi

JADWIGA TOOK him down to the basement. They passed huge whirring air conditioning units and thick cables humming with hot electricity.

Stainless steel double doors arched ahead. Doors like those on Eagle Lake's church.

Kazi's heart tripped.

The scent of blood teased his senses.

Where was Zaine? He'd be nearby, watching for threats... searching for Felix.

He wouldn't have to search for much longer if Jadwiga kept her word.

Jadwiga pushed through the metal doors and entered a lab just like the one on floor thirteen, like the one at Eagle Lake. But here, the work was still in progress. Electrical cables fed into it like veins to a central hub, then split off and fed dozens of pods, each one housing an unfinished nyktelios.

Felix would be safe. He'd be waiting...

Kazi's heart thumped too loudly, and a sharp, horrible thought tried to pry its way through all the others. He couldn't think it.

Two terrified men stood over a third, dead on the floor.

Kazi scanned the pods again, all of them full of unconscious men and women. Red tubes fed blood into their wrists and necks. One pod, near the back, was missing its door. It hung loose, broken. Its metal was a mangled wreck.

"Please..." one of the men begged.

The terrible, sharp little thought pierced Kazi's hope.

Where was Felix?

Jadwiga picked the blubbering man up and threw him down onto the floor, shattering his skull. The second tried to flee—Jadwiga was on him, embracing him, her teeth in his throat. She ripped flesh and muscle, silencing his screams.

"What is this?" Kazi asked. He didn't understand, didn't want to understand. Felix wasn't here. "You gave your word..." he said. His heart raced, hot and heavy, its every beat trying to tell him something. Something he didn't want to know. "I've seen your foul experiments, seen Vesna's identical attempts to create an army, and I killed all those. I'll kill yours now if you do not take me to Felix!"

She turned slowly, her mouth splashed with scarlet blood. "He isn't here."

Then why had she brought him...

Her gaze flicked to the broken pod. The shattered door, the fallen body... He drifted toward the pod. Tubes hung from inside, dripping blood. Jadwiga's blood. The soapy scent was Felix's.

By Nyx... what has she done!

Rage cooled, freezing behind an emotional wall.

"Kazimierz, he will be close."

Her voice was far away. The world and his place in it shrank to a small, sharp point.

"He is to be a gift for my blood prince." His sire's smile twitched, uncertain. "A true brother in blood. One Mikalis cannot take from us."

She'd touched Felix. She'd poisoned him. She'd taken his freedom, his control, *his life.* She'd destroyed him.

And now Kazi would destroy her.

Ice hardened around his heart, crushing it. By the queen of chaos, by all that was darkness, by the mother of time and order, the beginner of worlds—he was going to rip his sire apart.

The monster within roared through his veins, dragging power from ancient depths. More power than Kazi had known existed. It scorched his soul, setting him ablaze, and changed him. Muscles shifted and stretched. Two great weights tore from his back, through his clothes, bursting from his flesh.

His roar shook the air, and when he lunged, he *flew*, slamming into Jadwiga.

He flung her through a wall, crumbling it around her. With a snarl, he whipped his head around, tore open the nearest pod and sank his teeth into the unborn nyk, filling its veins with venom. Its blood tasted of her, rich and vicious. He'd destroy them all!

Claws raked down his back.

He rocked, grabbed the dying nyk and flung it at his sire. She screeched, bared her fangs and came at him—wings hunched at her back, her mouth twisted around fangs. He wasn't afraid, didn't feel anything. He snatched her out of the air by the neck, spun and slammed her into the next pod, sending sparks and blood raining. She writhed, wings flapping, claws raking his arms.

With his free hand, he punched the nyk behind her, shattering its face, and Jadwiga screamed.

He'd make her watch every single one of her children die.

He tossed her away, tore the next pod's door open and slashed his claws across the sleeping nyk's throat. It wasn't enough. He'd kill them all and it wouldn't be enough. Because their deaths wouldn't bring Felix back.

"Kazimir, my prince." Jadwiga laughed on her knees. She clung to a table and tried to heave herself to her feet. Her wings flapped out of sync, the left one bent and broken. He looked at her and saw weakness. He saw betrayal. And he saw the woman who had slain the brightest light in his life.

"Yes," she laughed, "this is your truth. This is what he hides from you! You are terrible. You are darkness. You are everything the great goddess made us, and he is the enemy."

A pod hissed, and its occupant inside twitched and bucked, coming to life. Kazi ripped its cables free, tore off the door and noosed the cables around the waking nyk's throat. He threw the half-mad creature at Jadwiga and yanked, snapping the cables tight, shattering its neck.

Her unfinished child slumped to the floor between them.

Tears brimmed in her silver nyktelios eyes. "You are magnificent."

No, he was a monster.

He lunged, claws reaching, fangs bared, new wings spread. A flicker of realization sparked in his sire's eyes. This was her end. She screeched and flapped, desperate to escape. He caught her leg, dragged her down into his arms and sank his teeth into her neck. Venom pumped.

A punch to his chest tossed him back. He struck a wall, plowed through it, and tumbled to the floor in one of the hotel's opulent hallways. Someone screamed. Other people ran.

He had no time for them.

A flap of his wing righted him onto his feet. He flew through dust and rubble, and slammed into Jadwiga. She twisted, dislodging his hold, and flung him to the floor. He bucked, moving fast, no time for thought—and tore through the air at her again.

He raked his claws across her neck. She roared and lashed, biting, tearing strips off his skin. They fought and raged, and the world around them crumbled, shattered, broke apart. It seemed as though the land itself trembled.

She tried to escape through a collapsed section in the ceiling, pouncing for the hole.

Kazi thrust his wings down and launched after her into another room in the hotel. She howled, flung a table and a lamp, and smashed a window into another hallway. Kazi stalked her, growing more powerful with every cut he gave her, every bite he tore from her.

The hotel quaked around them.

She ran and stumbled, and he stalked until her steps slowed and her body began to fail her. Her skin sizzled, bubbling away.

His venom brought her down.

"It does not die with me, blood prince," she panted and held out her hand as though to stop him.

He slammed a boot down onto her chest, pinning her to the floor. She grabbed his leg, claws digging into his thigh. "Nyx will have her vengeance, and there is nothing the Brotherhood can do to stop her."

Kazi leaned in, braced a forearm on his knee and spread his wings behind him. His sire was fading, and somewhere inside him, regret sparked, but he also knew vengeance. And right now, it reigned.

"We will never stop until you and your kind are gone from this earth. Nyx made a mistake. We are the correction."

Jadwiga's mouth twitched and quivered. But she still found a smile.

Kazi dropped to his knees and tore into her throat, pumping venom until he had none left to give. The witch who had stolen him from his life, turned him into a monster, taken thousands of lives by his hands—she clutched at him as her immortal soul disintegrated. And with her last breath, she whispered. "Erebus lives."

Her body collapsed and spilled through his fingers and arms like dried sand.

Kazi froze, twitched.

The ice-cold rage thawed, freeing him from its grasp. He slumped, surrounded by black sand, and listened as the real world ebbed back in. Fire alarms wailed. People screamed. The hotel groaned, bits of it crumbling.

Felix...

He had to find Felix...

Even knowing what he had become…

He staggered, and as the last vestiges of power recoiled inside him, the wings he'd been given slammed into his back, burrowing beneath his skin.

Still a part of him, just… elsewhere until needed again.

"Wings, huh…?" Zaine stood at the end of the hallway. "I reckon a pay raise comes with those."

Kazi almost smiled. This prick was all right. Sometimes. Rarely. He scuffed through the black dust and approached Zaine. "It's over. I just…" He couldn't tell him. Couldn't say the words. "Felix isn't there."

"Yeah, I picked up his scent on the lower floor, near the back of the building. Looks as though he escaped all on his own. We'll find him."

The building gave a structural, disconcerting groan.

"Doesn't sound good…"

"No." Kazi pushed on ahead, through the door and down the next corridor toward the main reception area. Zaine didn't know about the pod. He didn't need to know Felix had been… turned. They'd find him, and Felix would be all right. He'd fled. That was all.

They dashed through the hotel's main doors and stopped.

A huge crowd lined the road, filling every sidewalk and blocking the street. So many it seemed as though the whole town had turned out. And each and every person stared.

"You're the one who's used to an audience…" Zaine said under his breath.

There had to be a thousand people staring back at them. Not moving, not talking. No phones raised, no shouts or accusations. Nothing. Normal people did not behave this way.

Feeders.

All of them.

"Mikalis would kill them all," Kazi whispered.

Zaine's sidelong glance held a lot of doubt for a Brotherhood vampire whose job it was to kill nyktelios and erase all traces they'd ever existed, including their feeders. "Or... hear me out... we run?"

There was a big difference between killing a few nyk-addicted feeders and a whole town of people who didn't seem all that out of their minds, apart from the silent staring.

A man in the front row bowed his head and turned away.

Kazi narrowed his eyes.

Another bowed her head and turned her back. She left.

A third, a fourth, and then like a ripple through a lake, they began to disperse.

"Holy shit, something went right for once." Zaine jogged down the steps, heading left toward the corner of the building. "Your man's scent is back here."

Kazi followed, glancing back at the townsfolk's strange retreat. Feeders were rabid. They fought for their master and most would lay down their lives to protect them. But these people had just... thanked him? Perhaps they'd been weary of her reign.

"Here..." Zaine stopped by a patch of disturbed snow under an open window. Loping footfalls tracked back toward the cabin.

"Looks as though he's running..." Zaine wandered alongside the tracks.

That was normal, wasn't it? To run from this? But it didn't feel right. It didn't feel like Felix. He'd reported from war zones. He wouldn't run. He'd have been in the thick of it.

"You coming?" Zaine asked, checking behind him to see if Kazi followed. "He can't be too far ahead."

What would they find at the end of the tracks? The man Kazi loved or a nyk?

If Felix was a nyk, Zaine would try to kill him.

And Kazi would have to kill Zaine.

CHAPTER 41

azi

ZAINE CROUCHED beside the tracks leading past the cabin steps. "He didn't go in."

The tracks led into the forest. Kazi followed them, keeping his gaze ahead.

Zaine fell quiet, but his glances turned sharp, his mind working. If he suspected Felix of being a nyk, then he'd be watching his back too...

The snow-muffled forest wrapped around them. They picked up their pace, racing deeper into the cold darkness.

Kazi knew where Felix was headed. If he raced on ahead and tried to out-sprint Zaine, the Brotherhood member would know something was wrong.

The footprints in the snow ended outside an all-too-familiar cave opening. Perhaps it was Jadwiga's blood pulling Felix back, or perhaps it was just by chance that he'd returned to the very place Kazi had been reborn in.

Zaine stopped outside, his back to Kazi. He studied where the vegetation had been pulled down, exposing the yawning cave mouth.

"Something you want to tell me, Kazi?" He turned his head. Blue eyes shone in the dark. "Like how Felix may not be himself?"

Kazi waded through the snow. "We don't know what he is."

Zaine's glare rode him as he stepped up to the cave entrance. Water dripped somewhere inside the darkness, the *plink-plink* echoing in an otherwise thick silence.

Felix was in there. Kazi could smell him, smell Jadwiga, too, in his blood. Perhaps he wasn't all the way turned. Maybe he'd escaped the pod before too much of her blood had poisoned him.

As soon as Kazi took a step inside, he'd know Felix's fate. Right now, as he wavered outside, there was still hope. Still a chance Felix was all right.

Kazi gritted his teeth. If Nyx had taken him, by whatever gods remained, he'd burn the world...

"Kazi?" Zaine whispered.

Kazi stepped inside.

Oppressive silence wrapped around him. Only the water's *plink-plink* broke it.

Grief, fear, regret—it all tried to claw up Kazi's throat and choke him. "Felix?"

A blur rushed from the dark. Kazi shot out a hand, locked his fingers under Felix's jaw and flung him against the cave wall, pinning him there.

Felix's eyes burned silver. Fangs dripped venom. He hissed, lost to the madness of hunger, the same as Kazi had been in this cave so long ago.

He knew.

Felix was gone.

Jadwiga was dead, but she'd still won.

Kazi's heart shattered.

Felix bucked, and his teeth snapped together. He clawed at Kazi's forearm, growling like a rabid creature.

Nothing human remained in his eyes, nothing of the man he loved.

Kazi searched his gaze. He just needed one little spark, just a hint of Felix, one fragment, and maybe he could be saved. But there was nothing. Hunger and madness glared back.

"Kill him," Zaine said.

Kazi fought the quiver of his lip and tilted his head, fighting the agony swallowing his heart. Felix growled and thrashed his head. Foaming drool slipped down his chin.

"I can't," Kazi whispered, unsure if he'd spoken aloud.

"I know... I will."

"No."

"Kazi—"

"No!" He flung a hand behind him, holding Zaine back. "Don't." It hurt. Everything hurt. Every breath, every thought... His whole body wanted to collapse around him. Because he knew it was over. What he'd had with Felix, the brilliant thing they'd begun... it was gone.

"I can..." Kazi swallowed. "I can keep him here."

"Kazi—"

"Nobody has to know. I'll keep him here and bring blood... He can drink from me. It doesn't matter now. He can take as much as he wants—"

"Kazi, stop."

"Zaine..." he growled, breathing hard through his fangs. Zaine's face held no anger, no hate or disgust. If anything, his expression was pained too. Kazi couldn't stand to see that amount of compassion on his friend's face. "It wasn't enough..." Kazi said and faced Felix again, still hoping... Felix stilled, perhaps sensing he couldn't escape. His cold eyes looked back at Kazi. "We didn't have a chance to make it work. We had weeks. That's no time, Z. No time at all." Cool tears wet Kazi's face. His heart was breaking over and over, not healing. He could heal almost anything, but not that.

"But you had that," Zaine said.

Weeks... Kazi had known love for weeks, after searching for it for a thousand years. How could he let it go now? "I can't do this. I can't let *you* do this."

Felix lunged, almost tearing himself free of Kazi's grip.

Kazi spun and threw him toward the back of the cave—away from Zaine. But the momentum stumbled Kazi. Unbalanced, lost, he fell to his knees. Grief, so like hunger, ate him up inside. "I'll stay," he begged. "I'll stay here with him. Zaine, I can do that..."

"Kazi." Zaine's voice was soft, heavy with heartbreak. "Felix wouldn't want this."

Oh, by Nyx, why? Why had she given him this wonderful, brilliant chance at love, only to rip it away? They could have had decades, not weeks. Weeks were nothing. Kazi had drifted from century to century, moving like a ghost through the eras, to now feeling alive again. And for what?

Mikalis was right.

Love was cruel. It was devastating. It was torture.

"I did this. I killed him." He sobbed, then growled, filling with hate. Hate didn't hurt like grief did. Hate was easier to bear. "*I wish we'd never met.*"

"I know..." Zaine breathed. And maybe he did know. He'd killed his lover too, before meeting Eric.

Zaine's heavy hand landed on Kazi's shoulder. "It must end here."

No. Damn him. Damn the Brotherhood and Mikalis. Why did it have to end? Kazi whirled, launched at Zaine and drove him backward. "Don't touch him!"

Zaine raised his hands and bared his teeth. He didn't fight. He could. His eyes brimmed with tears too. Damn him. He knew this agony.

Kazi unlocked his grip and staggered backward.

His heart was gone, dead in his chest, his body cold and hollow. "I'll do it."

"You don't have to."

"I do." He swayed and swept the tears from his face. "It has to be me."

Felix knelt near the back of the cave, where the water dripped, hunched over and watching like the rabid animal he was. *Not Felix.* A nyktelios.

Just another nyk that needed putting down.

Not Felix, who'd dropped a can of soup in a Maine gas station and tried to hide it. Not Felix, whose beautiful baby girl would never know what had happened to her father. Not Felix, whose smile was both shy and sly, more sly now that he knew what he wanted. Felix, who had recently begun to live without fear. Felix, who quivered and moaned, coming undone in Kazi's arms.

Not the Felix Kazi loved.

He stumbled toward him. His vision blurred. He blinked the tears away. None took their place. He couldn't feel, not anymore. The world was colorless again. Empty.

Felix looked up.

"I'm sorry, baby... I couldn't save you."

Felix tensed to lunge, to escape. Kazi rushed in, scooped him into his arms, and plunged his teeth deep into his neck. Venom spilled, venom that would find its way through his veins and burn Jadwiga's poison right out of him, turning his body to dust. Felix fought, but Kazi wrapped him tighter, crushing him close, breathing him in, absorbing his warmth as his heart slowed.

Kazi withdrew his fangs and sank to his knees, trapping Felix close. He trembled in Kazi's arms, his body failing rapidly. It wouldn't be long now.

The creature dying in his arms was no longer Felix. Felix had died alone, trapped behind glass as nyktelios blood had poured into him, and Kazi would never forgive himself for that. He should have been with him in the end. He'd have stayed with him. They would have grown older, and when Felix passed, Kazi would have been beside him. He would never have been alone again.

But Kazi had failed. He'd promised to protect him. He'd have given his immortal life to save him, but it was too late.

A new sound joined the thudding of Felix's slowing heart. A

thump through the air. Rotor blades... coming closer. The Brotherhood's chopper, perhaps, or human authorities.

"Kazi... we have to go."

He laid Felix in his arms and looked into his open but unseeing eyes.

He'd given him a piece of his soul—wasn't even sure when it had happened. And maybe Felix had given him a piece of his own in return, because Kazi still felt him close, even as he passed from this world. He was still part of Kazi. And Kazi would keep that piece of him close, forever.

"Kazi," Zaine urged. "I'm sorry... They're here. We have to go."

He laid Felix down and pressed a hand to his chest, feeling the last beats of his weak heart under his palm.

He skimmed Felix's lips with his fingertips, then placed a kiss there. "We'll meet again, you and me. In whatever comes next. I promise you this, Felix Quaid."

The beat of multiple helicopter blades drummed the air, summoning Kazi outside. He staggered from the cave and shielded his eyes against the snow whipped up by the black helicopter's blades.

The Brotherhood was here.

And he could no longer find it in him to care.

CHAPTER 42

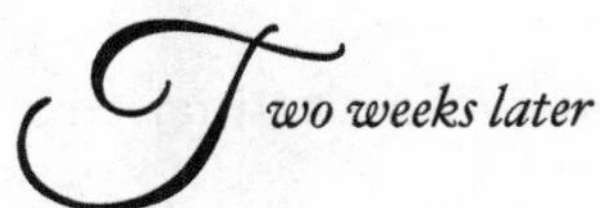
wo weeks later

Kazi

The bar's chatter, music and chinking of glasses swirled around him in a fog. He didn't really listen. Nothing touched him. No part of this world was real anymore. Just colorless monotony.

He'd left a part of himself inside that cave. Perhaps his heart.

He heard its beat in his chest now, but it didn't sound the same.

Nothing sounded the same.

The world was a dull, gray place, all its veins sucked dry.

"Hey, aren't you that Kazimir guy from Insta?"

Kazi leveled his glare on the man who'd asked.

"My mistake." He snorted and raised his hands, backing off.

"Right choice."

If one more person asked him about the publicity stunt in Zakopane, he'd throw them over the damn bar.

It had all been covered up with typical Brotherhood ease. Vampires in a ski resort? What a joke. Just a publicity stunt, a crazy photoshoot to garner more likes. The fact that Kazi was a vampire in this fake photoshoot ensured the likes and comments kept streaming in. It was a bit too on the nose, but in the age of the internet, nobody believed the truth anyway. The internet *was* the truth.

Although he'd drawn the line when some smart-ass had decided to ask him if he sparkled. He'd blocked and deleted the dick. It had probably been Zaine anyway, using a fake account.

He hadn't seen Zaine, hadn't seen anyone.

The London Blackrose Brotherhood—the European hub—had let him go, but told him to stay close, unconvinced he wasn't about to turn nyk and burn all of London down around them.

He might have done, if he'd cared.

A man propped himself on the stool next to Kazi and raised a hand, capturing the bartender's attention.

Kazi's instincts tingled. There was another predator in the room. He swirled his whiskey. "Mikalis." And took a sip, looking over when the Brotherhood leader didn't reply.

Mikalis hadn't changed. He never did. His fashion changed to fit the era, his dialect and mannerisms changed, like it did for them all, but his face was the same ancient handsome, the eyes the same Aegean blue.

Kazi knew better than to blame him for anything that had happened. Nothing was ever his fault.

"Quite the mess you made in Poland."

"If you want an apology, you'll be waiting a long time."

The bartender left Mikalis's drink. Mikalis raised it to his lips and took a sip, in no rush, as though he had all the time in the world.

Kazi could have raged at him, demanded to know where he'd been all this time, thrown him across the bar, but nothing he said or did would change a damn thing. So instead he cupped his hands around his glass. "You should lock me up."

"Elaborate," Mikalis said.

"Containment. Like you would have in New York. They must have the same here, in London. Lock me away. Take me out of the game."

"What are you really asking? Because if you believe you're a risk to the population, then I will act, but if you want to hide from the pain, then the last thing you need is to be alone."

Kazi swirled his drink and stared into its golden whirlpool. "And what if it's both?"

Mikalis sighed. "There are too few of us to lose you. Something has changed. In all the time I've been working to curb the nyktelios threat, they have never been this bold. Their numbers are rising at a pace we can't keep up with. The tide is turning. The Brotherhood needs you, Kazimir. *I* need you."

Damn him. He knew Kazi would never say no. "I need some time."

"Time is no longer something we have an abundance of. Regardless, that's not why I'm here."

Kazi raised an eyebrow. What was he going to ask of him? A mission, probably. There was no better way to shake off this malaise than to throw him back into work.

"What I am about to say will alarm you," Mikalis said. "I ask that you remember where we are."

That sounded ominous. "In a London bar?"

"Precisely." He danced his fingers down his glass and cast his gaze over the people around them. "Hmm, in fact, let's do this another way. Finish your drink. Come with me." He downed his own drink and stood.

Kazi finished up, paid the tab, and left the bar, walking the short distance to Mikalis's sleek, gray sports car—either a rental or belonging to the London brothers. They drove through central London, along the embankment, passing the sprawling Parliament building with its iconic clocktower. Kazi stayed quiet, watching London's sparkling city lights fly past the window.

"I know grief," Mikalis finally said. He slowed the car to a halt alongside a glass-fronted office building. "I know how it sucks all the purpose from life. This is why we must not care. Grief is one of the few things that has the power to destroy us."

"And the Brotherhood is all," Kazi said. He knew the spiel. He'd heard it a thousand times, spoken to others if not himself. He'd survive this like he'd survived everything else. It was inevitable, even if he sometimes wished it wasn't.

Mikalis left the car and strode to the building, leaving Kazi to catch up. A swipe of a black card unlocked the main door and the elevator at the back of a shiny, glass-and-marble reception area.

Kazi entered the elevator beside him.

"For once, I am grateful I can spare one of my own some of that agony."

Kazi side-eyed the Brotherhood leader. What was this? Some kind of cryptic lesson in managing grief? He'd prefer to do without the talk and get back to work.

The elevator door opened into a bland corridor. Nobody was around. The whole damn building felt empty.

"What is this place?"

"Plan B." He smiled. When Mikalis smiled, someone was either about to have their ass handed to them or win the lottery. It could go either way. Kazi had broken every Brotherhood rule. Multiple times. Technically, he'd gone nyk. Mikalis wasn't known for his tolerance. Kazi *should* be locked up. But there was something else happening here.

They stopped at a locked door. No windows. Mikalis swiped his card again, and the door hissed open.

Kazi entered the brightly lit room behind Mikalis. Glass made up the entire left wall, creating a huge window into another room. Cameras monitored the adjacent room.

A room with one occupant.

Kazi's heart shattered anew. He pressed his palms to the glass. "No... it's not possible."

Felix hopped off the bed, looking scruffy, as always, in oversized pajamas with the sleeves rolled up. His hair was a mess, his chin shadowed with the beginning of a beard. He smiled in that shy, sly way he was so good at. "Hey."

CHAPTER 43

elix

He hadn't expected to be so nervous.

Two weeks they'd kept him holed up behind the glass like a goldfish in a bowl. Two weeks of tests and monitoring. Two weeks of staring at white walls, wondering if they would ever let him out.

Then Mikalis had come, explained everything, and now this...

Kazi stood behind the glass, dressed all in black, his blue eyes the brightest thing about him. Felix hopped off the bed and approached the glass, kinda weirded out by *everything*.

"Hey."

Kazi's eyes widened.

He hadn't known.

They hadn't told him Felix was alive.

Bastards. Felix fixed his glare on Mikalis. "You're a real piece of work."

Mikalis dipped his chin and took a step back. "There was no use in telling Kazimir you lived until we were sure you would survive."

"*What the fuck.*" Kazi bowed his head. His shoulders heaved. When he looked up, tears wet his cheeks. A sharp fragment of a memory tore through Felix's mind—a cold place and Kazi's tears sparkling like ice on his cheeks. He didn't remember much, but that place had been bad. He didn't want to know what had happened there, although he saw some of it in Kazi's eyes now.

Felix pressed his hands to the glass, opposite Kazi's, desperate to feel his touch again. "Hey, baby. I'm okay." His heart hurt to see him in pain. Mikalis should have told him he was alive, although he'd been told he'd been about as close to death as anyone could get. He was immune to Kazi's venom but susceptible to nyk blood. Mix that with the anomaly in his blood, and all three quirks had fought it out inside him.

Kazi shuddered. "He's not nyk?" he growled.

"No," Mikalis replied. "Although we had to be sure. He's fine, remarkably so. As far as we can ascertain, your venom and his own blood—"

Kazi flew through the door into Felix's room. Strong, warm arms clamped around Felix's waist, lifting him off his feet. "I thought I'd lost you—I watched you die."

Kazi dropped him back to his feet and cupped his face. He stared deep into Felix's eyes, searching for something. His breaths stuttered. Then his mouth was on Felix's, his tongue tasting. Felix melted in his grip, kissing him back, a little scared but mostly just fucking relieved.

"I'll er... return later to debrief you both." Mikalis cleared his throat.

Kazi pulled from the kiss. "Turn the damn cameras off."

"Of course," Mikalis agreed, and Felix caught the leader's knowing smile before the door clicked closed behind him.

Kazi scooped Felix off his feet and propped his ass on his hands, moving so fast it left Felix dizzy. He laughed and wrapped his legs around Kazi, kissing him back. Needing to feel him, his skin, his warmth, he brought his hands between them, stroking his chest under his shirt.

Kazi trembled, but not from the cold.

Fear shone in Kazi's eyes. Tears too. Felix cupped his face in his hands. "I saw you... in that cold place... I couldn't get to you."

He turned his face away, but Felix drew him back. "You were there, so I knew whatever happened, it was going to be okay. I knew you'd keep me safe. And you did."

Kazi's face crumpled. "Felix, I killed you." He blinked wet lashes, dislodging more tears. "I'm so sorry. I had to—forgive me."

Felix's heart swelled. This man *loved* him. Real love. And Felix loved him back, he knew, because only love hurt like this. "You *saved* me." He wiped Kazi's tears away.

Kazi buried his face against Felix's neck and sobbed, losing himself. If Felix could have taken his hurt from him, he would have. But all he could do was wrap his arms around him and hold him so damn close that his sobs became Felix's too. "I love you, Kazimir." His voice shook, and he didn't care. "I love you. I don't know what that means for us, but I love you." He blinked through his own tears. "I was lost, but I found you—I fuckin' love you, Kazi."

Kazi sank to the floor, pulling Felix into his lap. Sobs racked him, and maybe he cried for more than Felix. Maybe there was a whole lot he'd lost too, and he was only now letting himself grieve. Felix held him, told him he was loved and that whatever happened, it was going to be all right.

He wasn't ever leaving him. His place was by his side.

Forever.

"I love you," Kazi whispered, his voice torn. "I don't know how else to say it. Words aren't enough." He grabbed his hand and pressed it to his chest. "There... You're there, inside me. A piece of me. And when you were gone, half of me was gone too."

Felix carefully unbuttoned Kazi's shirt and kissed him on the chest, over his wounded heart. "Maybe I was always there and you're what brought me back?"

"Maybe..." Kazi stroked Felix's hair from his face.

The kiss this time was a soft promise. Felix swept his mouth slowly over Kazi's, relishing how he gasped and trembled. He nudged his neck, kissed him there too, and relished his shudder. He pulled Kazi's collar down his shoulders, kissing each new inch of exposed skin.

He was unreal—a forbidden, mysterious myth that Felix had captured in his hands. "Make love to me."

Kazi drew him close, chest to chest, and cradled him there as he lifted him onto the bed.

Felix stretched out, sprawled shamelessly beneath Kazi's gaze.

Kazi lifted Felix's top over his head and kissed trails down his chest, flicking his nipples. Felix laughed and moaned, somehow together. The pants went next, and Kazi's smart mouth sealed around Felix's dick in such bliss that he almost forgot to mention the moisturizer in the cabinet drawer would make the perfect lubricant.

After that, nothing else mattered, just Kazi's hands on him, his hot mouth teasing, his teeth pinching. When Kazi's cock touched his hole, he whimpered for more. And Kazi was in him, and everywhere—a part of him, making Felix's body burn with his every touch. Felix watched Kazi's face and saw the truth in the tears on his cheeks. Felix had never wanted to hurt him. He wished he hadn't, wished he'd spared him that pain.

But they were here, together, and that meant everything.

It meant anything was possible.

Felix had died, and Kazi had brought him back.

Together, anything was possible.

CHAPTER 44

azi

HE ACHED to hold him closer, to breathe him in and love him and keep him safe in a world that had already proven deadly. As he stroked in and out, driving Felix toward breathless ecstasy, he vowed to live for this man and this man only. Kazi wasn't Brotherhood, not anymore. He wasn't nyktelios. He was Kazi, Felix's other half.

Felix shivered around Kazi's cock, his muscles tight and slick, his body like a home Kazi only now knew existed.

He fell forward, bracing an arm over his shoulder, and kissed his breathless gasps away, then peered into the eyes of the man who had captured his heart.

Felix smiled that half smile, and it was all Kazi could do not to spill in that moment.

He pushed up, grasped Felix's dick, and stroked in time with his rhythmic thrusts, riding his body, perhaps his soul too. Felix writhed and gasped, clutched at the bed sheets and bit his own lip.

And when he came, he moaned long and hard, and spilled his cum into Kazi's hand. The spiraling pleasure tipped Kazi over its edge until he came deep inside his man, sharing his body and soul.

He braced over Felix and kissed him slowly, relishing the taste and feel of a man who was his—not owned, but given.

Felix broke the kiss with a smile. "Let's stay like this forever?"

Kazi nudged his nose. He rolled onto the bed beside him and tucked Felix close, where he fit so perfectly. He rested his cheek against his shoulder and clung to him, too afraid to let him go lest he vanish again. "For you... yes."

"Wait..." Felix twisted in his arms and hooked a leg over Kazi's hip. "You mean that? You and me... You'd... walk away from them?"

"I will if that's what you want."

Felix's gaze skimmed Kazi's face, searching for doubts he wouldn't find.

"I'm just gonna say it... What about when I'm old? When my memory goes? When we can't... you know... do this anymore?"

Kazi twined their fingers together. "You're already grumpy, so—"

"Wow." He laughed.

"I love you in here." He shifted, freed his arm trapped beneath them and poked Felix's chest. "Hearts are immortal."

"Yeah but... they're not, really. Mine isn't."

Just the thought of losing him again made Kazi want to rage at the world. He pushed the panic away and kissed his knuckles. "Worry about the future tomorrow."

"Yeah, sure. Okay." But he was still worrying now.

"Live for the precious little moments, baby," Kazi whispered. "You'll be surprised how long you can make them last."

His smile returned, and so did the warmth in Kazi's chest. They lay side by side, content in the quiet.

"I don't want you to leave the Brotherhood," Felix said. "I've seen the worst of the nyktelios. They need to be stopped. I can't take you from that fight. You're too good at it."

"Then... will you fight it with me?"

"If you want me to?"

"Always."

Then it was settled. Kazi would ask Mikalis if Felix could join them. Mikalis had already said he needed Kazi, so that was his price. Felix would become Brotherhood too, for as long as he wanted, just like Eric was.

They dozed the next few hours away, then woke, tangled in each other's limbs, desperate and hungry all over again. But the bliss could not last. Mikalis had given them a reprieve. But he'd need answers, the same as Kazi needed answers.

Felix had somehow been *cured*. But being a nyk was incurable.

If Felix could be cured, then what about the rest of them?

What if the Brotherhood could be cured too?

Kazi wouldn't be the only one asking these questions. They'd all need answers.

~

"I SWEAR, Mikalis stationed me here as punishment for helping you." Zaine glowered, rising from the chair outside the steel door. When his glower landed on Felix, it softened. "Hey, you look a lot better than when we last met." He extended his hand, and Felix gave it a friendly shake. "Glad you're still with the living, Felix."

"Thanks, yeah." Felix rubbed the back of his neck. "I'm not sure how, but here I am."

Zaine caught Kazi's hard glare for touching his man and raised his hands in surrender. "C'mon, the British lot have given us use of this building for whatever we want. While you two have been reacquainting yourselves with each other, Mikalis has summoned everyone here."

"Who's checked in?" Kazi asked.

"Everyone... Well, kinda everyone... You'll see."

He led the way down quiet corridors into a plain conference room full of cheap chairs around a fake beech table. Storm stood at one end, reliable and predictable, as always. Raiden tapped on a laptop on the table. Aiko flicked his knives, bored as he leaned against the back wall.

Mikalis hadn't arrived, and neither had Octavius.

Felix wandered toward the view of the sparkling Thames at night through the windows. Kazi followed, instinctively keeping him close. He wasn't sure he'd let him out of his sights ever again.

Eric arrived, and Zaine scooped him up, planting a heated kiss on the man's neck that had Storm clearing his throat. "For fuck's sake, Z. No need to remind those of us who aren't getting any how we aren't getting any."

Zaine mumbled something in Eric's ear that had the man blushing and playfully shoving him away. Kazi watched, relieved Zaine had Eric. Knowing grief as he did now, it was a wonder Zaine had ever recovered from losing his first love. To find a second love proved he truly was a lucky son of a bitch.

"All right." Mikalis swept into the room. "We're all here. Let's begin... By now, you are all aware of Felix's miraculous cure. From what we understand, which admittedly isn't enough"—he stopped at the head of the table—"due to Felix's immunity to nyk venom, when Kazimir attempted to kill him, his venom instead reacted with Felix's unique genetic make-up, already altered by nyk blood, and essentially neutralized Jadwiga's attempt to turn him, reversing it. He... *healed* the turning."

"He healed from being a nyk?" Aiko asked, lifting his chin. "Has that ever happened?"

"No. Never."

They all shared concerned glances.

"So," Zaine raised a hand. "Let me get this straight. If Eric gets turned, my venom will cure him?"

Mikalis turned to Raiden, who nodded, and said, "In theory, yes."

"You've tested this?" Zaine asked.

Raiden prodded his glasses up his nose. "I've taken samples of nyk blood and Felix's blood, and we have Kazi's stored," Raiden explained. "Together, they create a reaction that neutralizes the nyk blood, rendering it inactive."

"So, let's be clear about this. There's a cure?"

Raiden lifted a finger, slowing Zaine's trail of thought. "Not an entire cure, just a cure for those with the same blood anomaly as Eric and Felix, should any nyk attempt to turn them. It won't cure us."

"You've tried?" Zaine asked. "You've mixed it all up in test tubes and you've tried, right? Because if you're telling me there's a ticket to being human out there, I'm taking it."

Mikalis straightened. "There's no cure for us."

"No offense, but *you* would say that."

Mikalis narrowed his eyes. "You believe I wouldn't want you cured?"

"I don't know what the fuck to believe with you."

Something sharp and dangerous passed between Mikalis and Zaine, only softened by Eric's hand on Zaine's arm, drawing him back. An awkward silence settled in the room.

Kazi caught Felix's concerned gaze.

"If you don't want to be here, then I don't want you here," Mikalis said. "You know where the door is."

"No, it's not... I'm good." Zaine backed down. "I just... This is big, that's all. This means something."

"Speaking of not wanting someone here," Kazi said. "Where's Octavius?"

Another ripple of tension spread through the room. They all knew something Kazi clearly didn't.

"Before we get to that, may I finish what I was saying regarding our recent new additions?" Mikalis said.

"Of course." Kazi sensed he was walking on thin ice. Something had happened to Octavius while he'd been dealing with his sire in Poland.

"Now..." Mikalis drew in a deep breath and looked each of them in the eyes. "I have kept information from you because I didn't want it to lead to false hope. But Storm and I discussed it. It's only fair you know."

"You're getting married?" Zaine quipped.

Aiko snickered, and Kazi fought a laugh back behind a grin. Eric and Felix shared a glance, still gauging the temperature in the room.

"Ha. Ha," Storm grumbled and showed Zaine his middle finger.

Mikalis lifted his gaze toward the ceiling. "Nyx, give me strength." But his lips found a smile. "Eric and Felix are experiencing fundamental physical changes. Whether it's due to your personal circumstances, your intimacy, or something we aren't yet aware of, they are both able to heal significant damage, and if our calculations are correct, they'll stop aging in the next six months."

"What?" they both said at once.

Felix approached the table in front of Kazi. "What does this mean?"

Raiden glanced around the room, noticed everyone was staring at him, and stood up. "You won't age. You'll heal almost any wound, besides decapitation or the removal of your heart."

"But that's not possible."

"You're in a room full of vampires, buddy," Storm said.

Kazi heard Felix swallow, and when he stepped back, Kazi folded his arms around him, tucking him under his chin. "It means, baby, we'll have forever." He was glad he'd whispered it, because any louder and Felix would have heard how his voice trembled.

"How?" Eric asked.

"That's the question, isn't it?" Raiden smiled. "We don't know. I have some theories. I'm working on finding out more. When I know, with certainty, I'll get you that information."

"As I've previously made clear," Mikalis said, "both Eric and Felix are under my protection. Given these discoveries, that is even more important. They're Brotherhood. And frankly, we need them. *I* need all of you. We are being attacked and undermined. Pillars we thought immovable have fallen. Our ranks have been breached. Atlas has been compromised. Not just for the US, but worldwide.

We are blind at a time when nyks have never been more organized."

A sinking sensation pulled at Kazi's gut. "Where's Octavius?"

Mikalis took a breath and held it, then blinked away. "Octavius is to be found and brought to me, preferably alive, but his ashes will suffice."

Kazi's heart sank. "What happened?"

"He's a traitor," Storm growled. "He's been working against us for months, possibly years."

"Against us how?" Zaine asked.

Storm worked his tongue around his teeth, as though to slot his fangs back into place. "The raid on Sebastien's nest in New York... Octavius sabotaged our comms."

"That prick," Zaine sneered.

"He deleted the footage of the Nyxians entering the parking garage and ambushing you, Kazi, delaying our efforts to find you."

It didn't seem possible. Octavius was as cold as ice, but he'd been a Blackrose Brotherhood member for almost as long as Storm. Nobody liked him, but they all trusted and respected him. "Are you sure?"

Storm turned his head toward Mikalis, deferring to him.

He nodded slowly. "Raiden recovered footage of Octavius entering the labs, taking the chip Kazi imported inside, and using it to download a virus into Atlas's heart. He was working with the Nyxians to sabotage us at every level. That's why the whole of Atlas went dark, and why we had to abandon New York. The attack came from *within*. It came from one of our own, where we're the most vulnerable."

Mikalis didn't show it, but he was hurting. His entire existence revolved around the Brotherhood. Every waking moment, every decision, every choice, every beat of his heart, if he had one. The Brotherhood was his, to his very core, and Octavius had torn out a piece of it. The others may not have seen the hurt in their leader, but Kazi had known him long enough to read the fine lines around his eyes and the press of his lips.

"Memento mori," Kazi said.

"Memento mori," the others echoed.

Mikalis nodded. "The Brotherhood comes first. Going forward, we will do things differently. Storm will contact you with nyktelios sightings. You will have limited resources to neutralize them. There will be no central hub, no base of operations. Once you leave here, assume you're on your own. I will assist when and where I am able. Do not rely on me to save your asses. I cannot be on multiple continents at once, and I have an urgent situation to deal with back on the East Coast."

"We're going old school," Storm said, adding a rare smirk.

"We always did do our best work in the dark," Mikalis added. A wicked glimmer in his eyes caught the ambient light and devoured it. "Questions?"

Silence. Aiko flicked his knives and smiled as though he couldn't wait to sink his teeth into the next nyk case. Eric and Zaine stood side by side, stronger together, and Raiden scooped up his laptop, eager to get back to test tubes and graphs.

Kazi kept Felix close.

Storm studied them all, proud, stalwart.

"Yeah, I got a question," Zaine said. All eyes turned to him. "When do I get wings?"

CHAPTER 45

elix

THEY WALKED the sparkling Thames waterfront at night. A wintery chill tried to whisper around Felix. He shivered and hooked his arm with Kazi's, absorbing his warmth.

Everything Mikalis had said was... a lot. Maybe he should have feared the changes happening around him and inside him. But he didn't feel afraid. With Kazi at his side, and knowing he might be able to keep up with the Brotherhood, he figured he was exactly where he was supposed to be.

"You okay?" Kazi's voice rumbled.

"Yeah, I'm good." He smiled up at him, alleviating some of the worry on his face. "I get the impression things aren't normally this dire?"

"Not normally, no." Kazi gazed ahead at the long, wide path stretching down the Thames in front of them. "Mikalis is worried, which usually means we should be worried."

"Having one of your own turn against you must be tough."

Kazi's cheek twitched. "Mikalis is the way he is because without him, without the Brotherhood, we'd be the same as the nyktelios we fight. But he's not made of stone. This has hurt him. Hurt us."

The Brotherhood wasn't good, and now he understood why. Good couldn't do the things they had to. But they had goodness in them, more than they let on. It just took an outsider like Felix to see it.

"You don't have to be part of this, despite what he says." Kazi stopped their stroll beside the river's edge and admired the swirling Thames waters. He drew Felix snug against his side and leaned on a railing. "I meant what I said before. Fractured as we are, you could walk away. He's stretched too thin to track you down."

Felix gripped the rail, one arm still hooked in Kazi's. "And what would I do?"

"I could pull some strings and get your old job back, just so long as you don't go digging in the Brotherhood."

Not long ago, he'd have been tempted. But he'd seen too much, been part of the impossible, and to go back to that old life, he'd have to leave Kazi, the man he loved. "Would you come with me?" he asked, testing the water.

"Yes."

He hadn't even hesitated. Damn, this man was amazing. "I can't take you from them, from this. It's too important. Maybe together we can make a difference, you and me? It's the right thing to do."

"I think so too."

Felix grinned and pulled Kazi closer. "Then it's settled. This is us now."

"This is us." Kazi gazed over the wide, dark river. The wind ruffled his hair, and for a few moments, Felix saw the ancient prince in his profile, a young man with a world of possibilities in front of him. Of course, that man no longer existed, like the Felix from before he'd met Kazi was long gone. They'd both changed for the better, despite the pain it had taken to get there.

"Oh, I er... bought you something." He'd almost forgotten the gift tucked in his coat pocket. "You know when we were in

Zakopane and I er… I mentioned your name meant something… on Urban Dictionary?" He couldn't look him in the eye. "Well, while I was recovering for a few weeks here, they let me have internet privileges. I'm pretty sure they were monitoring everything I did though, so I'm er… I hope you er…" He pulled the mug from his pocket, no longer sure if it was funny, or foolish, or if he'd just embarrassed Kazi in front of his UK brethren.

Kazi took the mug, his face unreadable. Printed on it was Urban Dictionary's definition of a Kazi: *A man with an enormous penis. Knows how to please sexually. A love/sex god.*

Kazi arched an eyebrow. "It's accurate." His smile bloomed, the real, brilliant, dazzling smile that was all for Felix, and he chuckled. "It's perfect, thank you." He planted a soft kiss on Felix's head. And now Felix wondered if he'd just stroked his ego even more, if such a thing were possible.

"Unfortunately, I don't have a gift for you, but you may want to use this to call home." He handed over a phone. "Rosa will be missing you."

The thoughtfulness punched Felix in the gut. "Yeah, thanks," he croaked. He pulled from Kazi's arm and dialed Julia's number. "Shit, what time is it there?" Maybe he should hang up. Was it too late? What if Rosa was asleep?

"Early afternoon," Kazi said softly. "You've got this, Felix."

Yeah, he had this. Mostly.

"Hello?" Julia answered.

Felix cleared his throat. "Hey, Julia, it's me."

She ranted at him—the last she'd heard from him was right after Mikalis had attacked the house. He let her get it all out, and then he told her what he could, told her he was safe and that he might not see her or Rosa again for a while.

"Are you with Kazimir?" she asked.

Kazi had drifted farther down the path, but not far, and when Felix raised his gaze, he smiled back, all dramatic and perfect in his long dark coat and loose black hair.

"Yeah, I'm with Kazi."

"Good," Julia said. "Maybe he can make you happy."

Guilt tried to choke him again. He'd spent his whole life making mistake after mistake. That ended now. "I think so."

"*Are* you happy, Felix?"

God, he was. He had everything he'd ever wanted and was free because of it. "Yeah, I am."

"Well then, I'm glad, for you and for him. But don't forget about us, huh?"

"I won't."

"Okay..." Her voice quivered. "Rosa wants to speak with you."

"Put her on."

"Here she is, and Felix... I love you."

"I know, and I'm sorry."

The line crackled, and muffled voices sounded. "Hey, Daddy! I won a drawing competition today. There was another girl who drew a cat in a drawer, but I drew a horse. And mine was way better."

"That's great, sweetheart."

Damn, he was going to miss them. She talked some more about her picture and her day, and the more she talked, the more he knew he had to help the Brotherhood hold back the tide, because if they failed, Rosa's world would vanish.

"Is Mister Kazi there?"

"He is... How'd you know?"

"Momma says you are boyfriends now."

"I guess, yeah, we are. Is that okay?"

"Will he come around again?" she asked, because two men being boyfriends didn't matter to her, as it shouldn't.

"Maybe." He caught Kazi's growing smile. He was listening in. "Would you like that?"

"Yeah! I want him to do the funny voices, the ones you're terrible at. Can you put him on?"

Way to dent his ego. "I er..."

Kazi sauntered back and held out his hand.

"Sure, sweetheart."

"Honey," Kazi drawled, then plowed into a discussion about

coloring and how Rosa was going to be an artist. Naturally, Kazi wanted her to draw *him* on a horse. And it had to be the biggest, most dramatic horse. He was a natural around kids, or so Felix thought until the topic of conversation turned to sabotaging the other entrants in any future drawing competitions.

"Wait, I'd better go. Your daddy is frowning." Kazi paused, then added, "Rosa says we have to visit for Thanksgiving."

Felix wasn't sure why he was even part of this conversation now; they clearly had everything planned. He laughed, and Kazi told her they would and said goodbye. He handed the phone back. "Be good, baby girl. Be strong..." Felix told her.

"I will, Daddy."

He hung up and welcomed Kazi's arm looping around him. "She's like you," Kazi whispered and fluttered a soft kiss on his lips. "She'll fight all the monsters."

"I'm hoping we make it so she doesn't have to."

"We will. The Brotherhood is a long way from beaten. We have a few tricks up our sleeves."

"I can't wait to see those." He laughed, then threw his arms around his neck and relished Kazi's hot touch on his lips. The kiss broke apart, leaving them breathless and hungry for more. "These tricks... Are they anything like the wings Zaine's jealous of?"

Kazi snorted. "The wings were a surprise, even for me."

"There's no vampire manual?"

"It's more of a fuck-around-and-find-out scenario."

"Then you got an upgrade."

Kazi's grin faded. "They came when I knew I'd lost you, as though Nyx herself had reached from the dark and touched me with her gifts."

"Maybe she did?"

"Perhaps." Kazi bumped his forehead against Felix's and closed his eyes. He was remarkable, a monster with a heart. For a race that didn't care, they seemed to care a whole lot.

"I'm not going anywhere." He took Kazi's hand in his. The vampire opened his eyes, their blue as bright as any star over

London. "You're stuck with me forever. I hope you know that. I've got the weird blood to prove it."

"Baby, I wouldn't have it any other way."

He kissed him as though they were alone, kissed hard and hungrily, leaving no doubt who Kazi belonged to. Because it worked both ways. Felix was Kazi's, and Kazi was his. Two halves of a whole. And the whole was a love so bright it had survived the touch of darkness itself.

If there were powers at work to unleash an era of chaos on the world, Felix knew the Brotherhood would stand against it. And he'd stand with them, with Kazimir. Forever.

For all the Blackrose Brotherhood news, character art and new releases, sign up to Ariana's mailing list at:
www.ariananashbooks.com

ALSO BY ARIANA NASH

Sign up to Ariana's newsletter so you don't miss all the news.

www.ariananashbooks.com

***

Shadows of London

(Five book urban fantasy series)

A sexy assassin, a billionaire boss with secrets, and magic bubbling up through the streets of London. All in a days work for artifact agent, John "Dom" Domenici.

Start the Shadows of London series with Twisted Pretty Things

***

Silk & Steel Series

(Complete four book dark fantasy series)

Elf assassin Eroan, falls for the dragon prince Lysander, in this heart-shattering star-crossed lovers tale.

"(Silk & Steel) will appeal to fans of CS Pacat's Captive Prince and Jex Lane's Beautiful Monsters." *R. A. Steffan, author of The Last Vampire.*

"A few pages in and I'm already hooked." *- Jex Lane, author of Beautiful Monsters.*

"The characters yank, twist, and shatter your heartstrings." -

Goodreads review

Start the adventure with Silk & Steel, Silk & Steel #1

ABOUT THE AUTHOR

Born to wolves, Rainbow Award winner Ariana Nash only ventures from the Cornish moors when the moon is fat and the night alive with myths and legends. She captures those myths in glass jars and returning home, weaves them into stories filled with forbidden desires, fantasy realms, and wicked delights.

Sign up to her newsletter and get a free ebook here: https://www.subscribepage.com/silk-steel

Printed in the USA
CPSIA information can be obtained
at www.ICGtesting.com
LVHW042100261023
762248LV00031B/341/J

9 781739 467241